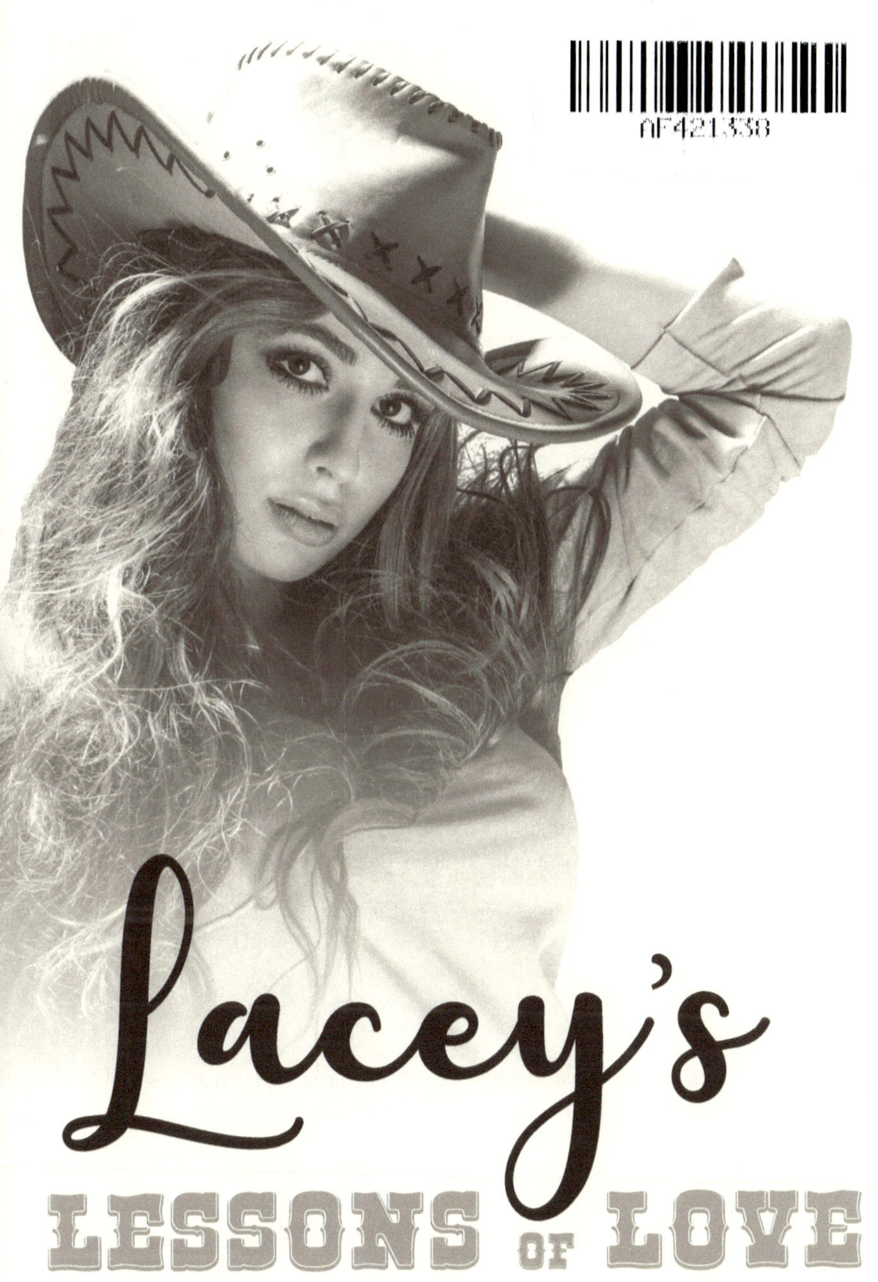
Lacey's
LESSONS OF LOVE
BOOK ONE
TAMMY LOUGH

Publisher's Note:
This is a work of fiction. Names, characters, places, and incidents
are a product of the author's imagination. Locales and public names
are sometimes used for atmospheric purposes. Any resemblance to actual people,
living or dead, or to businesses, companies, events, institutions, or locales
is completely coincidental.

Editor: Peggie Ireland
Cover and Interior Design: Rebecca Finkel, F + P Graphic Design, FPGD.com
Book Consultant: Judith Briles, TheBookShepherd.com

Published by Cottage Porch Books

Books may be purchased in quantity by contacting the publisher
through the author's website: www.TammyLough.com

Library of Congress Control Number: data on file
ISBN KDP softcover: 979-8-9868733-0-5
ISBN IS paperback: 979-8-9868733-2-9
ISBN eBook: 979-8-9868733-1-2
ISBN audiobook: 979-8-9868733-3-6

Romance | Romantic Comedy | Historical Romance | Women's Fiction

First Edition
Printed in the USA

In loving memory of two special angels.

My dad and brother:

Bill & Kelly Coan

"I will hold you in my heart,

until I can hold you in heaven."

To my cherished family who I love

beyond imagination:

Margie and Ken Rastberger, Judie Macinka,

David Lough, Christopher Lough,

Riley Lough, Brianna Lough,

Mason Lough, and Wendy Seip Coan

For those who refuse to allow

disability to steal their happy!

Even on the most challenging of days.

1-800-FIGHT-MS

ROCK SPRINGS, NEBRASKA

1873

acey Autumn Kendall clenched her hands into tight fists around the scrap metal bars of the jail cell. After taking a deep breath to fuel her volume, she rattled the bars and hollered at the deputy, "How dare the sheriff lock me in a blasted cell. When I get outta this pickle, I'm gonna give him a piece of my mind, that's fer dang-fire sure." She stepped toward the window, then turned. "Hey, speakin' of pickles, I ain't had nothin' to eat yet. You got any vittles?"

The deputy fiddled with a stack of newsprint. "Well, look here," he said and cleared his throat. "A fella named Levi, says here Levi Strauss and Jacob Davis got them a U.S. patent for blue jeans with," he said, leaning closer to the print, "copper rivets. Sellin' for $1.12. One fella said —"

"What in Sam's tarnation is keepin' m' pa so stinkin' long?" Lacey interrupted, her boots clippity-clopping atop the worn wood floor as she scurried to the cell window. Fingers on the sill, she hoisted on her tiptoes to look up and down rut-riddled Pigtail Alley. *Ain't nothin' stirrin' in this town 'cept dust.* Beyond the deep roadside ditch, a herd of cattle grazed in the crisp, chilled air among three-foot-tall grasses. She eyeballed the yellow-centered flowers in a nearby patch of sagebrush before taking aim and spitting a stream of tobacco. Returning to the cell door, she called out, "You sure you sent word to my pa? Or is you lyin' through yer jagged, yeller teeth?"

The deputy licked his thumb, pinched his lips tight, and scraped the top of the well-worn oak desk. He peered under his fingernail like he'd found something worthy of an eyebrow-knitting stare.

"Excuse me," Lacey hollered. "I'm talkin' to yeh and yeh best pay attention." She didn't like him ignorin' her one bit. "Don't make me kick yer butt, Leroy. I did it on the south side of Miss Wilbur's learnin' room nearin' eight years ago, and I'll do it again. Only take me 'bout half a second."

The deputy sprang from his chair like his hips caught fire and stabbed his index finger in her direction. "I done told you three times. Sheriff Billy Ray rode out to your place over two hours ago and spoke to your pa. Now, be still and wait."

She grabbed the bars and pointed to an imaginary spot on the floor outside her cell. "Come stand right there, Leroy. I got me a hankerin' to fix yer face."

"I swear, if you don't hold your tongue and hush up. I'm going to —"

The jailhouse door opened with a loud creak and Leroy snapped to attention. "Mr. Kendall, thank the good Lord you're here." He breathed a sigh of relief, grabbed a ring of skeleton keys from his desk and darted to Lacey's cell.

Rueben Augustus Kendall raised his right hand. "Not so fast, Leroy." He stepped forward and crossed sun-weathered arms over his chest.

Lacey's eyes grew wide as she glanced at the keys to freedom, then back to her pa. Lifting her voice an octave, she lined it with all the sweetness she could muster. "Pa? Go on now and tell Leroy to unlock my cell."

Rueben removed his black, ten-gallon hat and pointed the brim in his daughter's direction. He emphasized each word as he approached her cell. "You best listen to me, jailbird."

Lacey triple-checked the latch on her cell. T'was locked tighter than the butt cheeks on a bull spotting a horse fly.

Pa rubbed his salt and pepper whiskers with a work-worn hand. "I didn't do you no favors raisin' you alongside yer brothers. You act like some sorta hellcat gettin' yerself locked in a cell. I spoke to Sheriff Billy Ray and guess how much jail time he's givin' yeh?"

"I reckon a week or three, maybe."

"You reckon a week or three, do yeh? How does six months sound?"

"Six months? That ain't fair. I didn't *mean* to shoot ole Uncle Chester. Heck, I barely aimed."

"It ain't fair? Hell, if it ain't fair. You shot yer great-uncle Chester in the butt-ox, Lacey." He jutted his finger toward the front door. "A few minutes ago, I was fixin' to pay yer bail, and had m'hand on the doorknob. I heard you spewin' such an ear-torchin' spray of words, heck, there's a murderin' bank robber gettin' hung out in the square, and yeh made *him* blush."

"Well, I'm hotter'n a skillet a'frog legs, and you ain't helpin' one bit." She nodded toward the deputy. "And he won't get off his lazy butt and unlock m'dang cell. Walk on over there and take a look-see at Leroy's teeth." She put a finger in each corner of her mouth and pulled her lips apart to make a hideous face. "His green fangs would scare the stink off a skunk."

"All right, enough," Pa said. "Let me tell you somethin' else. When I took a gander around the back of the jailhouse and had to duck to miss that wad of chewin' tobacco yeh let fly through the bars of yer window, I made my decision."

"Whaddya mean by decision?" She scratched a spot under her dusty brown cowboy hat. "There ain't no decision except let me outta here. Right now!"

"I know you show a dreadful mad when your feathers get ruffled, Lacey, but go on and throw the biggest hissy storm yeh wanna." He walked to her cell and pointed his index finger an inch from her nose. "I will tell you how it's gonna be."

"How it's gonna be? How it's gonna be is you're gonna pay my bail and get me the hell outta here. I want a shot or two a'whiskey before I get dealt in over at the Cactus Rose."

"It's mornin', Lacey. Hell's fire, it ain't even nine o'clock yet."

"Well, ain't that ripe! I'm fixin' to get started an hour late." She pumped her fist at the deputy. "Thanks, Leroy."

"Lacey, I will do what I should have done years ago when yer ma, God rest her soul, went to be with the Lord. I'm sending yeh to live with yer Aunt Molly."

She stared straight into Pa's gray eyes. "You wouldn't dare send me away to that old bat." A thought crossed her mind, and she perked. "Anyhow, yeh ain't got the money to send me to London."

"I ain't sendin' yeh to London. Your Aunt Molly retired from that high falutin' lady school. She's over yonder in Montana, and I wired her a telegram. Yer gonna live with her fer six months and learn how to be a lady."

"Montana?" She eyed her pa's expression. "Six months? Have you popped yer shine cork?" Beads of sweat broke out on her forehead. "I won't go. I refuse." She brushed her hands together like knocking dust from her palms. "And that's that —"

"That's that, is it?" Rueben gave his hat a quick dip her way before returning it to his head. "Sweet dreams, darlin'. Enjoy yer six months behind bars." He moseyed through the jailhouse and straight toward the entrance.

"Pa!" She kicked the lower bars with the toe of her pointed boot. "Git yerself back over here and let's talk about this fer a spell."

He returned to her cell and stood silent as a wind-blown feather, then grabbed the bars with both hands and shook them like he intended to break them in two. He spoke slow and precise. "I will say this one time, and there ain't gonna be no hagglin'. You best listen close to what I tell you, or I walk out of here. And, let me be clear." He pointed to the front of the jailhouse. "If I go out that door, it won't make me no never-mind if you sit here till rot sets in. I ain't comin' back fer six months."

Lacey glanced at her pa's fists gripping the bars and attempted to lighten his mood — and maybe her six-month sentence with Aunt Molly. "You got yer knuckles wrapped 'round them bars so tight, Pa, they's white as ole Chester's butt cheeks when he dropped his drawers to see what was burnin' a hole in his ass."

Seeing how Pa wasn't cracking even the hint of a smile, she wondered if he was bluffing, or what kind of hand he held behind his straight-lipped poker face. She tried another tactic. "Okay," she said and grabbed the bars. "I call yer bluff. What kinda deal yeh got fer me?"

"Oh no, I ain't got no deal. You done run outta deals, jailbird. Now"— he slapped his hands atop her clenched fists. "Listen up little missy. All I better hear out of yer sassy trap is yes, sir. Do ya' agree on goin' to Montana fer six months to live with yer Aunt Molly and learn how to be a lady?" He cupped a palm behind his ear awaiting her reply.

She hemmed and hawed, took a deep breath and let it out in a great big huff, rolled her eyes a time or three, and kicked the bars near eight times, a ninth for good measure. Maybe if she forced a tear or two.

"I'm waitin', and I ain't heard yeh say yessir, Pa. You got less than four seconds before I…three…two —"

"Oh, yessir, Pa, iffin' I gotta."

"You gotta. Go on now," he said to the deputy with a fluttering of his fingers. "Open the little birdie's cage and set her free."

Rueben held an iron grip on Lacey's wrist as he sprinted her down the wood-planked walkway with such speed her feet struggled to keep up. A trio of ladyfolk waved fans under their noses as they passed with a wide swath. Lacey raised her fist at them before slamming it into her palm.

"Whoa, Pa," Lacey said pointing toward the familiar saloon. "Where the hell is you takin' me? I hitched Buckeye at the Cactus Rose."

"You ain't gonna be needin' yer horse."

"Whaddya mean, I ain't gonna be needin' m'horse? I need m'horse ever' day."

Rueben slowed. "I mean where yer goin', you ain't gonna be needin' yer horse."

"And just where do yeh think I'm goin'?"

"See that stagecoach over yonder?"

Lacey peered past him with a squint. "Yessum. What does that stagecoach hafta do with me? You meanin' I leave today?"

"I sure 'nuff do. I talked to the driver and he ain't movin' on fer near a couple hours. You got plenty of time fer Miss Aimee t'git yeh all fixed up."

She dug the heels of her boots into a dust-filled crack in the wood plank. "Gits me what?"

Rueben's eyes narrowed to slits. "I talked to Miss Aimee over at the hotel. That woman, she's got good solid horse-sense. You ain't ridin' no stagecoach and gettin' on no train with a buncha decent folk to Montana and meetin' yer Aunt Molly lookin' like a wildcat tomboy. She's a proper lady, and after takin' one good look, she'd probly leave you standin' with yer carpetbag."

Lacey held her chin high and squinted in the sunlight. "What's Miss Aimee meanin' to do to me?"

"She's gonna clean yeh up, and fix yeh some is all."

"I'll take a bath, but I ain't wearin' no stinkin' dress." She stared into his smoldering gray eyes. She didn't care if Pa got mad, she wasn't wearing no dress. "I mean it. Don't you dare tell her to put me in no frilly-ass dress. Iffin' you do, I swear some-body's gonna end up dead."

Rueben stopped in his tracks and faced her. His well-lived-in facial furrows deepened to near cavernous proportions as he seethed through gritted teeth. "When yeh git outta that tub, 'lil darlin', you'll either put on what Miss Aimee sets out fer yeh or plan on passin' the time to Montana nekkid as a peeled tomater." He jabbed his finger a speck from her nose. "It's yer decision."

Lacey watched his lips form every word. He sounded like he meant it. Maybe she shoulda been nicer to her brothers. "Pa, I'm sorry 'bout pourin' tar in Luke's boots."

He quickened the pace.

"And the pie. Dousin' the cherry pie with cayenne pepper was a cruel thing to do to Jeremiah."

He walked faster and pulled tighter.

"And the outhouse. I never shoulda hitched ole Buckeye and tipped the outhouse over with Matthew inside unloadin' his mornin' constitution. I'm sorry."

The swirly-painted Miss Aimee's Hotel sign swinging on chains over the two-story brick building ignited a hornet's nest buzzing in Lacey's guts. She took a deep breath. "Pa?"

"What?"

"We got us a problem."

"Problem? I ain't got no problem."

"Maybe you ain't got no problem." She unhitched her overalls. "But my guts are brewin' a batch a'green apple grizzlies itchin' to see daylight."

*P*a pulled Lacey inside Miss Aimee's Hotel and she recalled the time she'd snuck inside to steal hard colored candy from the pretty parlor bowls. She'd marveled at the showiest place she'd ever stolen from. It was still sparklin' fancy.

"Lacey?" said a buxom woman as she stepped from a polished wood counter. Her full skirt barely cleared the narrow opening to the lobby. She approached Lacey and wrinkled her forehead. "Land's sake, girl. Your mama, she's got to be rolling over in her grave at the likes of you."

Lacey adjusted her soiled brown cowboy hat sitting low over her eyebrows and concealing every strand of tangled hair on her head.

Miss Aimee reached to lift the hat, peeked, and hurried to replace it.

Lacey figured she got a good look at what Pa called her rat's nest. She tired of messing with all the knots, so she kept it plastered under the hat.

"Mercy," Miss Aimee muttered and took a step back to eye the girl. "Your shirt must belong to one of your brothers the way it hangs from your shoulders like a feed sack." She cast a grimace toward Rueben. "And bib overalls for pity's sake? What are you thinking raising this girl like a farmhand?"

Lacey nibbled the outer corner of her lip and raised one eyebrow. Who did Miss Aimee try to impress with her showy done-up hair and layers of fancy, sewed-together threads? Her brothers would laugh her right off the farm if she put on airs like Miss Aimee.

"Sugar Belle, we have our work cut out for us," the woman said with a sigh. She cupped her fleshy hands around her mouth and called toward an arched opening. "Yoo-hoo, Sue Ellen, Mary Margaret?"

"Yes, Mother," the two youthful women sang in unison as they entered the shiny wood foyer. They flashed a quick, curious glance at their past schoolmate and halted midstep. Mary Margaret turned to whisper in her sister's ear, and they broke out in giggles.

"Enough, girls," Miss Aimee scolded. "Go upstairs and top off the tub with hot water. We have work to do."

Miss Aimee motioned for Rueben to sit in a sage-green wing chair. He complied and placed his hat over a knee.

"This way, Lacey." Miss Aimee pointed to a curved staircase, and after lifting her broad skirts, climbed the steps.

Lacey turned and cast a quick, pleading glance toward Pa. Her knuckles showed pale from holding a vise-like grip on the massive cherry banister. "Pa?" she said, shaking her head back and forth. "You know I never say please, but I'm sayin' it now. I'm beggin' you, don't make me do this."

He stopped whittling a gee-haw whammy-diddle and pointed at the top step with a demanding finger, his brow set in a deep furrow.

Lacey huffed and climbed the staircase like a gunslinger dawdling to her own hanging. She stopped to take a second gander at Pa, but he wasn't going to budge. She looked to see Miss Aimee staring down at her from the landing. "I'll be there when I'm good and ready," she hollered. "Yeh ain't gotta watch me like a doggone hawk eyeing a limpin' rabbit."

When she reached the top of the stairs, the woman led her to a back bedroom where a fancy-legged tub came close to overflowing with steamy water. The room reeked of soap. Lacey glanced at Miss Aimee before bolting toward the door.

"Lacey Kendall." The voice boomed behind her. "Strip."

She hesitated, then unbuttoned and removed the three-sizes-too-big shirt, dropped it, and gave it a defiant kick across the room. Her pouch of tobacco tumbled free of the pocket and glided across the floor until it hit the wall.

Miss Aimee shook her head and walked to snatch the chew.

Lacey expected a lecture, but after Miss Aimee fetched her lip-dip and turned back around, her mouth flew wide open like a toad drooling over a juicy fly. Lacey couldn't help but giggle.

The woman dropped the near-empty pouch of tobacco on the floor and said, "Heavens, girl, you aren't wearing a set of stays?"

"Stay what?" *What in tarnation did Miss Aimee jabber about now?*

"Stays, girl." She clenched the sides of her generous bosom before skimming her hands down to ample hips. "They keep everything in place."

"Iffin' them stays is keepin' everything in place, I hate to think what would happen if they sprang loose." She took a few steps back in case and finished undressing. Holding the side of the tub, she stepped into the water and eased herself down until only the tips of her shoulders remained exposed. A slight wave of bath water and soap bubbles escaped over the rim and spilled onto the floor.

Miss Aimee's daughters each held a cloth and a bar of soap. Kneeling on opposite sides of the tub, they scrubbed off the surface dirt before going after the deep, ground-in grime.

Their foreheads scrunched, and their lips tightened into circles like drawstrings were getting pulled. "Ouch, watch what you're doin'. You don't hafta scrub m'dang skin off." Lacey looked first to her left, then to her right at the women attempting to skin her alive. "Ouch, I said that hurts. Will you, ouch."

Mary Margaret lunged forward, plopped her thick hand on top of Lacey's head, and dunked her under the water. Lacey resurfaced, sputtering liquid and bubbles from her nose and mouth as she flailed her arms. "What the hell?"

"Here," Sue Ellen said and squirted cold liquid into her hair. "Hold still a minute and let us finish."

Lacey's head bobbed back and forth as the women's hands scrubbed from her scalp to the ends of her hair three times before dunking her for a final rinse. She climbed out of the tub and Mary Margaret wrapped her in a big, fluffy towel as Miss Aimee returned to the room with a fancy burgundy dress draped over her right arm. She held it and brushed away a few wrinkles, then laid it across a bright peach couch with a carved wood back raised much higher in the center. It was decorated with small blue, ivory, and pink flowers in weaved baskets and looked nothing like the brown couch back home full of lumps and covered with stains, rips, and bite marks.

Mary Margaret motioned for Lacey to sit on the bed while she took a dry towel and pressed it into her forming curls. "Do you know what I would give to have your beautiful curls? If you don't move your head around too much today," she said, "these curls will stay pretty through tomorrow, I bet."

Lacey rolled her eyes skyward and willed the woman to shut her trap talking about hair. So, she had curls? So what. If there were scissors, she'd cut her pretty curls off and tell Mary Margaret to stick them to her head with a finger full of hog snot. Then, she'd watch Mar-Mar pass out on the floor.

"Lacey Kendall, I declare," Miss Aimee said. "I don't know when I've ever seen such a lovely, luminous shade of brunette." She bounced a ringlet in her palm. "Your hair falls to your waist like twisted ribbons." She gave Lacey's cheeks a quick pinch. "Mercy me, who would have thought under all of that," she said pointing to the heap of clothing scattered across the floor, "such a beautiful, young lady would present herself?"

Lacey thought for sure she would puke right there where she sat. This woman gave her a bellyache with her goings on. She never thought of herself as pretty. Heck, if she so much as pondered pertyin' herself, her brothers dunked her in the hog trough to set her straight. Pa never had money to buy dresses and such, so she got whatever her older brothers outgrew. She looked at Miss Aimee holding a ridiculous looking piece of…. "What's that?"

"It is a corset. You are so tiny in the waist you certainly do not need it, but I promised your pa I would dress you like a lady, and all ladies wear one of these."

"Well, you best get that contraption outta my sight. It's burning holes right through my eyeballs." She nearly poked her eyes out demonstrating. "I ain't no lady, and I ain't wearin' no such torture contraption." She huffed and crossed her arms over her chest. "And you go right on and tell Pa I said so."

"Your pa also told me if you make a fuss," she said holding the garment in the air between them, "I am to send you back downstairs, and he will put you on the stagecoach naked as the day you were born. Sweetheart, I've known your pa for more years than I care to count, and he means what he says."

Lacey grumbled as she set her face in a scowl and allowed Miss Aimee to adjust the garment. The tight waist of the corset threatened to cut off her air tubes. "How am I supposed to breathe in this contraption? What'd you do, tie me in?"

Miss Aimee chuckled. "As a matter of fact, I did tie you in. That is how a corset fastens. You will get used to it, sugar."

I'll get used to it all right when I toss it from the stagecoach a mile outta town, sugar.

"Here now, step into this slip and the petticoat will flounce your dress out all nice and full." Miss Aimee tugged and pulled to get the seams where she wanted. "All right," the woman said, gathering the dress in her arms. "Reach for the ceiling."

Lacey gulped a breath and with eyes wide, shot her arms straight to the ceiling. "What'd I do? I swear, I ain't shot nobody else…today."

"For pity's sake, girl. I want to put this dress over your head, not arrest you."

Lacey brought her hands down and released an uneasy breath before hoisting her arms upward with an exaggerated eye roll. "Hurry and get this over with."

The soft, unfamiliar fabric floated over her skin and settled light as a butterfly. She bounced her fingers on a slight puff where the shoulder and sleeve met and trailed it to a fitted wrist cuff adorned with round pearl buttons. She touched the dome of one button and rubbed a tiny circle as if polishing a precious jewel to a radiant shine. Movement from her left prompted a sharp breath, followed by a terror-ridden scream. She pointed to the woman's hand. "Where the hell does that go?"

Miss Aimee startled and clutched her chest. "Oh, Lacey dear. This?" She held the item between two fingers. "This does not go anywhere on, or in you, for that matter. It's a hook, a button hook for fastening the buttons down the back of your dress for pity's sake. I am sorry for frightening you."

"Well, that thing," she said pointing to the button hook, "nearly scared the freckles off my nose."

"You don't have freckles on your nose."

"See what I mean?" *That was way too easy.*

"You, my dear Lacey, almost gave me a heart attack." Miss Aimee fastened the buttons in back and Sue Ellen entered the room with a rose-colored sash. She handed it to her mother who tied it around Lacey's waist. Miss Aimee took a few steps back to observe her creation. "Sweetheart, your pa will not recognize you. It is sinful, positively sinful what that shade of burgundy does to your dazzling eyes. I must say, I have never in all my days seen anyone with your eye color, except your ma, and now you. I'm guessing they are a deep violet. Did you realize when you smile, your eyes shine with tiny sparkles of lilac?"

One thought kept circling in Lacey's head. *Iffin' anybody sees me lookin' like this, I'll drown myself in Hostetter Creek.*

Miss Aimee took Lacey's hand and led her to a standing, rectangular mirror. The second her image reflected, she jerked to see who stood at her side. She gulped and with a slow motion returned her gaze to the looking glass and smoothed her palms over the material. The corset heightened her breasts, allowing the rounded tops to appear above the delicate lace of the bodice. The lace resembled a cobweb and she pressed and rolled it between her fingers. Her hands slid down the sides of the gown to her…waist? *Mercy, I've never had a waist, have I?* She fluttered her fingers over waves and curls in her dark, sun-streaked hair. Her curious hands traced along the sides of the burgundy dress. She drew a sharp inward breath and clawed her fingers to undo the tiny buttons marching down the back and demanded, "Take it off. I want it all off."

"Sweetheart." Miss Aimee hurried to place her palms on Lacey's shoulders. She looked into the girl's pleading eyes. "I know this must be difficult for you, and—she pointed to the ragged overalls and torn shirt strewn on the floor—"I am not blaming your pa for raising you like a boy. He did the best he knew, but you are a beautiful young lady." She wiped a wisp of hair from Lacey's cheek. "A beautiful young lady who should wear pretty dresses and"—she fondled Lacey's curls—"fancy hairstyles every day."

Even though she fought to contain them, Lacey's eyes filled with tears as Miss Aimee once again turned her to face the mirror. She knew Lacey Autumn Kendall, the Tomboy of Calhoun County, but she sure didn't recognize the lady whose stunning image stared back.

NEW HARMONY, MONTANA

1873

acey's eyes flew open when her head bumped against the inner wall of the stagecoach. She stared at her two traveling companions. An old man drooled tiny bubbles from the side of his mouth, and his wife snored like a razorback sow, her head bobbing to the rhythm of the coach.

She chuckled as a vision of Pa's jaw-dropping stare popped into her mind. *He hadn't recognized his own flesh and blood.* No wonder, she had hardly recognized *herself*. She smoothed her hand over the skirt of the burgundy dress and couldn't help noticing the fabric *was* a bit pretty, and soft. The lace edges reminded her of the way Ma prettied the cloth bookmarks she placed in her Bible.

She pushed aside a curtain the color of maple syrup and peeked outside. Thank goodness New Harmony appeared straight ahead. The train ride had been comfortable enough, she reckoned, but one more minute of the coach's stiff seat, and she was fixing to get out and walk.

She pulled out a pair of ivory gloves and a crochet-edged handkerchief Miss Aimee had stuffed into the flowered carpetbag along with a bunch of ridiculous dresses and what she called, pretties. Yeah, perty ugly. If Pa hadn't threatened to make her stay in Montana longer if she embarrassed her aunt, the gloves and handkerchief would have found use on her backside before getting tossed into the train's crapper. Lacey had taken her shirt and overalls from Miss Aimee's floor and crammed them inside the bag. *I ain't gonna dress like some sissy-prissy when I get to Aunt Molly's.*

When they came to a stop, Lacey watched the driver's dust-covered, black cowboy boots step down from his elevated seat. He opened the door and offered Lacey his hand for help. She passed him the carpetbag and stepped to the street, scanning the small group of folks greeting the arrivals, but saw no sign of Aunt Molly.

The driver tossed her carpetbag onto the planked walkway, and Lacey took a gander at her surroundings. Dust from passing horses swirled at her feet and crept like a soft brown cloud onto her dress. She viewed the words painted on wood signs hanging above the door of each establishment across the street: General Mercantile, Telegraph Office, Stardust Eatery, Fronie Helfrich's Boardinghouse, and Miss Clemmie's Café. Then this side: Bank of New Harmony, Sheriff's Office/Jail, Crystal Saloon, Blacksmith, and Livery. A white church with a red door and pointed steeple stood on the hillside beyond Miss Clemmie's. Lacey figured the large piece of land behind the church surrounded by a white picket fence probably held the town's dead folk.

The Montana sun shone from a clear blue sky and she wiped her brow with the sleeve of her dress, then used the handkerchief to dab beads of sweat from the tip of her nose and chin. She pulled the gloves off and fanned her face.

Aunt Molly, where are you? She tapped the tip of her fancy, laced-up boot before grabbing her carpetbag and taking a step toward the street.

"May I help you, ma'am?" said a deep-timbered voice at her side.

Oh, for criminy sakes, one of the local yokels wants to chitchat. She turned to tell him oh-so-politely to jump in the nearest creek but couldn't get her mouth to form actual words. With a hard swallow, her gaze traveled from the dark hair falling out beneath the man's black Stetson in waves around his sun-bronzed face to the rich outline of shoulders straining against a white linen shirt. She glanced at her dress searching for the wagon marks that surely must be there, signaling she'd been run over, died, and gone to heaven.

He looked devilishly handsome and more rugged than a cedar fence post. His eyes gleamed a startling crystal blue as endless as the Montana sky. The intensity of his gaze drew her close and her mouth went drier than cornbread cooling on a porch rail. *I'm gonna be needin' me some butter.*

He removed the Stetson. "Name's Brandon, Brandon Chandler."

Lacey struggled to speak and when her lips finally moved, she managed to say, "Lacey … umm, umm, Kendall. Lacey Autumn Kendall. *This man is twice as good lookin' as any I ever seen or dreamed about.* "Pleased to make your acquaintance." She hoped she hadn't said that good looking comment out loud, but she couldn't be sure of anything right now. Thank goodness she'd listened to what the polite church ladies said whenever new folks showed up to hear about Jesus.

"The pleasure is all mine, Miss Kendall. I have to say, you look a bit lost." He flashed her a gleaming smile before glancing at her carpetbag. "Are you new to these parts?"

"Yep. My aunt was 'spose to meet the stagecoach, but I reckon she's runnin' late. I'm fixin' to mosey across the street to wait fer her."

"Miss Kendall … Miss Kendall?" A tall, rail thin man scurried toward her waving a piece of paper.

"I'm Lacey Kendall," she said.

"Miss Kendall, I'm Horace Sparker from the telegraph office." The lanky man shuffled his feet and said, "I have a message for you. Well, I have a message for you if Rueben Augustus Kendall is a relation of yours?"

"Pa? Rueben Kendall is my pa, so I reckon it's fer me. What kinda message? What is it?"

"I overheard the driver." He motioned toward the stagecoach. "I heard him say you were a Kendall arriving from Nebraska, so I'll give the message to you." He toyed with the telegram's edges. "This here is from Joe, err, Joseph Jacobson. He's the president over there at the New Harmony Bank." He took a deep breath and sighed.

Lacey darted her hands onto her hips, carpetbag and all. "Mister, you're poppin' around like a fart in a skillet. Now, tell me what yer gonna tell me."

"Miss Kendall, I sure am sorry to bring you such terrible news —"

"Terrible news? What happened, what's wrong?" Lacey dropped her carpetbag and stared at the messenger. Every time he spoke, a thin line of spittle rose and fell between his top and bottom lips.

"Your aunt. I'm sorry, Miss Kendall, but your aunt, Miss Molly Kendall." He stopped, his gaze darting between Lacey and his boots, before saying, "I'm afraid she passed away four days ago."

"Died? Aunt Molly is," Lacey's voice broke, "d-d-dead?"

"I'm sure sorry, ma'am." He swayed from one foot to the other before handing her the telegram and rushing back across the street.

Lacey made swirls in the dirt with the tip of her boot and whispered, "This is awful, just awful."

Brandon's voice softened. "I'm sorry, ma'am."

Lacey jumped. She'd forgotten the handsome stranger stood beside her. "I'm at a loss fer words," she said. "I don't know what to say. Aunt Molly, dead? Land's sake."

"Would you like me to carry your bag to the boardinghouse for the night?"

"What? Excuse me?"

"Your bag." Brandon gestured to the flowered carpetbag. "You'll need a place to stay the night seeing how the stagecoach won't leave until early morning."

"And why in tarnation would I take the stagecoach in the mornin'?" Aunt Molly, God rest her soul, just provided her a ticket to freedom. Not only did this mean an escape from Pa's rules and her ornery brothers, but she'd live wherever Aunt Molly had a homestead and have the kind of life only imagined in her wildest dreams.

"Well," he said. "I thought —"

"You thought wrong," she interrupted. "I got every intention of stayin' on here." Lacey looked over her shoulder as a noisy wagon passed behind. "But I don't have the foggiest idea where Aunt Molly's homestead sits." She rocked back on the heels of her boots. "You wouldn't know how I could git a ride out to her place, wouldya?"

Brandon crossed thick, tanned arms over his chest. "I suppose, I could take you out there," he said. "But if I were you, I'd be hauling myself right back where I came from on the next stagecoach."

"But you aren't me, now are you?" The streamlined muscles of Brandon's arms threatened to bulge right through his shirt-sleeves, causing her insides to feel jittery. "And I don't recall askin' yer opinion on the matter." She reached for her bag. *Who does this handsome stranger think he is, telling me what to do?*

"I know we just met," Brandon said. "And I feel awkward bringing a business matter to you so soon, but I want to be the first to offer a handsome price for your aunt's land. A fair settlement I guarantee your family will accept with pleasure. In fact, I —"

"Aunt Molly's land? No, her land is not fer sale."

"Miss Kendall, you will reconsider when you hear my generous *cash* offer. I —"

"Chandler? Did you say yer name was Chandler?"

"Brandon Chandler." He nodded with a wink. "Please, call me Brandon."

"Well, Chandler, are you daft, drunk, or just plain stupid?" Lacey asked pointedly. "The Kendalls ain't gonna sell my aunt's property now, or ever. It ain't fer sale."

Brandon stared at her for a few seconds before a nerve in his jaw twitched. He snatched her carpetbag and swatted the powdered dust with a few vigorous hand sweeps. Without another word, he stormed across the street. "If you want a ride out to her place," he barked over his shoulder, "then get yourself over here. Your aunt's property is about two miles that way."

Lacey stared daggers at his retreating backside and would have liked to tar and feather the cowpoke right there in the street, but he might be the only ride out to Aunt Molly's place. *Why did he behave like such a rascal, anyways?* She lifted the flounced edges of her dress to sidestep what she swore the cowpoke led her straight toward — a rather large pile of steaming horse apples.

Brandon offered his hand as assistance to the wagon step and the narrow seat. Lacey thought he hesitated a moment longer than necessary before releasing his bold grip. A tingling warmth remained in her fingertips seconds after he tossed the carpetbag inside the wagon.

He climbed in and sat next to her, tightened the reins, and made a click-click sound to signal the pair of horses to trot. "This won't be too long of a ride, Miss Kendall. If you don't mind my asking, where do you call home?"

"Miss Kendall? You can call me that but I sure as hell ain't gonna call you mister anything. Whaddja wanna know? Oh yeah, Nebraska, that's where I call home, at least until now." She sighed before continuing. "I ain't seen Aunt Molly in years and can't believe she's dead." Her fingers traced the edges of the handkerchief Miss Aimee gifted to her. She thought about happy times spent with her aunt. "I'll hafta wire Pa and tell him what happened. Her brows drew together. " What happened, anyway?"

"Can't say." Brandon shrugged his shoulders. "Seems like it was her heart." His left eyebrow rose a fraction. "You're not serious about staying in Montana by yourself, are you?"

Lacey straightened her shoulders against the backboard. "I am. Aunt Molly lived here fer a spell alone, and I reckon she liked it fine."

After a stunned silence, Brandon cast a stern glance at Lacey's profile. "You know, there are mountain lions, grizzly bears, and the like out there in the woods. If I were you, I wouldn't stray too far from your aunt's cabin." He nodded at the carpetbag on the floor. "I see you didn't bring a shotgun or rifle. You got a revolver in your bag?"

"I gotta get some stuff." She stared out over the vast wilderness and made a purposeful shudder. "Mountain lions and bears? Land's sake."

Brandon cast a quick glance in her direction. "And coyote and lots of snakes. Yes indeed, about every kind of snake you can imagine. Poisonous too. All I can say is when you go outside, you best watch your step, especially after dark when you can't see those rascals until you've stepped on one and felt it slither under your foot, or worse yet, take a bite out of you. Now, there's a good-sized woodpile out by your aunt's smokehouse. Remember, snakes love sunning on stacks of wood."

She caught herself before pealing off a snort of laughter. *Did this thick-chested cowpoke think I ain't never chopped wood, or seen no danged snake? My mama didn't born me in the woods to be scared by a stinkin' owl.* Lacey folded her hands in her lap, glanced at Brandon, and decided to have a little fun. She managed a gasp. "Snakes?"

"Big, enormous snakes. One more thing. Wear thick gloves when you dig through the wood pile. Like I said, some are poisonous and have killed ranchers a lot heavier than me."

He turned his head, but Lacey didn't miss how his lips inched into a smile when he conveyed this horrendous news. *Wait till I tell him I've caught snakes, skinned 'em, and fried 'em for breakfast a time or two.*

The wagon bumped over the dirt road leading out of town, passing yellow daisies, mullein, purple corn-flower, and the brilliant blues and reds of Indian paintbrush. A few scattered chimneys spouted puffs of smoke and cows grazed on the plentiful prairie grasslands. The air smelled fresh with rich, hearty soil and pastured livestock.

Lacey smiled and decided New Harmony might not be such a bad place to live after all.

Brandon pointed as a homestead came into view. "There's your Aunt Molly's place," he said and kept his attention focused on her profile.

Lacey's hand slapped over her heart. "I'm so glad it ain't leanin' over. I fell asleep fer a spell on the stagecoach and got woken by the most dreadful nightmare. I seen the cabin pitched to one side like ours back home. I always feared it would fall and squish me while I slept."

The cabin appeared simple, yet comfortable. A short, straight chimney rose from the center of the left side and further back stood a stone smokehouse and the notorious woodpile. A faded red barn, in desperate need of repairs and a coat or two of paint, stood to the right. As they neared, Lacey noticed the handle of a storm cellar lid jutting from the ground between the cabin and the barn.

Brandon halted the horses and placed the reins on the footboard before stepping to the ground.

Not thinking how a long dress differed from the overalls she wore every day, Lacey stepped on the hem and lunged forward six arm-flailing steps before falling face-first into the dirt and sparse grass.

Brandon rushed to offer his hand. "Are you all right?"

With chin lifted, she looked the rascal straight in the eyes. "There'll be a frozen creek in hell 'afore I go arse over tit and don't come out swingin'." She swatted at his outreached hand. "Get outta my way." After standing, she snatched the hem of the soiled dress and gave it a good shaking as she stalked to the cabin.

Brandon quickened his pace and reached the door ahead of her. It creaked painfully on its hinges, and he winced while making a sweeping gesture to motion her inside.

She stepped onto the planked floor and smelled a faint hint of perfume. *Must be what Aunt Molly smelt like.* A fireplace stood against the left wall with a mantel clock, and black-bottomed pots and pans hung above the firebox on forged iron hooks. Poised at an angle facing the hearth's right corner sat a slat-backed rocker; a woven basket filled with multicolored scraps of fabric and sewing supplies rested on its seat as if left for just a moment. The kitchen beyond contained a pie safe and a cast iron range taking a portion of the back wall. Atop a sawbuck table rested a stack of blue and white multisized mixing bowls, a green kerosene lamp, and a candy bowl with a scalloped, gold-edged rim. A bed hugged the right side of the wall and at the foot rested a steamer trunk with thick, brown leather straps. She ran her hands over a multicolored biscuit quilt laying atop a feather mattress. It looked like the one Ma made before she and Pearl — the infant who would have been her baby sister — died in childbirth. An oval mirror on a stand held by fancy spindles for legs, and a tub for bathing, sat alongside the wall and completed the room.

"I'll be on my way and let you get settled," Brandon said, breaking the silence. He set her bag aside and turned to leave, stopping at the fireplace mantel to set the time and wind the clock. "My cabin is on the other side of the meadow," he said, pointing due south, "separated from your aunt's property by South Sunday Creek. I want to talk to you again about purchasing this property."

She opened her mouth to protest and he raised his hands in surrender.

"Not now." He tipped his Stetson. "For now, I'll take my leave and let you settle in." He walked across the threshold and closed the door.

First things first. Lacey opened the steamer trunk by the bed and laughed at the ridiculous dresses decorated with frilly lace and ribbons tied into bows. And gloves. Gloves were for working and fixing things, keeping hands warm come a cold day. Why on earth would anyone have a pair made of lace, much less a pair in darn near every color? Same with hats — some decorated fancy with feathers and streamers, three made from straw with nothing different about them except color. Why in tarnation did Aunt Molly think she needed these nonsense clothes and why wasn't there a pair of overalls and a flannel shirt among all this mess?

She rolled her eyes skyward, undressed, and pulled her good old faithful overalls and shirt from the carpetbag. She unpacked and tossed the clothes Miss Aimee insisted on sending with her into the trunk and slammed the lid shut. Pulling the sheets off the mattress, she went in search of a bucket and soap.

Outside, the pitcher pump splashed icy water into a chipped, white metal bucket with a rusted wire handle. She washed the linens, rinsed them in the water's flow, and hung them to dry on a line between two trees. After wiping her hands on the bib of her overalls, she snatched the empty bucket.

Turning toward the cabin, she stopped dead in her tracks and hurled the metal bucket at a tall, suited stranger standing directly in front of her. It whacked him straight upside the head before clanging onto the ground and taking a three-roll tumble.

"What the tarnation are you doin' on my property?" she demanded, crouching low, her hands becoming fighter's fists.

"Miss, I did not intend to startle you," the stranger said, rubbing above his right ear. "I am sorry…and, I promise, I am not here to cause harm."

Lacey thought he sure had a funny way of talking. He had a gaunt face and small, beady eyes like a blackbird. He wore a beige shirt with stitches of colorful threads sewn around the shoulders. A black vest hit about the waist, and he had more pockets than she'd ever seen. *Nobody needs all them pockets.* A gold watch and chain hung by an open slant in the material and attached to what looked like a fancy gold fishing hook. *I wonder why Mr. Fancy-Pants showed himself here? He sure 'nuff looks outta place.*

"I didn't hear anyone comin'," she managed to say. "You appeared outta nowhere and plum scared the living Jehoshaphat outta me." Lacey glanced around for a horse but didn't see hide nor hair of one. She stepped farther into the yard and glimpsed a shiny black buggy in the pasture behind the smokehouse.

"I did not intend to startle you, miss. The wildflowers invited further investigation, and I stopped to pick a bouquet. I saw you from across the meadow and chose to make your acquaintance."

He touched a hand to his chest. "Please, I beg of you, pardon my rude behavior. I am Winston Beaumont the Third, of Birmingham."

"Mr. Beaumont, you ain't gotta beg. I'm Lacey Autumn Kendall." She threw her middle name in there since his name sure sounded an awful lot more important than hers. "I'm new to these here parts," Lacey said. "I reckon I ain't real sure where Birmin-ham is…wait, ain't that in Alerbammer?"

He pulled on one end of his thin mustache. "No, Birmingham is a city in England."

She gulped. What in tarnation brought the man here from England? She couldn't tear her eyes from his pale fingertips as they smoothed the curled ends of his wiry mustache like he reckoned himself the biggest toad in the mud puddle. It looked like grease got plastered on it or something. Surely it ain't pine tar. Lacey forced herself to stop staring at the slick lip hair. "What brings you from Birmin-ham all the way to New Harmony?"

"A dear lady friend," the man answered. "I am here to visit a friend who taught in London at the Lady's School of Proper Decorum."

Lacey swore somebody tossed a hornet's nest into her mouth and it tumbled right down to her gut-sack. "This umm, this friend's name wouldn't be Molly Louise Kendall, would it?"

His face appeared unfamiliar with the smile attempting to form on his lips as he eased the grip on his mustache. "It most certainly would." He held his right palm over his heart. "Pray tell, have I the propitious good fortune to arrive at Miss Kendall's doorstep after the hideous directions I received in town?"

"Yessir, yeh sure 'nuff came across the Kendall place," Lacey said. Shoot, she just met the fella and already had to give him bad news. "But I'm afraid I got somethin' awful t'tell yeh, and I dunno how t'say it after yeh traveled all the way from London t'see Aunt Molly and everythin'." Lacey knew she rattled on, but she couldn't help herself. Pa called it one of her female diarrhea-of-the-mouth shortcomings.

"What? Tell me what?" He looked around in a dramatic display of panic. "I pray nothing detrimental has bestowed itself upon Mademoiselle Kendall."

"She is de…de…deceased is what she is." *Deceased sounds better than stiffer'n a barn door dead…and probly nicer than tit's up.*

"This cannot be," Beaumont gushed. "How dreadful. I do not know what to say. I am speechless."

"Yessiree, it came as quite a shock to me, too," Lacey said. "I came here all the way from Nebraska to stay with my aunt fer a spell, and only learned she was six feet under when I arrived. It's been quite a dreadful day." Lacey picked a wad of white puff from her eyelash. "Doggone blasted cottonwood tree," she murmured, gazing into the tall branches hanging above her head. "I reckon I'll be livin' here now."

"You will…" He seemed to choke on the words. "You will what?"

"I'm fixin' to stay on here. And mister," she said, scrunching her forehead, "you're gonna stand there a long time with yer mouth wide open like that 'afore a roasted chicken flies in?"

His hand flew to his mouth as his lips pinched shut and his squinty eyes squinted further.

"Heck, mister, there ain't nothin' for me back home but work and there's plenty of that to keep me busy 'round here. When 'ya plannin' to go back to, what'd you say? Birmin-ham?"

"I am uncertain of my itinerary," he said and took a step toward the smokehouse.

"Are yeh leavin', Mr. Beaumont?" She wondered why he'd traveled all this way to see Aunt Molly.

"I have a room at the boardinghouse in town," he answered. "We shall further our conversation another time."

"All right, then," she called. *What in tarnation makes him talk so highfalutin? The feller must think he's slicker'n snot on a glass doorknob.*

She watched him ride away, then reckoned it would be a good idea to search around a bit to see what sort of supplies she needed to buy. The freestanding pie shelf in the kitchen held four cooking bowls, two well-used pie tins, and an iron cornbread pan. A skillet sat tucked inside the cast iron range; it looked to be about a ten-incher. Along the west wall hung several narrow wood shelves holding glass jars filled with flour, sugar, and an assortment of herbs, coffee, tea, and oyster crackers, plus one scurrying mouse. Lacey lunged to catch the rodent as he ran between her boots and across the floor. She tried to wack him with a dryin' towel, but he ran under the door and straight to freedom. "I'm gonna get you later," she hollered before returning the towel. She noted salt, cayenne pepper, cinnamon, and nutmeg. Cooking utensils hung on hooks to the right of the cookstove along with two potholders.

Lacey reached for a vial of murky liquid, held it to her nose and sniffed. She jerked her head back at the overwhelming smell of the fluid, thinking it resembled a mixture of wood alcohol and vanilla. A bowl of what appeared to have been peaches and berries now served as a haven for a thousand or more fruit flies and plenty of fuzzy green mold.

She took the soiled bowl and vial outside and chucked the contents into the grass before deciding to take a gander inside the barn. Peering into the darkened enclosure, she took note of an old wagon, an assortment of tools and wood boards lying in disarray, and strewn containers she'd investigate later. She pulled the door shut and headed toward the smokehouse but found it empty. She had hoped there might be meat hanging to dry. Aunt Molly must have taken most of her meals in town.

Outside, the root cellar opened via a trap door built into the ground. Lacey clutched the iron handle and pulled the door straight toward the sky and over, allowing the hinges to lay it flush with the ground. She peered into the darkness below, then returned to the cabin to fetch the lantern. She returned to the narrow steps and watched as the glowing light cast eerie shadows that danced across the walls as she descended. The cellar, lined with shelves, held glass jars of fruits and vegetables, but nothing to cause a hooping and a hollering. Lacey spied jars of strawberry preserves and carried one back to the kitchen, along with two jars of green beans.

She hadn't been inside the cabin long before a brisk knock on the door startled her. She opened the barrier and recognized the telegraph officer from town.

"Miss Lacey?" He looked left, right, and kitty-corner, dang near everywhere except at her clothing.

She glanced at her oversized shirt and overalls. *Iffin' the townfolk think I'm gonna dress like some filly, I got news for 'em.*

"Hello again, Mr. …?"

"Sparker, Horace Sparker."

"Whaddya want?" She couldn't keep the annoyed tone from her voice.

"The will, Miss Lacey," he said to a hair on top of her head. "Your Aunt Molly left a will, and you need to be at the reading Friday afternoon. You are her next of kin, right?"

"Well, Pa is her brother, but he's back home in Nebraska. So, I reckon I am. Now, what time is this here readin'?"

"Two o'clock, and I can escort you to the bank if that would be to your liking?"

"I reckon I'll agree to yer offer. I got a hankerin' to look around a bit and seen my aunt's wagon in the barn. I need to buy a horse to pull it. I'll see you on Friday then, Mr. Sparker."

"Thank, thank you, Miss Lacey." He sprinted back to his buggy.

"Land's sake," Lacey murmured, returning to the cupboard. She'd need to visit the General Mercantile after the will reading. After opening the green beans and eating her fill, she snatched a handful of stale oyster crackers and dipped them in strawberry preserves. Her hunger temporarily satisfied, she went outside and brought in the dry sheets.

Lacey laid on the floor next to the bed and swiped her hand underneath as far back as she could reach. She yanked out every item her fingertips touched. *Aunt Molly, where did you hide your money?* Pa hardly gave her enough for the trip, much less to buy supplies. She grabbed one book, and then several more before mumbling the titles of Molly's hardbound treasures: *The American Toilet, Etiquette for Ladies, Godey's Lady's Book.* She tossed them aside, stood, and sat on the edge of the bed. *What's a buncha dang books gonna do fer me?* Putting the clean, dry sheets back on the bed, she tossed the quilt on top and nestled in for the night.

*L*acey woke early in the morning, her eyes mere slits as she grabbed her pillow and hurled it at the window.

"Shut up," she screamed at the constant chirping of baby birds nesting in the oak tree outside her window. Minutes later, after throwing the covers aside, she dressed in her shirt and overalls, then pulled her hair into a loose knot on top of her head. After eating a spoonful of preserves, she opened the cabin door and propped the straw broom in place.

Faint rhythmic hoofbeats coming from the soft grass of the meadow caught her attention and with a wedge of her hand, she shielded the bright sunshine. The rider sure looked like that handsome, annoying rascal from yesterday. Knowing she always had flyaway hairs, she gave her hands a good licking and patted down the sides of her head.

"Good morning," Brandon said as he dismounted and draped the black stallion's reins over a low tree limb. He patted the giant's neck and walked toward Lacey, gesturing at the horse. "Meet Thunder."

"He's a beauty," she said. "What brings you here so early in the mornin'?" *He sure is eyeballing my overalls funny.* "What you lookin' at?"

Brandon shook his head. "Nothing, it's nothing."

"So, whaddya want?" She bent to pull a tall piece of wild grass from the yard and stuck it in the corner of her mouth. Her gaze lingered on his blue eyes longer than she intended. She wanted to kick herself.

He tipped his Stetson and shrugged. "Does a neighbor have to want something to make a friendly visit?"

"I reckon not," Lacey said. "I reckon I ain't used to no social visits. Back where I come from, iffin' somebody calls on yeh come early mornin', it means yer backside is bein' hauled off to jail, or some poor bastard's gone tits up."

He furrowed his brow. "I, uh, did come by this morning with something on my mind." He propped his right foot on a tree stump, leaned forward, and removed the Stetson. He held it in his hand as if studying its creases. "Now, listen to what I have to say. I'm prepared to offer a substantial amount of *cash* for this land." His tone was matter of fact. "I'll even take it off your hands at a much higher price than what the property is worth. I —"

"Didn't I tell yeh it ain't fer sale?" she interrupted. "Now, just you listen fer a minute to what I have to say." She worked the blade of grass to the other side of her mouth. "Let me ask yeh somethin', Chandler. Are you unschooled, or dumb as a rock stupid?"

He dropped his foot from the stump, his voice now deep and strained. "Be reasonable, not to mention realistic." His left eyebrow raised higher than the right as he pointed his finger.

"When you arrived in New Harmony, the last thought on your mind was living alone in your aunt's cabin. The best thing for you to do is pack your bags and head back home to your pa. And you know it. You're just too stubborn to admit it." He replaced the Stetson as he walked in lengthy strides back to his horse.

"That's right. You go on and git the hell outta here," Lacey hollered. "I got work to do today, and none of it includes wastin' time talkin' to the likes of you." She stomped toward the cabin.

"Hear what I'm telling you," he called to her backside. "It's hard living out here. You'll sell and wish you'd high-tailed it out of these parts sooner."

Lacey turned when she reached the door and watched him ride from the property. "That's right. You go on, get off this here land." She snatched the propped broom and swept with renewed fire as her thoughts trailed back to his words. Bristling with anger, she swept the dust-caked threshold with the warning in his voice echoing in her ears. *Wish you'd high-tailed it outta these parts.* She vowed with a quiet firmness, "I'll show you, Brandon Chandler," and made another wild sweep with the broom.

She tidied the inside of the cabin, pulled the quilt on the bed, and then licked the remaining preserves from her breakfast spoon. *I sure am tired of eating nothin' but these gall darn preserves.*

Lacey took off toward South Sunday Creek after deciding not to waste a sunny day indoors, plus she needed to walk off some steam. The wispy tops of the tall grasses in the meadow swayed in tune to a gentle breeze and tickled her outstretched palms. She inhaled the honey-like sweetness of the flowers, sparking a distant memory of Ma's Sunday perfume. As a slight gust of wind rippled the grass, the bluebells appeared to nod agreement with this sudden recollection.

She missed Ma and her gentle ways. Soft-spoken, even to her rowdy brothers, she never raised her voice. But those boys sure walked a straight line. Lacey supposed it was that way because they adored her, and that if she mentioned misbehavior to Pa, he'd haul their soon-to-be-sore butts out to the woodshed for a solid whooping.

Lacey entered the tree line. The surrounding twigs crackled and crunched under her boots, and the scents turned earthy. Brown mushrooms grew aplenty near the base of several trees and she made note to pick a batch. A few rabbits scampered about searching for tender greens under the bristles and wisps of moss. She plucked a handful of plump blackberries from a bramble butted against a rusted wire fence and ate the juicy, sweet berries right then and there. As she made her way down a gentle embankment, the croaking of frogs alerted her that the creek would soon come into view. Breaking past the tree line, she shielded her eyes to deflect the millions of diamond glitters casting on the sparkling stream. The gemstone-blue water beckoned her for a quick dip and after her confrontation with Brandon, perhaps it would help ease her inner fire.

She swatted at two dragonflies whizzing past her head, glancing over one shoulder and then the other. She didn't figure anybody was around, or she'd have heard or seen them. The chirping songs of various birds and an occasional squirrel rustling among the branches were the only sounds. She pulled off her boots and overalls before undoing the top two buttons and bringing the shirt over her head. Small, darting fish tagged her legs as she entered the cool water. Invigorated, she eased toward the deeper water, submerging herself. Lacey stood to fan her hands through the water, sending gentle ripples around her body, then dove underneath.

Brandon crouched among the dense cattail reeds and foxtail barley on the opposite bank, not sure what to do. He'd rinsed out a bucket used to carry feed to the chickens when Lacey appeared out of nowhere on the other side of the creek. She cast several glances over her shoulders, but before he could call out to make his presence known, she'd stripped herself naked. Well, if he were being honest with himself, yes, he had time to call out to her. He didn't want to. The woman may dress like a boy, but no doubt possessed the body of one fine, desirable woman.

If she looked over and caught him staring — he chuckled to himself — if Lacey did see him, she would holler about getting the law out here to shoot him, or worse. He attempted to stand, but his legs betrayed him. Never had a woman made him weak in the knees. Silently, he scolded himself for remaining hidden, but wouldn't change a thing if it happened again. Plus, he couldn't stand and call out to her now even if he wanted to. With his physical reaction to this sensual woman, she'd think, hell, he didn't know what she'd think. He found her beauty intoxicating. When he realized he couldn't look away, he figured he better not only look but get away as fast as possible.

As he stood from his crouched position, she emerged from under the water not fourteen feet away. She tilted her head back and with her palms open, wiped wet strands of hair from her face, then cleared her eyes. Her incredible breasts gleamed with droplets of water and he found he couldn't move, didn't want to. Once again, her seductive image caused the messages in his brain to scatter like straw on a dance floor. His legs intended to follow the order to flee but his heart stopped the signal. Her perfect breasts rose and fell with each breath, their fullness streaked with water and kissed by a ribbon of sunshine he followed downward to a tiny, shapely waist disappearing beneath the surface of South Sunday Creek. What he wouldn't pay for a pair of glasses that penetrated water.

When Lacey opened her eyes, she released such a string of foul language, she had to invent some dirty words to finish her paragraph. A few of them — the likes of which she was sure Brandon's ears hadn't been privy to — she shouted before lowering neck deep into the water. "What the hell are you lookin' at, you slimy, sneaky son of a —"

Brandon raised his hands in defense and an easy smile played at the corners of his lips.

"How dare you? How dare you hide in the bushes like that!"

"How dare I nothing. I wasn't hiding from anyone." He grasped the handle of the feed bucket. "I was sitting here minding my business when you came traipsing over to the creek bed —"

"You shoulda made yer presence known."

"I would have," he said with a naughty-boy smile. "But you didn't give me a chance before shedding all your clothes."

Lacey eased further into the water as a hot blush crept onto her cheeks. "Of all the — you were starin' at my titties."

"Is that?"— Brandon pointed to her chest and waggled his finger back and forth —"what those are?" He chuckled. "I've seen bigger skeeter bites." He tipped his Stetson back, bent forward, and squinted. "Seriously? Those are your titties? Point to them, so I know I'm looking at the right freckles." He shrugged when she didn't comply. "If you say so. Now, if you'll excuse me, ma'am." He repositioned his Stetson, gave the brim a quick two-fingered good-bye tip, and threw her a lazy one-handed salute. "I have a lot of work to do today, and none of it includes wasting time talking to the likes of you." He took a step, adding, "Much less straining to see titties that don't exist."

"I'm gonna git the sheriff after you, and I'm gonna tell him to shoot yeh, and shoot yeh good, shoot yeh dead!" She glowered at his retreating form before releasing a long, shrieking, fist-pounding scream and retreating toward the bank, and her clothes. *I'll get even with that miserable rotten, no-good excuse fer a cowboy.* She scurried back to the cabin, her empty stomach growling with every maddening stomp.

acey reckoned since she was going into town for an important meeting, she would wear one of the dresses Miss Aimee packed in her carpetbag. She ran her hand over a soft, rose-colored dress with four loose, bouncy sections running around the whole thing. She put the dress over her head and since no one was watching, twirled in the mirror to see how it moved. She supposed dresses weren't *too* awful bad when there was nothing else to wear.

She peered out the window. A dark thundercloud released a heavy wall of rain about four miles out. *Horace, where are you?* The mantel clock showed pert-near two o'clock and she needed to be at the will reading at two o'clock sharp. She headed out to walk the distance when a buggy jostled over the hillside. *Finally.*

"I am rightfully sorry for arriving late, Miss Lacey," Horace said as he jumped from the buggy holding a rain-soaked umbrella and glancing at the sky. "I think the rains passed us, at least for now," he said and tossed the wet object under the seat. "You sure look pretty, Miss Lacey." He offered his hand to assist her onto the buggy before plopping next to her. "I had an urgent telegram to transcribe for Brandon Chandler, or I wouldn't have been running behind. It came in as I headed out the door of the telegraph office. I figured, since his place is yonder from yours, I would deliver it on my way over."

"A telegram?"

"Yes." He puffed like a regal rooster and stabbed both thumbs toward his chest. "I am the O-fficial telegraph officer in town."

Lacey wondered what kind of telegram Brandon had received. "I do hope everything is all right out at the Chandler place," she cooed. "Mercy, I'd hate to think something awful happened." She scrunched her eyebrows and feigned a mortified expression of concern.

"Miss Lacey, oh dear, I am sure everything is all right. Don't you go fretting one bit now."

"I can't help myself. I'm afraid this news has ruined my entire day." She forced a sniffle and fanned her face as if preparing for a faint.

Horace glanced over each shoulder and Lacey noticed his knees had started shaking. "I'm not supposed to say anything about no telegrams, Miss Lacey." He licked his lower lip and continued, "But seeing how upset you are, well, I can put you at ease. Brandon Chandler got the word…got word from his digging crew…the crew due out here next Monday." He pointed his chin forward. "That's all I can tell you."

Lacey's voice changed to a gentle purr. "Digging crew?"

"Yes." He glanced at Lacey and shifted in his seat. "He must think he is sitting on a gold mine or something. Heck, the land by South Sunday Creek is overflowing with milky quartz — that darn near whispers the promise of gold."

No wonder the scoundrel wants Aunt Molly's land. He thinks there's gold on the property. She didn't have the means to hire a crew to dig, nor could she expect to know the location of the gold. She'd have to outwit the greedy varmint to get the information.

When they reached town, Horace brought the buggy to a stop in front of the bank. He stumbled from the seat and scurried to help Lacey depart. She took his hand as Brandon was making his way down the walk escorting a proper-looking lady dressed in what appeared to be Sunday finery. The woman smiled at Brandon and cuddled up to him, her arm laced with his. *So, that's the kind of mess that twists Brandon's union suit.* Lacey allowed Horace to hold her hand an extra minute while she stepped to the walkway.

"Thank you. Why you are such a gentleman," Lacey said with a bright smile, hoping Brandon had noticed this exchange between Horace and herself. She released her grip and looked at the fancy etching scrawled on the door in front of her — *Bank of New Harmony*. Horace sidestepped to open the door, then followed Lacey inside.

"Miss Kendall, it is a pleasure to make your acquaintance," said a portly, redheaded man in a shiny, black-cherry vest, and striped trousers. "My name is Joseph Jacobson." The rotund banker walked toward her, a pocket watch in his left hand. He thrust the timepiece in front of his face in an exaggerated fashion and smirked.

"We's probly not more'n a minute or two behind schedule," Lacey said, hands on hips. "But, not nothin' a person with any *sense* would give a rat's ass about. So, banker Jacobson, whaddya want me fer?"

"A rat's wha — ?" He splayed chubby fingers over his heart and glanced at a co-worker. "Did I hear? Y-y-yes, I believe I did. Come, please, come into my office." He ushered her forward with a wave of his hand.

"Miss Lacey," Horace called to her retreating form, "I'll be right here waiting for you. Don't you worry about getting home, now, you hear? Don't you worry none."

Lacey stopped short. "Worried? Do I look worried, Horace? I wasn't worried when you was late coming t'fetch me, was I? No, I weren't, and I ain't worried now." She rolled her eyes, but realized the banker caused her anger, not Horace. Taking it out on him wasn't right. When she turned to apologize, the expression on Horace's face forced her to break out in a big smile. "Horace, you're grinnin' jis like a possum eaten' a sweet tater. I'm sorry fer snappin' atcha." She eyed Jacobson and proclaimed, "Why, if you were an inch taller, you'd be pert-near round, now wouldn't yeh?" She entered the banker's office.

"Please, have a seat," Jacobson said, shuffling sideways to pass beside her. He fanned his hand toward a black leather chair across from a big, fancy desk. He walked around the massive piece of furniture and barely sat before shuffling through a stack of papers. "Here we are." He pulled a document from the pile. "The Last Will and Testament of Molly Louise Kendall." He glanced at Lacey. "May I extend my condolences for your loss, Miss Kendall?"

"Thank you. It came as quite a shock, you know, her being dead and all." Lacey scrunched her eyebrows and rubbed her belly before focusing her attention outside the window. "Mr. Jacobson, can we shake a leg? My growling stomach's gittin' madder'n a bear with a sore ass."

"Actually," he said and stared at her for a second, "yes, Miss Kendall, I will communicate the information to you as quickly as possible to get you out of my — err, on your way." He cleared his throat. "She states her wishes clearly. Miss Molly Louise Kendall deeds her home and entire land tract to —"

"Pa," Lacey interrupted with a sigh. "He is her only living relative, you know, 'cept fer my ornery brothers." She leaned forward to rest her elbows on his desk and yawned. "Will Pa have trouble settlin' the paperwork from Nebraska?"

"Miss Kendall, you did not let me finish. Your aunt did not deed the land to your pa."

"What? Land's sakes, are yeh tellin' me the land will belong outside the Kendall kinfolk? Is that what yer tellin' me?" She stared into the banker's face and screeched, "Am I gonna hafta move back to Nebraska?"

He shrugged and cocked his head to the side. "I suppose that depends on you, Miss Kendall."

"Me? Why — what? Whaddya mean, me?"

"Well, it says *right here*." He pinched the top of the document, turned it, and scanned the words with his finger so she could read along. "Deeds her home and entire land tract to her niece, Lacey Autumn Kendall."

"What? She did what? She said what?"

"Yes. But it is conditional, Miss Kendall."

"Conditional, my skinny 'lil butt. You read her words." Lacey stood and pointed at the document. "I heard what you said. Aunt Molly deeds the whole shabang to me. HOT DANG!"

"Miss Kendall, please sit down and allow me to finish." He motioned to her vacated chair. "She specified her only niece,

Lacey Autumn Kendall, may live out her days in the cabin and homestead tract, if desired, but not as a lonely spinster like she did. She stipulates the deed will transfer to you free and clear if you become a married woman by the age of twenty. If not, the deed will transfer without prejudice to the adjacent landowner, Brandon Chandler, as compensation toward land conservation, preservation, and maintenance of years past and future."

Lacey merely stared at the man, her face blank, her heart pounding.

"Miss Kendall?" the banker said.

A soft gasp caught in her throat.

"Miss Kendall, are…are you, all right?"

Lacey fanned herself briskly. She had turned nineteen on her last birthday and in ten months, married?

"I gotta git hitched to inherit Aunt Molly's land? What in living tarnation was Aunt Molly thinkin'?" Her voice escalated. "And, and Brandon Chandler?" She stood and slammed her palms atop the desk, bent forward and screeched, "Was she polecat crazy?"

"Yes, ma'am. I mean, no ma'am, she wasn't polecat…umm, I mean, crazy. Per this last will and"— he pointed his finger straight at her nose —"I personally deemed her of sound mind. Word for word, Miss Kendall, those are her wishes."

"Does Chandler know 'bout Aunt Molly's will? About what it says and all?"

"Absolutely not. He knows nothing of your aunt's wishes and, I assure you, the intricacies and stipulations will remain confidential until, if needed, a second reading will take place with Mr. Chandler in attendance as a trustee."

"Over my dead body," she said, pointing her finger at the banker's nose, "will that haystack cowpoke own one speck of *my* duly inherited dirt." Lacey shook her hands at her sides in a futile attempt to stop them from trembling. A pounding heartbeat boomed in her temples. "Excuse me, banker Jacobson." She tapped her gloved index finger on the desk and bit her bottom lip. "I need some fresh air. I'll be in touch." Her legs weakened like soggy milk toast. She clenched the edge of his desk.

Hitched? If she didn't get hitched, her life consisted of Pa, farming chores, and her prankster brothers. *What about the gold*? Evidently, Brandon knew the location of those precious nuggets.

Jacobson walked to open the office door and asked, "Miss Kendall, are you going to be all right? Do you need assistance?"

"No, I'll be fine in a minute." With a creepy-crawly sensation in her legs, she re-entered the lobby. "Horace," she hollered, "I need to spend some time here in town. Is there a place we could meet later?"

"Sure, Miss Lacey. I would be happy to walk with you. Real happy."

"I'm sure you'd be happier'n a hog in a mud bath 'cept that don't mean yer walkin' with me." She teetered past him and called over her shoulder, "We'll meet at the General Mercantile in, how 'bout thirty minutes?"

"That will be fine. Just —" Horace called as the door clicked shut.

Lacey took a few hesitant steps down the walkway and stopped short when Brandon appeared carrying packages for *that* woman. How long did Miss Fancy-Dress think she needed to keep her hand on his forearm and giggle, for pity's sake? She turned back toward the bank as Winston Beaumont stepped into her path and startled the living daylights out of her.

"Miss Kendall, I have a matter of great importance —"

"Hang on to your britches fer a dang second and listen. That's the second time yeh scared the bedickens outta me. Make yer presence known 'afore sneakin' up on folks."

"Miss Kendall, please accept my humble apology. I had no intention —"

"Oh, fer land's sake, will yeh stop yackin' and tell me why yeh got in my way?"

"I have a matter to discuss and would prefer a private conversation. Where would you like to speak?"

A deep-gutted tummy growl planted an idea, and she motioned toward the Stardust Eatery. "Let's go there. I ain't et yet."

The wood floor of the restaurant creaked and popped as they walked to a table by the window covered with a white, heavily starched linen. A faded pair of red and white plaid curtains draped to the sides were secured by two oversized nails.

The waitress arrived at the table in a heartbeat. "Sorry, folks. It ain't lunch time yet. The only thing I can offer you is some good, strong coffee."

Winston nodded he'd have a cup. Lacey slammed the table with her palm and shook her head. "You ain't got no eats? And I could eat the south end of a north bound mule? Heck no, I ain't got no use fer black tar without no vittles to wash it down with."

"I'm sorry, miss." The woman hesitated a few seconds before fetching Winston a cup of the black liquid.

Lacey tossed her fan on the table, pulled the gloves off one finger at a time, and sat forward in the chair. *Why has this man traveled so far to see Aunt Molly?* She reckoned he wasn't old enough to be a beau.

Winston cleared his throat. "Have you met anyone from this village?"

"You mean here? Village? You callin' this bump in the road a village?" Lacey asked. "This here ain't no village. It's a town. A tee-oh-dubya-n town. And, as a matter of truth, I have. Yesterday, I met Horace Sparker." She pointed to the building across the street. "He's the telegraph officer and seems a little squirrely. Between you and me, iffin' his brains were leather, he wouldn't have enough to saddle a June bug." Lacey caught a glimpse of Brandon from the window. *Why the hell is he all spiffed up like he's goin' t'church or...or a'courtin'?* He stopped along the walkway with the snooty looking, well-uddered floozy.

Winston glanced out the window. "You know him?"

"Oh, him?" She waved her hand in a mock shoo-fly motion and shrugged. "That's Brandon Chandler. I met him yesterday when I arrived on the stagecoach. He took me out to Aunt Molly's cabin." Her attention returned to the sight outside. *What in tarnation could be so gall darn funny? Brandon and Miss Cantaloupe with their big, toothy smiles sure 'nuff looked like they were takin' a cotton to each other.*

"Lacey, your aunt and I were such jolly good friends. I loved her like a sister and will miss her dearly." He placed his hands on hers and cleared his throat. "I received a wire from her when I was in London. She asked me to come to New Harmony and start a school with her. A school for ladies." He sighed deeply and lowered his eyes.

Lacey slid her hands out from under his. "You sure 'nuff got clammy mitts," she said, crinkling her nose and wiping her hands on the tablecloth. "I don't get it," she said, cocking her head to the side. "Aunt Molly wanted to start a school in New Harmony? She didn't write Pa 'bout no school. Which reminds me, I gotta send a telegram off to Pa 'bout Aunt Molly dirt nappin' and all."

"Pa?" he asked.

"Yep, Pa back in Nebraska. She never mentioned him? Her brother? Rueben Augustus Kendall?"

"Yes, yes, of course she did." He took a sip of steaming coffee. "She spoke highly of her sibling."

"I don't know 'bout no sibling, but they's brother and sister. Nebraska," she said with a sigh. "Reckon I'll be headin' back there soon."

Winston's eyes perked wide. "Why? What makes you say that?"

"I just left the will readin'. Thought I'd stay on here, make this my home. Reckon I won't be inheritin' Aunt Molly's place after all."

His eyebrows headed north. "What did it say, Miss Kendall?"

She shook her head and frowned. "I gotta git hitched, I reckon. Because of Aunt Molly's wishes, I gotta git hitched to inherit her homestead."

He licked his lips. Twice.

The café door opened and Brandon stepped inside. The handsome man removed his black hat and still needed to duck to clear the archway. Lacey noticed his squared-off shoulders filled the ample entrance.

"Good day, Miss Kendall," Brandon said as he strode to their table.

She twisted a section of the tablecloth's hem between her fingers. She wasn't ready to see him yet; she needed time to think of a plan. Lost within a mesmerizing pool of blue eyes, a sensation akin to hot cider passed from the nape of her neck to the tips of her toes.

Brandon broke the silence. "I see you didn't take my advice. It's apparent you weren't on the stagecoach headed back to Rock Springs."

He looked incredibly imposing in a pressed and pleated black shirt sewn from material costing a lot more than anything she owned. Five flat, round buttons gleamed like gold nuggets against the garment. Lacey's gaze drifted to the slim waistline of his tailored pants before returning to the angular lines of his jaw, so distinct he appeared carved. She patted a bit of moisture from the side of her lip.

"No, I done told you I'm fixin' to stay on here," Lacey managed, and introduced the two men. She sensed a stiff, uncomfortable tension between them and reached for her gloves. "I suppose I should be on my way —"

Brandon raised his hands. "No need to leave on my account." He took a step back. "Good day, Winston. A pleasure to meet you, I'm sure." He turned and left the cafe.

Lacey quieted.

"Is something wrong?" Beaumont asked.

"No," she said. "The man is nothin' but a snake in the grass. He informed me, rather forcefully, he desires to buy Aunt Molly's homestead. Over my dead, pickled body will he get his hands on her land." She glanced at the time. "Heavens, I forgot about Horace." She stood and gathered her gloves and fan. "I intended on meetin' him some time ago."

Winston followed her out of the restaurant and Lacey watched Brandon assist "Miss Big Ole Titties" into his buggy and grab the reins.

As she and Winston stepped toward the street, Brandon's buggy passed and hit a sunken rut. The front wheel dipped hard, causing the muddy water inside to splash forcefully onto the front of Lacey's dress.

"Why, you miserable, rotten weasel. You did that on purpose." She turned toward Winston in disbelief. "Did you see him veer his buggy right toward that blasted mud hole?"

"I certainly did, Miss Kendall. Rest assured he will pay for this indignity."

Winston bid her adieu and she crossed the street to enter the telegraph office and send Pa the news of Aunt Molly's demise, then scurried to the General Mercantile. She gathered a few items from the shelves and picked out a shotgun, plus three boxes of shells. After promising Mr. Breedlove she'd make payment, he placed her items in a box and offered to hang onto her shotgun while she took the other purchases to Horace's buggy.

She mumbled a thank you and scurried out the door, stumbling over her feet and nearly losing her balance. There were a few small dirt clods in her path but nothing worth tripping over.

Horace waved her a big hello and sprinted to grab the box from Lacey's arms.

"I know I'm running behind," she said. "But it's too bad and can't be helped. I'll be right back." She hurried inside for her new gun, and on returning to the buggy, she handed it to Horace before hoisting herself into the seat.

"Shucks, Miss Lacey, this gun looks like it'd knock down a grizzly bear."

"I bought the right one then, didn't I?" After settling in her seat, he handed it to her outstretched arms. Horace glanced at the muck clinging to the hem of her dress and dripping around her boots and said nothing. However, he took a double-take when she broke open the double barrels on the shotgun and loaded it with shells.

When they reached the cabin, Horace carried her goods inside and placed them on the kitchen table. Lacey leaned the shotgun against the fireplace hearth and thanked him for taking her to town and bringing her home. As soon as the door shut, she removed the shawl and tossed it onto Aunt Molly's rocking chair. She made a dash for the bedroom and stripped out of the soiled dress, dropped it on the floor, and sat on the bed covers to absorb the banker's news.

Mercy sakes, married? She didn't want to lose this land, nor her freedom. If she married, she'd certainly be giving up her freedom, wouldn't she? Well, maybe so. Anything sounded better than going back home to live under Pa's rules. And she could never accept it if Brandon became the lawful owner of what should be *her* property. She gave the dried, dirt-clod encrusted dress a kick with the toe of her laced boot.

loud bang jarred Lacey from her thoughts. It sounded like it came from a spot next to the window, and the window was probably the intended mark. "Who's there?" Remaining perfectly still, she listened for sounds besides the wind and rain before shouting. "I said who's there, and you best be answerin' me." Not hearing a peep except her own quickened breaths, she snatched the lantern and tiptoed from the bedroom to the fireplace and the shotgun.

The lantern illuminated all but the far corners of the cabin, so she figured no one had come inside. To be certain, she lifted and pumped the shotgun, turning to point the firearm in every direction, her eyes keen for movement. Nothing. She scurried to the front door, flung it open, and hollered into the night, "Who's out there? I swear iffin' you don't answer me, I'll shoot yer no-good behind!"

The brim of a black Stetson disappeared around the southeast corner of the barn. "Chandler," she hollered. "What in Sam's tarnation are you doin' on my property? You get yourself over here, right now."

No answer.

She hustled through the rain toward the barn. The door stood ajar, though she clearly remembered closing it earlier in the day. One of the front wagon wheels lay tossed in a heap of dry straw. "You best show yer face," she yelled into the quiet. "I swear, I'm gonna tar and feather you from eyeball to butt cheek if yeh don't show yer theivin' face."

She stormed from the barn and swung the door behind her, jumping when it hit the soggy ground and covered her backside with cold, muddy water. She turned and lowered the lantern to see the door hinges were removed.

When she returned to the cabin, she stopped short. The glow from the lantern revealed scattered pieces of wood and the ax from the barn laying smack dab in the middle of the floor. The howling wind and rain forced her attention upward toward a jagged hole in the ceiling. *What in Sam's tarnation?* Lacey set the shotgun down and hurried to place a wash pan on the floor to catch the deluge of rain. She tossed Aunt Molly's shawl over her head, grabbed a box of shells and the shotgun, then ran through the gusting storm in the direction of Mr. Stetson's ranch.

So help me, Brandon Chandler, when I git my hands 'round yer neck.

Lacey cursed with every step as she trudged the rain soaked field. She held tight to the walking bridge over South Sunday Creek, stepping her boots gingerly over the slippery boards awash in mud and muck.

Finally, she saw a glowing lantern in Brandon's window. The wind swirled up a mighty force causing her to walk near sideways as she stepped to the door and beat the butt end of the shotgun against the wood barrier.

The second Brandon opened the door a severe gust of wind caused her to stumble forward, her nose planting into his broad chest, a chest akin to a brick wall. Yet that chest warmed her insides from her breasts clear down to her kneecaps. She attempted to regain her balance on the slippery stoop.

"Lacey?" Brandon stepped forward and steadied her. "There's a helluva storm coming." He looked at the shotgun and under his breath said, "And it looks like a bigger storm just landed on my doorstep."

She took a step back causing his grip to release from the top of her arms. "What's that supposed to mean?" She shoved the muzzle into his chest. "I ain't here on no social visit. What were you doin' out at my place this evening? And don't yeh go lyin' through yer teeth and tell me yeh weren't there cuz I seen yeh."

He cleared his throat and lowered the barrels of the shotgun with his index finger. His eyes held hers in a trance. "You saw *me*, or you saw someone? I'm afraid you're mistaken if you think it was me."

She stomped her boot and hurried the barrels back to his chest. "How dare yeh stand there like a lyin' skunk and say yeh weren't at my place. I seen yeh 'round the corner of my barn and — and yeh took the wheel off my wagon, stripped the barn door from its hinges, and cut a hole in m'dang roof with an ax." The rain now fell in torrents causing a mess of hair to stick to her face like corn silk. Lacey smeared it away and glared at him. "Fess up, I seen yeh."

The tone of his voice deepened as his blue-eyed gaze settled on hers. "You should have taken my advice and left town on the next stagecoach. I repeat, and you damn well better listen to me, I did *not* step foot on your property this evening. You did not see *me*.

"Listen, you," she seethed. "I don't have the patience, nor the desire, to put up with a cowpoke like you stoopin' to boyhood pranks. I warn yeh, yeh step one foot onto my property again and I'll —" Lacey set her chin in a stubborn line and cocked an eyebrow as she pumped the shotgun —"I'll shoot yeh, that's what I'll do. And the law? I'll get the law out here and, and they'll shoot yeh, too."

"You'll shoot me, will you?" His sudden burst of chuckles became a doubled over, hands on knees hee-haw.

His hearty laughter set her guts ablaze. A sudden bolt of lightning rattled the window glass nearly out of its frame, causing her to startle, and the shotgun discharged with a tremendous boom every bit as loud as the thunder that followed, but with the power of a double barrel's worth of buckshot. "Now look what you did. Yeh made my ears ring so loud they's hurtin'." She looked into Brandon's dark, smoldering eyes narrowed to a thin slit with a face full of red-hot rage, and a jaw tightening like a skeeter's backside in a nosedive.

"You wanton, out of control, hellcat crazy, backwoods she-devil. You could have," he said moving his hands erratically up, down, and across his chest, "shot me. Ya damn near did!"

Lacey's heart raced triple time. Any second, she might puke right there on top of his cowboy boots. Had the lightning not struck at the instant it had, she wouldn't have startled and pulled the trigger. But, had she not startled, she wouldn't have raised the gun and would have shot clear through his guts instead of shooting a bunch of holes in the porch roof. "I wouldn'ta had to shoot yeh if yeh hadn't laughed at me. It's yer own stupid fault."

"You need to go on and get yourself home." He clenched his teeth and pointed in the direction of Aunt Molly's cabin. "Yes, you need to go, and you need to go *right* now."

A bolt of lightning, like an exclamation mark, struck nearby, followed by a loud boom.

"Wait a minute." He inhaled an audible breath. "Come in. I'll take you home. I don't want you out walking in this storm, even if you did attempt to kill me."

"I'd rather get fried by lightnin' and go 'round with my clothes reekin' a'smoke than ride next to the likes of you."

"I'll be damned." He shook his head. "You're even more stubborn than I thought. Suit yourself. And good luck dodging the lightning."

The door slammed in her face.

After returning to her cabin, Lacey changed into three layers of dry clothes and wrapped herself in the thick biscuit quilt. Every piece of her shivered as she rocked in Aunt Molly's chair and repeatedly glanced at the hole in the ceiling. The wind had died down and the rain slowed to an occasional trickle.

"How dare that excuse fer a man call me backwoods?" She rocked faster. Visualizing Brandon, cozy in his dry cabin after causing her such grief, made her itch for retaliation. He deserved the same suffering she endured. A thought crossed her mind. She stomped her boot heels on the floor and the rocker came to an abrupt halt. An idea was brewing and since she was already soaking wet, it wouldn't hurt to get rained on a bit more. She ran to retrieve a couple of items from the kitchen, then scurried back to Brandon's ranch to carry out her plan.

The morning sun shined nice and bright through the hole in Lacey's ceiling and woke her from a fitful sleep. Thank goodness the wash pan hadn't filled and run over while she dozed. Maybe there'd be enough scrap wood in the barn to fix the roof. She dug for work clothes among the garments in Aunt Molly's chest. Finding not one suitable piece of clothing, she settled on a soft, yellow dress with only a touch of lace on the bodice. Glancing at the suck-it-in corset tossed on the floor, she decided it would be a freezing day in hell before she strapped herself into that contraption again. She best get her wet overalls hung on the line to dry or be stuck in a dress all day.

Brandon grabbed hold of *The Montana Post* from the dining table and made his morning trip to the privacy of the outhouse. He read an article about a new-fangled typewriting machine and finished his business with a corncob. His underside lit on fire without a flame and his eyes shot tear bullets.

"Lord have mercy. What the hell?" Brandon's voice echoed through the valley and faded out somewhere near South Sunday Creek. He threw the cayenne pepper-saturated corncob down the crapper, jumped off the seat, and raced as best he could with his union suit flap unfastened and pants around his ankles in desperate need of a bucket of cold water and the healing salve.

acey hung the last of her wet laundry onto the clothesline. The clomping hooves of an approaching horse grew louder as Brandon rode Thunder like a madman toward her cabin. *How dare he approach me after what he did?* She visualized wrapping her hands like a vice around the varmint's neck after his juvenile twilight prank.

Brandon halted Thunder a mere three yards from where she stood, kicking a cloud of dust onto her clean laundry.

"So, Chandler, I see it's wash day fer you, too."

"What are you talking about?"

"You threw dirt on my clean clothes." She plopped her hands on her hips and stared at the man. "And yer gonna clean 'em spotless."

His eyes held a squint and appeared dark and mysterious behind the brim of the Stetson. His massive hands held a white-knuckled grip on Thunder's reins and hell's fire if the man wasn't a fetching sight for her eyes. "What are yeh *doin'* here, anyway?"

Brandon tipped his Stetson forward, then removed it, causing stray curls to land on his forehead. "I've come to offer you a final deal for this land. I'm willing to offer you double —"

"Not for sale."

"I'm willing to offer you an exorbitant sum of money. I suggest —"

"No, and I suggest yeh stop askin' me somethin' I already told yeh ain't gonna happen. I'm gittin' plum sick of listenin' to yeh askin' 'bout it. It weren't fer sale, still ain't fer sale, never gonna be fer sale." She hitched up the hem of her dress with a short jerk and strutted toward the smokehouse.

Brandon dismounted and took long strides before reaching Lacey. He took hold of her arm and turned her to face him, mouth open but no words formed on his lips.

Her eyes met his in a standoff of determined will before she noticed him watching her chest rise and fall under the thin material of her dress. With feet shuffling, she brought her arm to her side, afraid Brandon would somehow know how fast her heart was beating, or that her spine tingled in such a pleasant way. She didn't know herself why she reacted like this, but she sure didn't want Brandon to get a hint of this strange sensation she was feeling.

"What in land's sake makes yeh so gung-ho 'bout acquiring my aunt's property, anyhow?"

He pointed his finger at her, his jawline set firm. "You'll sell. Mark my word, you'll sell or spend the rest of your days wishing you'd packed your"— he pointed at her dress —"fancy clothes and high-tailed it out of these parts before you get run out."

She snapped to attention and reacted to the angry challenge. "Are you threatenin' me?"

He leaned in so close, the warmth of his breath caressed her skin.

"You can take my words any way you please. I'm not accustomed to bending to the ways of a hick-girl's whims, and I'm not about to start now, or ever. Good day."

Lacey watched him ride from her property before she headed inside and gave the door a hearty slam. *He can say whatever he wants 'bout me. Why should I care?* She thought for a moment before stomping her boot onto the floor. *And the gall darn shifty didn't take my dirty clothes with him.*

She paced in front of the feather bed long after Brandon took his leave. It would serve the weasel right to trick him into a marriage of convenience, inherit the land like it said in Aunt Molly's will, and then dump his no-good butt like a weevil-infested flour sack. She wiped a damp spot from her cheek and realized it was a stream of tears. She kicked, half-tripping over the books laying on the bedroom floor. The covers peered at her: *Decorum: A Practical Treatise on Etiquette* and *Dress of the Best American Society*. She sat next to the reading material and flipped through the pages of *The American Toilet* and read the overlays, then read several columns of the *Godey's Lady's Book* until she fell fast asleep.

She awoke with a start as her hand flew to the top of her head. A sigh of relief escaped her lips when she realized it was only a horrible dream that Luke dumped a shovel of warm cow patties in her hair while Jeremiah and Matthew rolled in laughter. Drumming her fingers on the floor, she stared at the tall stack of books her aunt used for teaching at her prim and proper lady's school. She glanced at the trunk filled with pretty clothes. Lacey caught a glimpse of a shiny, peach-hued dress trimmed in ivory lace. She looked away. With the tip of her boot, she lifted a corner of her ratty work shirt strewn on the floor. The fabric lay mere inches from her fingers, but before she touched the familiar material, she drew her hand back. Again, she looked at the peach and lace garment, then back to the hand-me-down-twice shirt. Heck, she'd make a fool of herself if she went around putting on airs like some lady, when she was a poor farmer's daughter with no more knowledge of how to be a lady than some snotty-nosed boy.

She stood and walked to the storage chest. Her fingers fluttered through the vast assortment of colors, textures, buttons, laces, and trims. Lacey guessed wearing a dress wasn't *that* awful bad. Pulling out a royal-blue gown, her eyes closed in bliss as she held the soft, delicate fabric to her cheek. After tossing the gown on the bed, she turned to address the standing oval mirror. "All right, Lacey Autumn Kendall, either you high-tail it back to Pa and your miserable, rotten brothers, and spend the rest of your life as a housemaid and farmhand, or learn to be a lady, catch you a husband, and rightfully claim Aunt Molly's land for your own."

But, how in tarnation am I supposed to live until I get a husband? She didn't have any money and never held a job except for working on the farm with Pa and her brothers. She couldn't cook worth a darn. Sewing only resulted in pricked fingers and ragged hems. Once when trying to darn Pa's socks, the result was one large tube. She huffed and plopped onto the bed. The only thing she did well enough to earn money for was fixing things and working on a farm. Every available man would clamber for the hand of a woman who shoveled hog poop and plowed fields for a living. Well, maybe not, but she could make enough money to live if she found work as a farmhand. Most of the folks who visited back home never guessed the youngest son of Rueben Kendall was his only daughter.

She released a bottomless sigh. She'd never latch onto a husband. Then, something Pa always told her and her brothers popped into her mind —"don't tell me I cain't, tell me I'll try." *By golly, I'll learn to be the primmest and properest lady this side of the Miss'ssippi River.* Pulling the remaining books from under the feather bed, she decided to study every one of Aunt Molly's lessons. And didn't Mr. Beaumont say he taught with Aunt Molly at her lady school? Maybe he would help? Lacey shot out of the cabin and headed toward New Harmony.

"Miss Kendall, how nice to see you. What brings you here this afternoon?"

"Mr. Beaumont," she said, near out of breath, "you taught at that fancy lady school with Aunt Molly, right?"

"Yes, that is affirmative," he answered skeptically. "I taught students for fifteen years. Why?"

"Would you be willing to take me on as a student, you know, tutor me? I know this probly comes as quite a shock, but I could use me some lady lessons."

Winston flashed a big ole horse grin.

Lacey thought if she had a big enough candle flame, she could see all the way down to his gut sack.

"It would, why, it would be my pleasure."

"Let's start tomorrow evening, then. I'll look fer yeh after supper. I gotta be on my way. Good day, Mr. Beaumont," she said before making a beeline to the door.

♡ ♡ ♡

When Lacey wasn't tossing her covers on and off during the night, she lay awake listening to her stomach growl. She had to find work, and fast.

Early the next morning, she eagerly donned her overalls, shirt, and boots. Finding a straw hat in the storage chest, she yanked all the flowery decorations off, tucked her hair inside nice and tight, and set out to find a job. She walked the entire county, it seemed, then trudged down an incline toward a marsh filled with tall weeds and cattails. She scared three pheasants and hundreds of dragonflies before making her way to the homestead sitting directly next to hers.

Mercy sakes, she'd tried every farm within walking distance, and not one person showed interest in hiring an extra hand. She considered turning and following the creek back to the cabin but decided since she'd trekked all over the countryside, she may as well try the last farmhouse sitting a hair to the west of Aunt Molly's place.

Smoke poured from the chimney and faded into wisps as it rose into the crisp morning air. Other than the clucking sound arising from the chicken coop and the occasional whinny of a horse, the place was quiet. Rounding a corner of the barn, she noticed several broken planks of wood and a rusted-out door latch. A clothesline strung from one tree limb to another, but the clothing on the far side nearly touched the ground. Closer investigation revealed a broken branch too weak to serve its purpose.

Lacey stepped onto the broad front porch. The sound of forks scraping against plates proved why no one was milling about the farmyard. She curled her hand into a fist to knock and paused to take a deep breath. She looked toward the heavens and bit her lip. *Please, God. Please let 'em hire me.* A sudden thought made her eyes grow wide. She tiptoed off the porch, rounded the corner of the farmhouse, and ran all the way home.

ey young fella, what in Sam's tarnation are you doing on my property?" An elderly man called to Lacey driving a nail into the side of his barn. A woman Lacey figured to be his wife, stood beside him.

"Howdy folks," Lacey said in her best attempt at a deep voice. "I couldn't help but notice you all's barn needed fixin'." She pointed to the plank of wood she'd fetched from Aunt Molly's stockpile. Out of the corner of her eye, she watched the couple exchange curious glances. "I put a new latch here on your barn door and when I finish patchin' this section here, I'm fixin' to rewire yer clothesline over yonder."

The man ran a hand down his short, silver beard and eyed his wife. She shrugged and wiped her hands over the skirt of a bright crimson apron with a pattern of apples and cinnamon sticks.

"Young fella, do I know you?" The man cocked his head to the side and stared at Lacey's profile.

Lacey dropped a handful of nails onto the ground and stood. She sprinted toward the couple with her right hand extended. She hoped they didn't notice the leather glove reaching for a handshake fit two sizes too big, the top finger digits flattened like hotcakes. "Where's my manners?" She smiled and said, "The name's Mace Kendall. I'm stayin' with my sister, Lacey, for a spell. I decided to come over today and kindly introduce myself and by darned iffin' I didn't notice a few things in need of fixin' 'round here. I'd like to offer my services."

The woman cleared her throat and jabbed the man with an elbow. "My name is Sarah, and this here is my husband, Adam. Sarah and Adam Burke. Pleased to make your acquaintance, Mace." Her thin, wrinkled lips formed a quaint smile, as prim and proper as the silver bun pinned tight to the top of her head.

Adam sized the boy up and down. "Where'd you say you're from, boy?" Adam said. "I never heard of no Lacey Kendall."

"Over yonder." Lacey pointed toward the meadow. "My sister and I live at my aunt's old place. Molly Kendall was her name. She passed —"

"Oh heavens, Adam. This here is Molly Kendall's kin. Come on in and sit for a spell, youngin'." She clasped her hands together. "Follow me inside and have breakfast with us, there's always plenty to go around. I'm delighted to know we have neighbors again." She repeated to her husband, "This here's Molly's kinfolk."

"I heard you the first time," Adam said, swatting an invisible fly.

"Not only was Molly a dear neighbor, she was a good Christian woman," Sarah said. "I felt mighty sorry when I heard she'd passed on. You say you're looking for work?" She glanced over her shoulder. "Adam, we have plenty that needs fixing around here."

Adam grumbled as he scratched the side of his head and spit into the grass. "I can't pay you much."

"I can feed you good," Sarah added. "Why, you ain't got a lick of meat on them bones, young man. I'm going to enjoy putting some weight on you."

Lacey's stomach erupted in a long, deep growl as she followed Sarah into the cabin and the aroma of fried sausage and hot yeast biscuits hit her senses. The smell of vanilla and cinnamon promised future treats. She peeked at the stove where a fresh tray of sticky buns steamed and pinched herself to make sure she wasn't dreaming.

Sarah walked to the far wall and scooted a chair across the floor. She motioned for Lacey to take a seat at the table before retrieving a blue-speckled plate from the cupboard. She dished Lacey a piece of sausage and two biscuits.

Three hard knocks sounded on the door before it opened, and the top of a dark curly head popped in. "Morning all. Am I too late for breakfast?"

"Get yourself in here, Brandon. You're never too late for vittles in this house." Sarah bounded out of her chair and fetched a plate for the new arrival.

Lacey's stomach did a flip-flop. Of all the people to come calling this morning, why did it have to be Brandon? She lowered her head, propped her forehead with her right fist, and stared at her plate.

Sarah spoke excitedly as she sat. "Brandon, you need to meet our new neighbor. This here is Mace Kendall. He and his sister are living at Molly Kendall's old place."

Brandon's eyebrows raised as he looked at Lacey. He sat and said, "I met your sister. She didn't have anyone living with her that I could tell." He stabbed a piece of sausage with his fork.

"I arrived last night," Lacey answered, keeping her eyes cast downward.

"Mace is going to help Adam with chores around the farm. An extra set of hands will sure be welcome around here." Sarah jumped to fill the platter with another round of sausage.

"Mace," Sarah said when she returned and sat next to her newest guest. "Brandon is a godsend to us in our old age. Somehow, he finds time to help us out. Today, he and Adam are repairing a broken-down fence out back. I'm sure they could use an extra set of hands. Isn't that right, Adam?"

Lacey refrained from bolting upright in her chair. *Brandon works fer Adam and Sarah?*

Adam looked from his plate to Brandon, then at his wife. "It don't look to me that Mace here"— he cocked his head toward Lacey —"has enough muscle on them skinny arms to be much help, Sarah. Perhaps —"

"Nonsense, Adam," Sarah piped in. "A good day's work will be just the thing this boy needs to grow him some muscle. And a few good meals won't hurt, neither."

Lacey needed to think, and fast. "No, really," she said, "maybe Mr. Burke is right. Perhaps this isn't such a good idea I work here." She couldn't imagine pulling off such a farce with Brandon breathing down her neck all day. "I didn't realize when I offered my services, you already have a farmhand."

"A farmhand?" Adam momentarily choked on his eats. "No, Mace. Brandon isn't a farmhand, he's the owner. We rent this land from Brandon."

"I'll tell you what." Brandon wiped his mouth on a linen napkin. "It would help me out considerably to have someone take care of the daily upkeep of this property. I'll pay you out of my pocket, but you make damn sure what needs to get done, gets done." He pointed at Mace with a squint to his eyes. "And gets done right." He nodded in Adam's direction. "I'll help you with the bigger jobs," he said, "but leave the daily chores to Mace."

Sarah looked lovingly at Brandon as she placed her hand on top of his. "Brandon could have forced us to leave this farm years ago when we got too old to take proper care of it. Instead, he jumped right in to do a lot of the work himself to keep the value of the property intact. Like I said, he is a true godsend."

Lacey didn't dare look at this "godsend." If Brandon helped these nice folks, it wasn't because he was such a do-gooder. From what she knew of his character, it wasn't his sweet spirit, neither. *No, sir.*

She looked at Brandon and back to her plate, his glare burning a hole in her. Yes, he was staring right at her…titties? *Did my binding loosen?* Lacey took a quick peek at her chest and confirmed her breasts were indeed still bound tight like the band on a butter churn. He stared at her for another reason, then. *He's figuring out I don't look like a boy.* She needed to act quickly. She belched, long and loud, then hoisted her right hip and farted. "'Scuse me." She wiped her nose from the inner elbow of her shirt clear to the wrist.

Brandon pushed his chair from the table. "Adam, we best get busy if we're going to finish that fence today." He glared at Lacey. "You know, boy, I already don't like you." He threw his napkin onto the empty plate. "Probably because you look like your stubborn sister."

Lacey thanked Sarah for breakfast and followed the men to the barn where they loaded a wagon with supplies for the day. Adam got busy hitching the workhorse. Sarah came out shortly afterward carrying a basket full of eats for lunch. She threw a navy blanket into the wagon then patted the horse's head. "Good, sweet Old Nellie. She's getting to be almost as old as we are."

Adam positioned himself on the seat and took Old Nellie's reins. Lacey quickly sat next to him on the bit of available space left on the narrow seat. Brandon would have to ride in the back with the greasy tools. She wiped the smirk off her face when instead he grabbed hold of the buggy and hoisted himself next to her. His hard thigh pressed against hers so tight she knew how Miss Aimee's 'stays' felt, suckin' in her belly blubber. She flashed him a hostile glare and tried to wiggle her arm out from under the varmint's massive shoulder.

Heavy with sarcasm he said, "What's the matter, Mace? Am I crowding you?"

"It is a bit tight."

"Then," he said, stabbing his thumb backward, "get comfortable with the tools."

Deep ridges in the trail through the pasture threatened to bounce Lacey out of her seat and felt relieved when they reached the far end of the property. Adam pulled on the reins with a gentle "whoa" bringing the horse and wagon to a halt.

The warmth of Brandon's shoulder against Lacey's arm sent unexpected tingles throughout her body. She wondered what *that* was all about and relieved when Brandon climbed down from the seat to unload supplies from the wagon.

He stopped to peer at her. "Are you going to sit there all day twiddling your fingers or make yourself useful?"

She narrowed her eyes and climbed down as he handed over a picket and pointed his finger in the opposite direction. "Line these boards along the fence," he said and reached for another plank.

Lacey made several trips from the fence to the wagon and noticed the sweat on Brandon's face glistened as the rays of sunlight touched his bronzed skin. Only the tip of Lacey's nose had a few sprinkles of moisture she wiped with a gloved finger.

The afternoon air blazed like red-hot kindling against Lacey's back. She pulled the straw hat lower over her forehead and checked to see that her shirt stayed buttoned at the cuffs. She sure didn't want a sunburn. As she wondered if they would ever take a break, Adam strolled to where Lacey hammered the final nail into a fence post.

"Sarah fried some chicken for us and threw in scratch biscuits and cornbread," he said. "I've got everything over by the wagon."

"Sounds mighty good," Lacey called to his retreating form. "I'll be there right quick." She gave the nail a few more whacks for good measure, envisioning Brandon's nose with every solid wallop to the nail's head.

Brandon strode past her on his way to the wagon. "You can stop and eat if you want," he mumbled.

Lacey looked at him and rolled her eyes skyward. "No, perhaps I'll work all blasted day and maybe you'll get lucky and watch me drop dead from starvation."

"Suit yourself," he drawled.

Lacey bolted upright. "What's yer problem, Chandler?" She turned on her heel and was toe-to-toe with him in an instant, her head at his mid-chest. "I never done nothing to make you treat me bad."

No?" Brandon said. "You're Lacey Kendall's brother, right?"

"Yep, I sure 'nuff am. And mighty proud of it, too."

"That's enough reason for me." He spoke like a seething grizzly with a thorn wedged between his toes, spat on the ground, and resumed his walk.

"What you got against my sister?" Lacey walked double time, but Brandon's strides were twice as long. "She never did you no wrong."

"Your sister did wrong just by being born, in my opinion."

"You dislike Lacey that much?"

"That much. She's nothing but a conniving vixen without the faintest idea how to take care of a farm. She'll hang on to it to spite me."

"Lacey isn't staying on at Aunt Molly's old place to spite anyone. She's keeping it to make a home for herself. I'd, I mean, she'd rather rot than see it in the likes of yer hands."

Brandon took hold of the boy and shook him before throwing him to the ground. "That's the last time you'll talk to me like that. Do you understand?"

"I hear you all right," she said, flicking straw from her overalls. "I hear you loud and clear."

Two hours after lunch, they finished the job. After loading the tools back into the wagon, Brandon motioned for Lacey to hitch herself onto the wagon seat.

"I'll walk home from here," she called to Adam. As much as she longed to repeat the honeybee buzzing sensation of her thigh pressed tight alongside Brandon's, and anticipated reliving the experience, she had a much larger prize in mind. If she hit the jackpot, not only would the warmth of his thigh cause her legs to buzz and weaken, her entire body would purr like a satisfied kitten with a belly full of warm milk.

"Mace, hold on a minute." Adam held the lunch basket with the uneaten pieces of chicken and biscuits. Take this food home for you and your sister. Sarah always sends way too much and there will be double this amount on the cookstove."

"Don't mind if I do. Thank you, Mr. Burke." She took the basket. "I'll be at your place bright and early in the mornin'." She was miserably tired trudging through the meadow and looked forward to a hot bath and a good night's sleep.

Lacey pulled the tub in front of the fireplace and carried several buckets of hot water from the cookstove until it filled to near overflowing. She tossed a towel onto the arm of the rocking chair, undressed, and kicked her boots off. She swished the water and determined the temperature was perfect before stepping in and lowering herself until it lapped her shoulders.

A heavy knock startled her from a peaceful dream. The water had lost its warmth and her body shook like she'd dozed on a bed of ice. *How long did I sleep?* She glanced at the window and forced her shoulders deeper into the chilled liquid. "Who is it? Who's knocking on my door?"

"Lacey?" A deep voice boomed back. "It's Brandon. Open the door."

Oh, fer crying out loud. She looked at the dirty work clothes scattered across the floor. "Whaddya want?"

"Let me in. We *need* to talk."

"No, we don't *need* to talk just because you *want* to talk. I'm busy and you're gonna hafta skedaddle on outta here."

"Is Mace home?"

She slammed her fists into the water. "Are you talking a different language now or what the hell's your problem? I said, I'm taking a bath, so go away and leave me alone. I'll talk to you tomorrow."

"Simple question, Lacey. Is Mace home?"

"It ain't none of yer danged business, but no, he ain't here right now."

"If you don't open this door…I'll take the hinges off and open it myself."

"Is that so? Tell me, big, bad Brandon Chandler. Tell me what you reckon. Would you rather I shoot you in the chest, the stomach, or betwixt yer legs. You go on and think about it fer a minute while I load my gun." She put her hands on the bottom of the tub to lift herself out, the whole time keeping her sights on the dusty window. When a shadow crossed it, she shouted, "I see you trying to peek at me nekkid. You're a sick one, Chandler. Get outta here."

She sat back down and stretched to grab her towel draping it across the tub as a shield. "This is your final chance to keep yourself alive, or I'll get the law after yeh and they'll give yeh a good hangin' fer peepin' in m'window."

"Mighty tough sentence for knocking on a door. I'll take my chances with a judge. Here's what I propose. I'm going to give you two minutes to make yourself presentable before I kick the door open. I *am* the law as far as tonight is concerned. Now, let's try this again. Open the damn door, or I'm coming in."

She reached over the side of the tub and walked her fingers until she touched the heel of her boot, then inched it close enough to grab. With as much force as she could muster, she hurled it at the door. The heel struck the door with a tremendous clatter and she shouted, "The next time you hear that thumping sound it's gonna be your head saying *bye-bye now* to your shoulders."

"Rather than threaten me, I'd advise you to cover yourself. You better make it fast. You just wasted a whole minute."

Her mind flashed in a million directions as she half-climbed, half-bounded from the tub. She wrapped the towel around her and snatched the soiled clothing as she slipped and slid across the floor toward the bedroom. She threw a pink cotton nightgown over her head and managed to get her damp arms into the fitted sleeves.

When she opened the door with a mighty jerk, Brandon was standing all lazylike with his arms crossed over his chest and muscle ripped shoulder resting against the frame.

"What in fire and tarnation do yeh want? I suppose from now on yeh need to learn yerself some patience. Not everybody's gonna jump to yer demanding temper, includin' me."

He stared at her. For quite a few seconds, he stared.

Lacey bit her lower lip and followed his gaze downward until the reason for his interest became clear. The thin material clung to every curve of her body. She hadn't taken the time to put undergarments on, and Brandon's eyes traced every inch of her near nakedness.

"I . . . I uh." He stuttered and looked to an invisible spot above her head, then back to her chest.

She raised her chin and demanded. "What do yeh need to tell me of such importance it can't wait till tomorrow?"

"Mace." He stood like a tree trunk in the center of the doorway. "I want to discuss his piss-poor attitude."

"Mace? Why in Sam's tarnation ain't you talkin' t'Mace instead of gettin' me outta my nice, relaxin' bath? Huh?" She wrinkled her brow. "What about him, anyways? He ain't done you no wrong."

Brandon thrust his finger into the air, waggling it to emphasize his words. "You tell your wiry brother, you tell him, if he's going to work for me, he best get it through his thick skull who the boss is. And if he doesn't change his attitude, he can stay home tomorrow, and the next day, and the day after that!"

"Why must yeh be such a horse's ass?"

She slammed the door shut.

The man infuriated her more than anybody she'd ever known. If she had a wad of beef jerky, she could bite it clean in half without much yanking. She must learn to control her temper around Brandon, but he was such a rascal. No matter how bitter the taste, she'd bite her tongue, be nice to the varmint, and make him swoon like a heartsick possum in heat. But, if she started acting cordial, he may get suspicious and reckon she'd hidden a rotten egg in her basket. Heck, he'd probably snoop around and learn the particulars of Aunt Molly's will. *Mace.* Sure, that was it. She'd get under Brandon's skin through Mace. Happy for an answer, she skipped through the kitchen and twirled onto the feather bed.

"Good mornin', everyone," Lacey announced with a big smile as Sarah swung the kitchen door open to allow her entrance.

"Good morning, Mace. I'm thrilled you're eating breakfast with us." Sarah shut the door and retrieved a plate of biscuits from the stove, offering one to Mace as he neared the table. "It's my pleasure to put some meat on them bones."

"Well, thank you, Sarah. I sure hope it tastes as good as it looks." Lacey gave Brandon a playful punch on the arm as she passed his chair.

Once everyone sat, Adam said a prayer over the food. As soon as he said, "Can I hear an amen?"

Everybody said, "Amen."

Forks started poking into plates and Lacey said, "You folks eat like you ain't had vittles in a week of Sundays." She cleared her throat. "I wanna say something."

"Speak what's on your mind," Adam coaxed. "If you got something to say, you ain't gotta ask permission. Say it."

She met Brandon's eyes. "I want to apologize foer my behavior yesterday. I admit, I was a tad angry, Mr. Chandler, and it won't happen again."

Sarah looked at Mace with a wrinkled brow, then at Brandon. "Whatever for? What happened, Mace?"

"Well, I was mighty disrespectful out in the field yesterday, and I feel right poor 'bout it." She turned to Brandon. "Here you offered me a job and all, the least I shoulda done is showed my appreciation."

Brandon eyed the boy, his left brow rising a fraction. "Apology accepted," he said matter-of-factly before taking a swig of coffee. He stared into the cup for a second before setting it down. "I'll tell you what, I'll leave most of the chores for you to take care of, more than I figured on, but I'll swing by often to check on things." He took another swig of coffee. "I expect you to do the heavy chores for Adam and inform me when I'm needed. And I'm going to give you a hefty raise."

"You are? A raise in money? Thank you."

He eyed the boy for a minute. "I appreciate your honesty and integrity for recognizing your wrongdoing and apologizing to make it right. I will always reward good, hard workers…and honesty. You lie to me one time, one time, Mace, and I'll fire you on the spot and never trust another word coming out of your mouth. Got it?"

Lacey shook her head. "Yessir. I got it. I don't know what to say 'cept thank you."

"You're welcome."

Lacey chewed on her lower lip. If Brandon wasn't going to be around much during the day, she'd better hurry her plan into action. She stretched her arms and released a large sigh. "I'm sure sorry fer runnin' late this mornin', Sarah. My sister went on an early mornin' buggy ride. I reckon all that fence work yesterday plum tuckered me out. I slept right past the roosters crowin'."

Brandon stabbed his fork into a chunk of sausage like it needed a good killing before eating.

"Heck," Lacey continued with intense pleasure, leaning forward with a sunny cheerfulness. "Sis stayed awake bakin' pies till all hours of the night. Mmm, Mmm, did they smell good. I had a dickens of a time fallin' asleep with all the good smellin' eats cookin'."

Sarah said, "So your sister has a beau?" She held her fork midbite and scooted to the front of her chair.

"Yes, ma'am. I suppose so, anyhow. I didn't see who came for her, but she packed a basket heaping with eats and wore the prettiest dress I ever did see. I thought it was a little, well, a lot too revealing right here." She pointed to her chest. "But I didn't say anything." She whispered loud enough for Brandon to hear, "I won't swear by it, but I think she put flowers in her bath water last night."

Sarah's eyes grew wide until Adam shot her a disapproving glare. A blush rose high on her cheeks as she fingered the hem of her apron.

Brandon gulped the last of his breakfast and shot Lacey a scalding glare before he said thanks to Sarah and reached for his hat. The door shut behind him with a solid thud.

Early morning buggy ride? Baking pies and putting flowers in her bath water? Brandon commanded Thunder to a full run. Planning to check properties northwest of his cabin, he decided to ride near the McAllister's farm. This took him past several picnic spots, but he didn't happen upon Lacey and her beau. He wondered who in tarnation she had met and remembered seeing her with that no-good Horace Sparker. The thought put his mind at ease. Horace was a harmless enough fellow, certainly no match for himself, but he'd still like to squeeze the man's skinny little turkey neck.

Brandon reasoned he'd take a ride through town on his way home. He'd check in at the telegraph office in case there was word from the digging crew. Moreover, maybe someone would be eager to talk about why Horace was absent. When he walked into the telegram office, his blood ran cold when Horace greeted him from behind the office counter. He stormed back outside before the man finished saying good afternoon and hit the Crystal Saloon's swinging doors with such force they bounced back like a tightly coiled spring. "Give me a double bourbon, Rusty." He scowled and lodged his boot atop the footrail.

"Mace," Adam said after they finished pasturing the horses, "there's a bucket right inside the barn door. You milk Daisy and Rose before the girls burst. Then, gather eggs for Sarah."

A gulp caught in Lacey's throat. "I don't uh —"

"Oh, and don't forget to feed the chickens and slop the hogs," he continued. "They'll be mighty hungry by the time you get to them."

Lacey wiped the clammy beads of sweat that formed on her nose and forehead. Milk the cows, feed the chickens, and slop the hogs? *Land's sake.* She reckoned herself prime for whitewashing, mending fences, and such, but she sure didn't have any experience with livestock.

She opened the barn door and found the metal milk pail dangling from a hook. She took it by the wire handle and inched her way toward the cows. A sudden, deep moo caused her to jump nearly out of her skin. She headed in the direction of a stall with the word *Daisy* scrawled above in black paint. A three-legged stool, red with more chips than paint, sat in front of a division between Daisy and Rose.

"Good cow," Lacey cooed as she inched sideways down the narrow space between Daisy and the side of the stall. She set the stool down and eyed the situation, then moved the stool back about a foot. "Jesus, Mary, Joseph, and all the Saints," she whispered before taking a seat. She inched her hand forward and drew it back several times before forcing herself to grasp a cold teat. She squeezed. Nothing happened. She squeezed again and then shook the udder like a rattle. Again, no milk. Lacey squeezed, pulled, shook, and finally when she squeezed and pulled at the same time, success. She hummed a tune while filling the bucket with milk, then turned her attention to Rose.

She found an empty bucket and entered the next stall, set Daisy's full-to-the-brim bucket aside and noticed Rose seemed a bit feistier than Daisy. She neared the cow and readied herself for milking. After setting the stool down, she reached for an udder. Even after feeling all around the cow's belly, she couldn't locate one. Suddenly, Rose gave a tremendous bellow and her hind leg kicked out, sending the bucket of Daisy's milk catapulting, and splashing the walls of the stall.

A gentle *moo* sounded behind her and she turned to see the word *Rose* carved out with a sharp stick above the entry to another stall. *Iffin' that's Rose, then what cow is this?* Her hand jerked from under the cow's belly when she realized this cow was no cow at all.

"Criminy Jehoshaphat," she hollered and bolted from the stall. When her heart stopped beating like a scared rabbit, she glanced around the barn to see if anyone witnessed her mistake before doubling over in laughter. After milking Rose, Lacey took the bucket into the farmhouse and handed it to Sarah with an apology for spilling the brunt of Daisy's milk. Then, she threw feed to the chickens and slopped the hogs before searching for Adam.

Brandon rode out to the Burke's place and halted Thunder next to Mace. He stared down at the boy.

Mace stopped twisting the chicken wire he worked on, looked at the man on horseback, and squinted. "Howdy, Mr. Chandler. I'm darn near finished with this chicken coop. I'm thinking it'll be done pert near lunch time."

"You're doing good work, boy." He dismounted and his shadow loomed over Mace.

"I sure hope to get all these chores done before supper. Lacey promised she'd fix a special meal tonight. There ain't many women can cook eats like my sister." He stood suddenly and looked at his pocket watch. "Oh darn, I told Lacey I'd skedaddle to the Mercantile and get some white beans and a bag of flour for fried fatcakes. I'll fetch it for her real quick and come right back, iffin that's okay, Mr. Chandler?"

"Sure," Brandon answered. "Sure, go ahead."

"I'll be back 'afore you can chew a wad, Mr. Chandler," Lacey called over her shoulder and scampered, giggling across the green pasture. She hoped he'd spend the rest of the day trying to clear his mind of a delicious, steaming crock of bean soup and sizzling, fried fatcakes.

Lacey returned in no time, a wide grin across her face. "Well, looks like I'll be begging Sarah to eat with her and Adam tonight."

"Why is that?"

"Lacey invited company for supper and asked me to find something to do for the evening. I do believe this fella's courting my sister."

Brandon clenched his jaw as he turned and took Thunder's reins.

Lacey caught her breath as he rode away. She'd run back to her cabin and pull the curtains closed, light the kitchen lantern so it would be aglow after dark, then high-tail it back to the Burke's farm. If Brandon got nosey and went snooping this evening, he would certainly believe she entertained a guest. She knelt to twist the final strands of wire on the chicken coop.

Later that evening, after Brandon checked on his property, he led Thunder back toward his cabin. Taking a short side trip over a gully to the northwest, he couldn't help noticing the faint glow coming from Lacey's cabin. His knuckles turned white where he gripped the reins, and his breath burned in his throat. He stabled Thunder and entered his cabin but couldn't concentrate on cooking supper. Visions of thick, golden bean soup and fried fatcakes danced in his head.

Brandon muttered under his breath as he opened the cabin door and looked upward at a hail of shooting stars in what his mother called, "heavenly sparks glistening like an angel's celebratory bonfire." Wishing he were sharing dinner with someone special this evening, he sat to watch the incredible theater in the sky.

Upon her return home, Lacey pushed herself through the door of the cabin and fell into the rocking chair like a flaccid rope of licorice. After finishing her chores, Sarah had insisted she stay for dinner. Her plan was working exactly as she had hoped. Every free moment she read from Aunt Molly's lady books and thanked the heavens for free meals with the Burkes.

A knock sounded on the cabin door. *Who in tarnation?* Lacey rose, peeked out the front window and sighed before opening the door. "Mr. Beaumont, I forgot all 'bout you comin' over this evenin'."

She noticed his mouth fell open as his beady eyes settled on her overalls.

Lacey glanced at her ragged clothing and said, "Somethin' wrong?" When he didn't answer, she directed him to the kitchen table and Aunt Molly's teaching books.

"Shall we begin?" Winston stated as he made a show of wiping crumbs from the seat of his chair before sitting. He rummaged through the books Lacey had stacked on the table.

She pulled out a chair, spun it around and straddled the seat, arms crossed along the top.

"Miss Kendall, please," Winston begged.

"What?" She stood. "You want somethin' t'drink?"

Winston stood and righted her chair with the table before thrusting a finger at the empty seat. "Sit down and pay close attention to my lips."

"Yer lips?" Lacey plopped into the chair and glanced at his face, then looked away. She glanced again but the last thing she could do is focus her attention on his dry, thin lip flappers lying there under straight-as-an-arrow chopped off mustache hairs. *Ew!*

"You possess a dreadful vocabulary," he said, shaking his head with angst. "Furthermore, ladies do not curse, chew tobacco, dress in," he said and swallowed hard with a sour face as he appeared to heave the next word, "overalls. Nor do they drop themselves into a sitting position or walk like a clumsy stockyard beast."

"I take offense to that," Lacey said. "There ain't a dang thing wrong with my overalls. They's comfy and I kin get 'em right-near dirty as I wanna."

Winston's mouth dropped open and he released a deep breath. "Vocabulary. Calm yourself and please, let us proceed with vocabulary."

"What in tarnation is vocah-balary?"

"As I assumed."

Three hours passed before Lacey knew the basics of correct diction. He lifted one of the smaller books from the table and walked to place it square on her head.

"Wha —?"

"Until you learn to walk proper, rather than appearing intoxicated, you will practice proper posture by balancing a book on your head."

Lacey reached for her head.

"Leave it," he ordered. "It will force you to walk like a lady. Now walk."

The book wobbled several times, and she reached to steady it before making her way across the room.

"Sit," he said.

She pointed upward. "With this stupid book on my head?"

"With the book." He stood and placed his hands on her shoulders to gently ease her down. "Sit."

Lacey's knees bent as she lowered herself toward the chair. The book crashed to the floor in a flutter of rustling pages.

"Stand and try again." His slick mustache hairs appeared to tremble.

"It's stupid," she moaned.

He showed his teeth.

She huffed, snatched the book from the floor, and placed it back on her head. It crashed to the floor long before her bottom touched the chair.

"I'll practice later. I promise," Lacey said into glaring eyes.

"Sit."

She plopped into the chair.

Winston cringed. "Gently, Lacey. A lady eases herself gently into a chair." He shook his head. "Now, either cross your legs or press your knees together."

She pressed her knees together.

"Place your hands in your lap." He glanced around the room. "Where are your gloves and fan?"

"Right over there." She pointed to a stack of rumpled linens.

He walked to retrieve the gloves and held them in front of her face. "Before I allow you one more lesson"— he pointed to the wrinkled stack —"you will press, fold, and place each of those garments in its designated place. Now, put these on."

She groaned and put them on.

"Now, pay attention. I am going to show you how to remove them in the fashion of a lady."

"Take 'em off? You're gonna stand in my kitchen and tell me how to take off a pair of dang gloves? Are you drunk?"

"I am trying to show you. And no, I am not drunk. The *correct* way to —"

"To take off my gloves?"

His lips pursed. "I will take my leave and you can continue to carry on with your poor diction and bad manners. Or, listen, follow my guidance, and learn how to become ladylike. Is that not what you asked of my services?"

"All right." She raised her hands in surrender as her eyes rolled almost audibly toward the ceiling. "I'm tryin', err, trying."

"Now, follow my instructions for removing gloves. Gently pull the fabric from the tip of each gloved finger on your left hand with the tips of your right fingers. Grasp the material and pull them off. Then do the same to the other hand. And I want you to smile. A lady appears to enjoy herself, even when she is miserable."

"That's plum crazy."

"That is the way it is," he said and pulled a beautiful ivory fan with delicate multi-colored flowers and golden, scalloped edges from his pocket. He handed it to Lacey and sat across from her.

"Well, it's stupid anyway," she said, running a finger over the edge of the fan. "This sure is perty."

"You distract too easily. Now, place the gloves in your lap and flick open the fan. Yes, it is made of silk and is," he spelled out, "p-r-e-t-t-y, pretty...not perty. Gently, fan your face."

"I ain't hot."

"Lacey."

"Well, I ain't."

"It does not matter if you are hot, or not. And it *isn't* hot."

"That's what I said. It *isn't* hot."

"You said it aint...." Winston held his breath as he turned as red as a sugar beet.

She drew the fan across her cheek before waving it in front of her face.

"Not like that," he shouted.

Lacey startled. "Why in tarnation not?"

He leaned close to her face. "That particular fan movement implies you are"— his voice lowered —"a willing participant."

"Nooo." Her eyes grew wide.

"Yes."

She threw the fan on the floor. "I'll never learn all this stupid lady business."

"I think we have learned enough for one evening." He rose from his chair. "Practice both walking and sitting with a book balanced on your head." He pointed toward the table. "Read all you can of your aunt's manuals."

Winston wrote more rules of the fan, and to Lacey's relief, he let himself out the door.

What have I gotten myself into? She sat the book on her head and took four steps before it hit the floor. "Stupid book." She kicked it to the far corner of the kitchen, plopped into the rocking chair and took inventory of herself. Yes, her shirt looked filthy, and dirt was plastered on every speck of her overalls. Deep grass stains filled in where the dirt left off. She'd have to find the energy to scrub some of the grime away and hang them to dry or, she chuckled, go to work the next day buck naked. Giddy with sleepiness, she envisioned the Burkes shocked faces if she arrived naked and bent forward laughing.

The laughter caught in her throat when she heard a loud banging on her door. "Who is it?" She sprang from the rocking chair.

"It's Brandon. Open the door. I need to speak with you."

"Oh mercy." She glanced at her clothes. "This isn't a good time, Brandon. Umm, I can't see you right now." Thank goodness, she'd closed the curtain so the varmint couldn't peek.

His voice boomed through the locked door. "I know you're entertaining a guest this evening. This will only take a minute." He banged his fist against the barrier with double the effort.

"Hold on a blasted second," Lacey hollered before snatching her straw hat from the floor and stripping off her clothes as she hurried to the bedroom. She grabbed a mint-green dress and threw it over her head, reached for a hairbrush, and then opted to let it hang loose. She pinched her cheeks the way Miss Aimee did.

Opening the door a smidgen, she peeked through the slit. Brandon's jaw was set in a granite-like scowl and his eyes appeared dark and brooding.

"Let me in." He placed the palm of his hand on the door and attempted to peek inside. Lacey did the best she could to shield his view of the empty room.

"I have *company* this evening." She cast a quick smile along with a wink toward the inside of the cabin. "As I *told* you, this is not a good time for, for you to visit." Lacey scrunched her nose and waved her hand in the air between them. "Lord have mercy, you've been nippin' at the 'shine, ain't you?"

His brows drew together in an angry frown as he forced the door wide enough to reach her arm and pull her into the night.

"What are you doing? Let me go." She jerked her arm in the hopes of freeing it from his grasp, then dug her boot heels into the grass, but he held a vicelike grip. She tugged on her arm. "Let. Me. Go."

When they reached a patch of clover nestled under the cottonwood tree, Brandon turned and gazed into Lacey's eyes. He lifted his index finger and placed it under her chin while he eased his lips closer. With a gentle pressure to the small of her back, he pulled her as near to his body as a second skin and tilted her chin upward. As his lips pressed to hers, his fingertips moved across her cheeks wispier than a feather's caress. His breath quickened like a wild beast about to ravage its prey as he released a ragged groan like he succumbed to the fiery passion of primal lust. He pressed into her body and Lacey's heart raced as an internal flame gathered momentum from deep within and rose to match the inferno emanating from his need.

Lacey inhaled sharply and took a wavering step backward. Her eyes smoldered with a fire akin to the blaze on her lips. "How dare you. How dare you kiss me like that." She swung her right arm back to gather momentum and delivered a solid punch into Brandon's stomach. "You miserable, rotten bird turd."

As her words sank in, the moment of escalating passion evolved into a burst of laughter. "Bird turd?"

Lacey furrowed her brow and stared at the man. "Stop that. Stop laughing." Her hands curled back into fists as she watched his display of amusement.

Brandon raised both arms in mock surrender. "Oh no, please…bird turd?"

Lacey clamped her jaw tight and stared as he walked, still chuckling, toward Thunder. He landed like a stone made of muscle into the saddle and rode from her property, bits of laughter fading into the night as he crested the gully near South Sunday Creek.

She returned to the cabin and the comfort of her rocking chair. *How dare that miserable, rotten, sensuous-kissing man whose lips meld perfectly with mine, force himself upon me?* She drew a finger to her buzzing lips, still warm from the intensity of his kiss. Closing her eyes, she relived the moment in her mind and an intense flame rose from within her body. She replayed the scene over and over, not wanting the moments of passion to fade from her memory.

Forcing herself to get busy, she gathered her dirty work clothes from the bedroom floor, lit her lantern, and took them outside to scrub and rinse in the wash pan. She returned to the cabin and hung them over kitchen chairs to dry. Donning a nightgown and returning all except one of Aunt Molly's books from the kitchen table to the floor next to her bed, she chose a culinary volume to review. *One day, I may hafta cook an actual meal.*

Lacey couldn't concentrate on reading. Her fingertips trailed to lips that continued to sear like the bottom of a pressing iron. She lay the book on the floor and paced. *How dare he kiss me like that? How dare he kiss me at all? And the nerve of the man to think he can stroll over any time he feels like it, and demand I see him.* She sure would like to show that raccoon a thing or two. *That's it.* Lacey scurried into the kitchen and threw an apron over her nightgown. She took a piece of string from the pantry shelf and tucked it into one of the two front apron pockets, each adorned with three embroidered cherries with black stems. She lit the lantern and bolted outside.

After digging the scarred hinges from the dirt near the barn door, she took them inside the barn and tossed them onto the ground. Searching a bit, she found several planks of wood, a handful of nails, and a hammer. She felt thankful for paying atten-tion when her brothers made box traps. Matthew and Jeremiah loved to coon hunt and she'd sneak out and let the critters go before they checked traps in the early morning. They would whine, gripe, and complain to Pa during breakfast about never catching any critters.

She didn't have a piece of wood wide enough for the lid, so she nailed several smaller pieces together with cross boards. After attaching the barn door hinges to the lid, she drove a nail into the hinged side of the box and retrieved the string from her pocket. She passed the string through a nail hole and tied it to the bottom of the trap. The other end of the string she let dangle. Stepping aside, Lacey surveyed her work.

"There you go, Mr. Raccoon," she said to the cobwebs. "That should keep you from gittin' a free meal and scurrying back home without so much as a howdy-do."

Lacey dragged the trap outside and left it next to the barn before returning to the cabin for bait. Thank goodness Mr. Burke sent the extra fried chicken and biscuits home with her. What coon could resist such a picnic? Lacey crammed the pockets of her apron full of the tasty eats and scurried back outside. Pulling the trap across the field proved more difficult than she had imagined, but Brandon certainly deserved the biggest critter this county offered.

Deciding on a spot near South Sunday Creek next to a hollow log, Lacey propped the box open with a stick and tested it several times to be certain it wasn't *too* secure. She smashed a piece of biscuit around a chicken leg and tied it to the dangling string, then to the stick. She returned to the cabin and crawled under her quilt.

The early morning sun cast golden sparkles of light shooting and scattering through the bottoms of the trees as Lacey hurried to check her trap. The 'coon's nails scratched the inside of the box and the critter's paw stuck out, reaching for freedom. Yep, she'd caught herself one mad-as-hell raccoon. *Perfect.* By the time she dragged the hefty trap through the field and to the far side of Brandon's barn, exhaustion had seeped into her bones. He'd be at the Burkes eating breakfast about now, so she better hurry. Brandon's cabin looked quiet, nothing stirred, and the surrounding woods were still. Lacey eyed his property for movement before dragging the box trap to his front door.

"All right, varmint," she informed the raccoon. "I've told you what I want you to do. Now don't let Lacey down." She opened the door to Brandon's cabin and pulled the 'coon trap inside the room. "Okay, my 'lil bandit, don't be shy. Make yourself right at home." After opening the lid, the raccoon bolted from the box like its hind end got lit with firecrackers and took off for the kitchen. Lacey hollered over her shoulder, "You have a real fun day now, you hear?" She pulled the empty trap outside and slammed the cabin door with all her might in case he needed more riling. Lacey hid the trap in her barn and headed to the Burkes' cabin. Visions of Brandon returning home to the raccoon's havoc excited her almost more than she could stand.

"Morning all," she sang merrily and found her place at the table.

"Good morning, Mace," Sarah and Adam said in unison.

"Sorry, I'm a few minutes late for breakfast." She was near out of breath from running like the dickens to change clothes and get over to the Burkes. "But Lacey asked me to help knead dough for tonight's supper. She's sure 'nuff taking a mighty liking to this new beau. Heck, her fella's coming over again this evening."

Brandon scowled as he reached for a bowl filled with steaming fried potatoes and onions.

"Yep, I don't think I've ever seen my sister so smitten with a fella. No, sir."

Everyone startled when Brandon opened his hand and let his fork drop with a loud clang onto his plate. He glowered at Mace. "Is there something we can discuss besides your sister's escapades?"

Adam and Sarah exchanged glances.

"Gee, I'm sorry. I haven't seen Lacey this happy, well, maybe never before." She took a plate of bacon from Sarah. "I guess it's rubbing off on me a 'lil, too. Heck, I'm wondering if she's gonna get hitched." Lacey forked a pancake and passed the plate to Adam.

"I guess your sister will be attending the corn festival this evening with her beau?" Sarah asked.

"Huh?" *What in tarnation did she say?*

"The corn festival. The townfolk hold it every year, and I don't think anyone ever misses it unless they're sick. Why, it's a yearly highlight for the entire county."

"I truly don't know, ma'am. I doubt iffin' Lacey knows 'bout it. I'll surely mention it." Lacey squirmed. She didn't count on a social event where Brandon would expect to see her with a beau.

Brandon needed to get off the Burke's farm. He couldn't look at Mace without thinking of Lacey, and when he thought of Lacey, he thought of her with a beau. His hands gripped the reins until his knuckles knotted into tight fists.

Thunder barely halted outside the cabin before Brandon dismounted. He shouldn't have kissed her. A big mistake. Now he needed more, much more. And, if Mace told the truth, some no-good swine was sparking Lacey.

He opened the front door and before he fully stepped inside, got an eyeful of *what in the world is that?* He stopped, stepped backward, and promptly closed the door. After blinking a few times and wiping his eyes, he shook the *that can't be* image from his mind. He reopened the door and within two seconds his heart hammered in a rapid rhythm like a starving woodpecker drumming for a juice-filled ant.

The inside of the cabin resembled a floating cloud of white… flour? It covered every square inch and everything in-between those inches. Confusion racked his brain as he waved his hand in a futile attempt to clear the hazy air. He stepped to the fireplace and wiped his hand across the mantel, sending ant-hill-sized mounds of flour scattering, dusting his clothes, and drifting to the floor. Brandon took a step back and came this close to falling face first as his boots were stuck near solid to the floor. He could not raise either boot more than a few inches. Trailed between his boot and the floor were thick, streaming, globs of honey. The more he fought to get unstuck, the more the streams of honey became long, sticky webs. He untied and removed his boots, then attempted to avoid getting honey on his socks.

He dared to look in the kitchen. The door to the pie safe swung freely on its metal hinges, the shelves stripped bare. Jars of preserves lay smashed on the floor, the contents spread like a sea of thin strawberry, blueberry, and blackberry goo. Animal tracks covered the floor in dancing patterns through piles of sugar, flour, and unidentified gunk. He squatted and took a good look at the paw prints. *What? How did a raccoon get in here?*

As he visually absorbed the enormous mess, it appeared the 'coon had sat on his haunches and thrown eggs for game points. The busted yolks splattered the walls and came within inches of reaching the ceiling in some spots. He stepped to the bedroom and welcoming him were shards of glass from a shattered bottle lying amidst a pool of his favorite whiskey. Crouched atop his bed with a union suit dangling over the top of his soon-to-be-dead furry head, crouched a madder-than-hades, hissing 'coon.

"I'm going to nail your hide to the barn door," Brandon threatened, moistening his lips. "You've breathed your last breath." The second he lunged, the 'coon lunged back at breakneck speed and ran straight for the kitchen. Brandon stayed a hair away from its tail and attempted to sink his hands into its furry coat. The 'coon slipped and slid over the gooey mess on top of the cookstove, then dove for the floor and attempted to get traction under its clawed feet. Instead, it ran a mock mile, his busy feet never leaving the same spot. Brandon stretched to reach the 'coon but lost his balance when his sock slid through a thick glob of sticky muck. He landed on the floor with a hard thud and the 'coon turned to stare Brandon down. After releasing a mighty screech, the critter sailed through the air, its sharp claws settling on Brandon's face. Sharp pain seared the flesh of his nose like embedded alcohol-soaked needles as he bolted upright, sending the 'coon scurrying out the open front door and into the woods.

Lacey hurried home as soon as her workday finished. *Corn Festival?* Adam mentioned a barn dance, too. It certainly sounded like a hoot. If anyone asked, she would say her beau couldn't make it. Simple.

She decided on a sapphire dress with a sweetheart-shaped bodice that fell from her waist in what Winston called alternate folds of cashmere and satin with worsted lace trim and velvet ribbon. What he had called "dressing in elegance." If appearing elegant, or even delightfully sinful would get Brandon's attention this evening, then so be it.

Fire and tarnation. I'm becoming a lady.

Lacey scanned the crowd at the barn dance. *Where is he?* Her foot tapped impatiently on the straw-covered floor. She turned to see Horace Sparker walking in her direction.

"Miss Lacey, I'm so doggone glad to see your pretty face." He wore a grin the size of a watermelon slice.

"A pleasure to see you, Horace," she managed to say. She peeked at the folks on the dance floor, sighed, and wondered if Brandon was dancing with the fancy lady from town.

"Shucks, Miss Lacey," Horace said, following her gaze. "If you wanted to dance, why didn't you say so?"

Before she could protest, he clasped her wrist and pulled her among the dancers.

Brandon opened the barn door to the festivities and stepped inside. He crossed his arms over his chest and scanned the crowd. He'd find out which scoundrel was behind the havoc in his cabin. He had spent most of the day making a path through his kitchen. The no-good raccoon had the nerve to return to his porch for another meal as he'd headed for the dance. If only his gun had been two steps closer.

A hand settling on Brandon's arm caused him to turn and break into a wide smile at the familiar face.

"Good evening, Brandon," his sister said. "My goodness, why such a sour face?" Her brows raised as she added, "And what did you do to your nose?"

Brandon leaned toward her and planted a kiss on her cheek. "I got into a raccoon fight, and the 'coon won," he answered gruffly.

Brandon searched the dance floor, and Rachael stifled a chuckle. "Looking for anyone in particular?"

"Just looking," he said before spotting Lacey.

Brandon strained to see around the swirling dancers in the center of the barn. John Petitjean called the square dance and dang it, as soon as Lacey met with one man, another whisked her away. *She looked beautiful.* Her dress twirled like spinning sapphires as she danced to the music. He shifted his weight. How could anyone's smile be so alluring? He must learn her beau's name and choke the miserable —

"Hello, Brandon." Sarah Burke interrupted his thoughts. "And, Rachael dear, how nice to see you again."

The two women exchanged a friendly hug and Rachael asked, "How is Mr. Burke?"

"Just fine, thank you," Sarah answered. "He slaughtered a hog this afternoon and feels a bit poorly in the shoulders but wanted to join in the festivities all the same."

Sarah looked at the woman on the dance floor who so intently held Brandon's attention. "I don't have to wonder who that beautiful lady is," she said. "Can you believe the resemblance between Mace and his sister, Lacey? It is uncanny." She glanced around the room. "Speaking of Mace, have you seen him?"

Brandon didn't hear her comment. *A beautiful angel.* An angel glided on the dance floor with a bright smile. Glistening tresses flowed behind her as an unfamiliar man spoke to Lacey and led her in a two-step. Brandon's blood turned into a raging inferno as the idiot pulled her close and whispered in her ear. He stormed across the dance floor, with determination obvious in his stride. As he neared Lacey and her partner, he reached for her arm.

♡ ♡ ♡

"Git yer, I mean get your hands off of me," she said and attempted to pull her forearm free of Brandon's iron grasp. "For your information," her hand fanned toward the man at her side, "I accepted a dance with this gentleman, and I intend to finish it."

Her confused dancing partner shuffled from one foot to the other until Brandon's unblinking scowl convinced him to make a beeline for the refreshment table.

"My dear lady." Brandon took Lacey in his arms without missing a dance step. "You seem to be in a pleasant mood this evening, and I can think of nothing I would rather do than dance with the most beautiful woman in New Harmony."

"What? What are you up to?"

"Up to, my dear? Nothing more than attempting to satisfy my desire to dance with you."

"Your desire? All right, that's it. Fess up," Lacey said, lowering one hand to her hip. "You been smoking wacky weed out behind the Burkes' place, haven't you?"

Brandon chuckled. "I don't need any assistance from 'wacky weed' to realize what a beautiful and charming woman you are." He placed his right hand on the small of her back and whisked her among the dancers.

Lacey hadn't missed seeing the exchange, and kiss, between Brandon and the dark-haired woman — the one she'd seen him walking beside in town. She nodded toward the group standing by the door. "I see your lady friend has arrived."

He glanced over his shoulder. "Who? Do you mean Rachael?"

"How would I know if I mean Rachael when I've never met her? I'm talking about the lady over there holding an umbrella."

She nodded toward a woman wearing a peach dress, carrying a flowered parasol.

Brandon looked again and grinned. "Yes, that's Rachael. She's a seamstress at the General Mercantile and just so happens to be my sister."

"Yer, I mean, your sister? Oh…I didn't know you had family."

"True, neither one of us has talked much about our families." He chuckled as he said, "Here you didn't think I had family, and I'm one of twelve."

Lacey's voice rose an octave. "Twelve?"

"Yes, you heard me right, twelve. In school, we were known as the "Chandler Dozen.""

Lacey placed her hand over her heart. "I can't imagine having such a big family to feed. My ma died giving birth to my baby sister, Pearl Rose. Neither made it," she said swallowing hard. "So, it's just Pa, and my three older brothers, Matthew, Luke, and Jeremiah.

"Rachael's three years younger and lives here in town. She comes out to the ranch once or twice a week for a visit and takes pleasure in cooking me a hearty meal. And, I have to say, I take greater pleasure in eating it," he said with a chuckle. "Everyone else, they're scattered all around. Mom and Dad, they aren't too far away. They live in Billings."

The song ended, and Brandon ushered Lacey to a table of refreshments. "Apple cider?" He offered her a mug of the warm liquid.

"I'd like that, thank you."

"Let's go for a walk. I could use some fresh air." Brandon touched her elbow and they walked into the night.

Fresh air? Maybe that will jar the real Brandon awake. *Why in tarnation is he being so nice, even talking about his family. I don't know…but I like it.* Feeling light as a feather, she glanced at her shoes to see if her boots touched the floor, or if she truly walked on air. The day she stepped off the stagecoach and met Brandon, she thought he was the most handsome man she'd ever laid her cotton-picking eyes upon. Aunt Molly's will stipulation or not, she dreamed of being Mrs. Brandon Chandler. Heck, she only invented a beau to test Brandon's reaction.

Her thoughts halted when the kerosene lamps from the barn dance became a distant haze. Brandon slowed and as he turned, he took Lacey's free hand in his. He curled his finger under her chin and tilted her face upward.

She looked into eyes that swam in a deep pool of desire. His gaze held hers as gentle as a caress and as lustful as any sin. His warm lips pressed upon hers. Softly…gently he kissed her. Lacey wanted Brandon to press into her lips with more force and she encircled the tops of his broad shoulders as he continued this sweet, desirable torture. Finally, his mouth possessed hers like he would consume her with his lustful kiss. His hands feathered lightly down the sides of her body, then moved to encompass her waist. Lacey's knees weakened as his breathing turned raw and husky and his eyes captured hers in a lustful gaze.

Is this how love feels? Could Brandon love a…a backwoods tomboy like me?

He crushed her body close to his and traced the tip of his tongue along the soft outline of her lips. His voice became a hoarse whisper. "Lacey, I want you."

Could this be true? She had only dreamed of a moment like this. His kiss eased for a fraction of a second before Lacey drew him closer with her arms and returned the same passion Brandon revealed to her. *I'm in love with Brandon Chandler.*

His sensual touch, his full lips and exploring tongue, sent welcome shivers of desire coursing through her body, and sending the pit of her stomach into a wild, out-of-control spiral. Brandon eased her onto nature's pallet of fall leaves, which Lacey perceived as a featherbed while in his loving, muscular arms. He kissed the pulsing hollow at the base of her throat causing a wave of sweet, tortuous heat to bolt down Lacey's spine. "Sweet heaven," she whispered before drawing his lips to hers and kissing him like a lover, savoring every precious moment.

"Miss Lacey, are you hurt?" The lovers bolted upright to the panicked voice standing a mere three feet away. "Should I holler for Doc Petitjean?" Horace Sparker's flesh appeared white as Christmas linen. "Did you fall, or swoon, Miss Lacey?"

She took one look at Brandon's clenched jaw and knew if she didn't say something, he would kill the man and make kindling out of him. She stood and brushed leaves from her dress. "Horace, I'm fine. Brandon, err, helping me look for, umm for my umm, my necklace. It unfastened and, being dark and all, we were feeling for it with our hands. I'll, uh, come out tomorrow when it's daylight and look for it," she said before scurrying back toward the barn.

Winston Beaumont's hands shook so violently he dropped his cup of warm apple cider. He stepped over the rapidly spreading puddle and stared in the direction of the barn door. Brandon and Lacey left the dance over twenty minutes previous and still had not returned. He overheard Horace Sparker inquiring as to Lacey's whereabouts and casually mentioned he had seen her walk outside.

He paced. How long was it going to take the imbecile to find them? Finally, Lacey came rushing through the door, the Chandler fellow following close behind. He reached for the flask from his pocket. A swig of scotch was in order.

Brandon placed his hand on Lacey's elbow and ushered her to the dance floor. A smile washed over her face when she realized this was a couple's two-step. She did not want any other woman within spitting distance of Brandon.

"Would you like something to drink?" he asked when the dance finished.

"Yes, I would," she answered and walked with him to the refreshment table where he poured them each a glass of sweet apple cider.

Lacey took the cup of punch Brandon offered and noticed his fingers lingered atop hers for a second before reaching for his glass. As they enjoyed watching the dancers, he casually reached to hold her hand. The feel of Brandon's flesh upon hers sent renewed shivers down her spine. She noticed Winston Beaumont nearing the table and when he reached for a glass, she said, "Good evening, Mr. Beaumont. "Are you enjoying yourself?"

"I most certainly am," he answered, and was obvious about staring with distaste directly at the hand Brandon held.

Lacey wished he would stop carrying on about the sudden intimacy between her and Brandon.

"Dear," Brandon said, "whenever you are ready to leave, I'll escort you home."

Sarah Burke walked toward them, and Lacey's guts did a quick somersault.

"You must be Lacey," Sarah said as she neared the group, a bright smile on her face. "I have heard so much about you from your brother, Mace."

"It's a pleasure to meet you, ma'am," Lacey said. "Mace sure is grateful for you and Mr. Burke giving him a job."

"Mace?" Winston Beaumont's eyebrows headed north.

Lacey squirmed. "Yes, my brother. He is stayin' with me fer a spell."

Sarah Burke started jabbering again. "I can't believe the resemblance between you and Mace. It is uncanny how much the two of you look alike. I declare. I saw you on the dance floor and had no doubt you were related."

Lacey forced herself to stop fidgeting. Winston watched her every move. His nose and forehead were scrunched, and one eyebrow shot higher than the other.

"Brandon," she said stifling a forced yawn. I'm ready to leave if you are?" She cast a quick glance at Winston who continued to stare. "Yes, it's time I head home," Lacey repeated and cast a wave over her shoulder. "As Pa would say: Time to pee on the fire and call in the dogs. Goodnight, Mrs. Burke. Such…"

"Hey, slow down, girl," Brandon said as he hurried his steps. "What's the rush?"

Lacey took a deep breath. She couldn't get away from Sarah Burke's questions nor the curious stares she received from Beaumont fast enough.

"I'm sorry, Brandon." she said, reaching for his outstretched hand. "I guess that sweet apple cider gave me a sudden burst of energy." She slowed to walk beside him.

"Lacey?"

They turned at the sound of Sarah Burke's voice and Lacey's insides went taut as chicken wire.

"I wondered if you and Mace would enjoy a few pounds of fresh bacon? Adam slaughtered a hog and we have more than enough for the two of us. You can hang it in your smokehouse, dear, and come winter you'll be glad to have it."

Lacey relaxed and said, "That would be nice." She'd never turn down smoked bacon. "Oh, but just a second." Lacey turned to Brandon. "I noticed there are a few cracks in the smokehouse floor. The meat will spoil iffin', I mean, if it isn't sealed properly."

"I have some coal tar in my barn," Brandon offered. "We can stop on the way to your cabin and I'll grab it. It will only take a few minutes to spread it over the floor, and day after tomorrow you can hang the bacon."

"That will be wonderful," Lacey said. "And thank you, Mrs. Burke."

"You're welcome, dear, and please call me Sarah." She waved goodbye as Brandon assisted Lacey onto the seat of his buggy.

The buggy jolted as Brandon snapped the reins. He sure seemed to be in a hurry, Lacey thought, and wondered if he expected an invitation inside for coffee after he spread the coal tar.

It only took him a minute to sprint into his barn and grab the bucket of tar, a flat knife, and a lantern.

When they arrived at Lacey's cabin, her mind raced. *What'd I do with my dirty work clothes?* She bit her lip. *What 'bout the straw hat I wore to the Burkes? Was it on the table, or stuffed under my bed?* As soon as the buggy came to a stop, Lacey quickly stepped down. "I'll be right back to help you with the coal tar," she called and hurried to the cabin door.

"You stay inside," Brandon said. "I'll spread the tar. It will only take a minute, and then I'll join you."

Lacey cast a glance over her shoulder as she brushed a hand over the tiny gathers near the waistline of her dress. She noticed the smile forming on Brandon's lips certainly took on a rather sensuous flame. She bolted into the cabin.

Twenty minutes later, Brandon opened the door and peeked inside. "I didn't see any need to knock since you were expecting me," he said with a devilish grin.

"Th…thank you for the ride home," Lacey stuttered as she scurried to stand beside him. She reached for the door handle.

"Whoa, wait just a minute, girl." Brandon said, wrapping his arms around her waist. "What's the big hurry?"

She tried to keep her attention on him but found herself looking around every corner and crevice for her dirty *Mace* clothing or any stray item she may have missed.

He lifted her chin with a finger. "What's wrong?" He looked over his shoulder before returning his attention to her eyes. "Relax, you seem preoccupied."

"I suppose all the dancing and fresh air made me sleepy. My bed is gonna feel perty…pretty darn good tonight." She squeezed past Brandon to open the door.

Brandon followed her onto the stoop and touched her arm lightly. He brushed a kiss across her lips and when he spoke, his voice sounded husky. "I had hoped we could spend more time together this evening, seeing how we were interrupted." His lips on hers prevented further conversation. As he kissed her, he wrapped his arms around her waist and drew her close. He kissed her eyelids before reclaiming her lips in a hungry kiss.

Lacey's pulse danced a quick two-step as his lips pressed firmer and more demanding, his breaths developing an urgency that sent tingles surging through her body. A smoldering heat penetrated her dress and swirled around her insides a few dozen times and repeated. She melted in his arms and returned his passion. The moment ended abruptly when her palms pushed against Brandon's chest. "I'm sorry," she said, her breathing heavy, "but, we hafta stop. We must stop, now. I'm a lady."

Brandon inhaled deeply and released an audible breath. "Yes, you *are* a lady, dear. No doubt about it, you are one fine lady."

She looked into his eyes and smiled. "Goodnight," she whispered and closed the door. Watching from the window as the buggy rolled out of sight, tears of happiness streamed down her cheeks. Brandon stole her heart, and it appeared she stole his, too. Realizing how easy it was to tell him she had become a lady, she twirled in a circle, holding herself in a hug. All of her worrying for nothing.

Someone knocked forcefully on the door to Brandon's cabin.

"What do you want at this hour?" He opened the barrier and looked at the weasel on his stoop.

"Please, pardon the inconvenience, Mr. Chandler. I am concerned about Miss Kendall," Winston Beaumont said. "I must say…I fear for her life."

"What are you talking about?" Brandon asked with skepticism. "Lacey isn't in any danger. I left her cabin not more than fifteen minutes ago and there wasn't any sign of trouble."

"Not immediate danger, Mr. Chandler." He placed an index finger on his hollow cheek. "I see you are unaware of Miss Kendall's employment status."

"Employment status?"

"I see by your inquisitive reaction you are not aware of Lacey's dire situation either. Perhaps I have made a mistake by coming to speak to you." He tipped the brim of his hat forward as he added, "Please excuse me, Mr. Chandler, and I shall be on my way."

"What are you talking about? What dire situation?"

Winston shook his head with pity and said, "Miss Kendall, the poor girl works as a laborer at the Burke's farm. The lass is posing as a boy to earn enough money to eat."

Thunder roared. Or was it the surge of blood crashing through his temples?

"Of course, bless her dear heart," Winston continued, "because of her aunt's will stipulation, she must do something until she finds a husband, *any* husband, in order to inherit her deceased Aunt Molly's homestead."

Brandon never remembered feeling more confused than at this moment. "I think you best come inside, Beaumont. I don't have the foggiest idea what you are talking about."

Winston slithered inside and stood next to a table piled with a mound of soiled clothing.

A moment later, Brandon turned to hand his visitor a shot glass and said, "You have my attention, Beaumont. Start talking."

The rider's lips formed a cynical smile as he rode to Lacey's cabin, halting on the outskirts of her land. He stopped to pat his left pocket before dipping a finger inside and running it lightly over the gold button. *Here I come, Miss Kendall.*

He rode to her smokehouse and dismounted before unbuckling a pouch from the saddle. He pulled out a rag and a tin of kerosene. The smokehouse door opened without a sound and the air reeked with the smell of coal tar. Walking to the far corner, he slid down on one knee and soaked the rag with kerosene before tossing it on the floor. Striking and throwing a lit match on top of the rag caused it to erupt into a blaze of fire.

When he stood and turned to dash outside, his boots stuck to the sticky muck and he doubled over as his hands slapped soundly onto the tarred floor. "What the heck?" Each step was a struggle, but he managed to inch himself outside to safety as flames shot high into the night sky, the embers crackling and falling to the ground like confetti ablaze. He hurried back to his horse through the black shadows created by Lacey's enormous cottonwood tree.

$\heartsuit\ \heartsuit\ \heartsuit$

Engrossed in reading, Lacey didn't smell smoke until it seeped in around her windows. She opened the door of the cabin and released a shrill scream. Fire emerged thunderous from the smokehouse and the grass was ablaze with a breeze blowing it to within minutes of reaching the cabin. The smell of kerosene hung heavy in the air.

Lacey screamed as loud as her lungs would allow as she dashed outside to find her large, speckled wash pan. The pump handle on the well couldn't keep pace with her frantic movements. She threw the pan full of water onto the fire and realized in terror that no amount of effort on her part would control the blaze. As the tongues of fire crept closer to the cabin, she bolted inside and ran to her bedroom. Seeing the heavy chamber pot on the floor, she snatched it and hurled it through the window. Next, she threw handfuls of clothing, quilts, and Aunt Molly's lady's books through the opening. She raced to salvage items until the heat became unbearable and forced her to retreat to the yard. Lacey dropped to her knees near the clothesline, the tears streaming down her cheeks as the cabin crackled and weakened under the immense heat of the relentless flames.

"If it's the last deed I do," she vowed, staring blankly at her destroyed refuge, "I'll tie the hanging noose on the monster responsible for this."

After gathering her salvaged possessions and placing them far from the fire, she walked toward the smokehouse and stopped short. Something on the ground caught her eye. From where she stood, it looked like a gold coin. Curious, she bent to pick it from the embers. When her fingertips touched the coin, it seared her flesh. Then it seared her heart. No, it was not a gold coin, it was a button. And not just any button…the button from Brandon Chandler's fancy black shirt.

The sound of distant wagon wheels snapped Lacey's attention back to the dire threat at hand. Hot, crackling flames and thick smoke rolled from the cabin. Adam and Sarah Burke's wagon came over the hillside as three men on horseback neared her property at breakneck speed. The riders dismounted, and Adam brought his team of horses to a halt.

Adam jumped from the wagon seat and hollered to Sarah and Lacey to fetch the buckets he'd thrown into the back. The new arrivals formed a line to the pump and as fast as the buckets filled, the sloshing containers were handed from one person to the next and the water thrown onto the flames.

The smoldering heat threatened to melt Lacey's clothing to her skin along with the black soot that had already adhered. The last of the fire signaled its departure with a cloud of black smoke, and Lacey used the sleeve of her dress to wipe her brow before collapsing in Sarah's arms. She squinted as one of the men walked toward her. Soot and sweat plastered his thick arms and hair clung to his forehead in matted disarray. The life seemed to flow from Lacey's soul as she slid to the ground. *How dare he approach me after what he did*? Lacey shook with rage as she looked into the eyes of the devil himself — Brandon Chandler.

"Lacey, oh heaven's girl," Sarah said.

Sarah's voice sounded far away as if coming from the bottom of a pickle barrel. *Why was everything happening in slow motion?* Lacey attempted to stand, her eyes never leaving Brandon's. Her breath came in short, raspy waves — her throat raw.

"Lacey, are you all right?" Brandon wiped his forehead across the length of his shirt sleeve.

She squinted against the harsh sound of a thousand bells ringing in spiraling waves within her head. She could barely hear. *Why did everything sound so muted and distant?*

The bells stopped. Voices once again became clear. Lacey screamed like a woman possessed as she lunged forward with outstretched hands and scrunched her fingers around his neck.

Sarah screamed, "Lacey, oh my, what ever are you doing? Adam, Adam come quick!"

Sarah's hands pressed on Lacey's shoulders to pull her from the demon, but she kept a tight grip. Visions of Brandon in a pine box kept her focused on her task. He attempted to peel her fingers from his neck, but with the same determination, she continued to squeeze until her wrists became so sore, she had to let loose.

Brandon brought his hands to his neck and attempted to talk, but only a raspy hoarseness emerged. "What's wrong with you? You about"— he rubbed his neck —"you about killed me."

Sarah sounded frantic. "Lacey, where is Mace? I think it may be a good idea if Mace were here." She embraced Lacey, and with Adam's assistance, they helped her to their wagon.

Lacey stared intently at Brandon as they led her away and repeatedly mouthed I hate you…I hate you…."

Adam helped Lacey into the back of his wagon and set her belongings by her feet before signaling the team of horses to giddyap. Brandon became the size of a speck of ash before Lacey finally allowed herself to blink his image away.

Sarah turned in her seat and said, "Honey, you and Mace stay on the farm with us until you get yourselves settled again."

Lacey snapped to attention. She needed to think, and fast. "Miss Fronie's Boardinghouse," she said. "Mace can meet me there. He headed over to the Crystal Saloon this evening, and I want to be the one to tell him about the fire." Her growling stomach ached to be Sarah's dinner guest, but what about the fictitious Mace? "I wouldn't dream of imposing on the two of you."

Sarah reached to touch Lacey's arm. "It would be no imposition at all, dear. We'd be glad to have the two of you."

Lacey patted the woman's hand. "Thank you, but please, you've already done so much." She spoke with as much conviction as she could. "Fronie's will do just fine."

Adam and Sarah kindly helped to carry her belongings into Fronie's and now Lacey fancied a soft bed and a pillow to cry into.

"Miss Kendall?"

Lacey took a deep breath as she turned to the sound of Winston Beaumont's voice.

"Yes, it's me, Mr. Beaumont," she said over the pile of clothing in her arms. She blurted, "My cabin's been burnt to the ground, and I'll be staying at the boardinghouse fer…for a spell." Miss Fronie gave me a room." She opened her hand and displayed a key in her palm.

"Why, that is simply incredulous," he said, his eyes wide as a pop-eye fish. "Your cabin — burned?"

She pursed her lips and blew the air out slowly. "Yes, the cabin. And no, I didn't start the fire on the cookstove. It was deliberately set." Visions of Brandon's shiny gold button coursed through her mind.

"Lacey." He touched her hand with the tips of his buffed fingernails. "I am so sorry to hear this dreadful news. If there is anything, anything I can do to help." He reached to take the bulk of clothing from her arms. "Let me carry this for you."

Lacey nodded toward the front desk. "There is something you can do. I'll carry these clothes upstairs, but the books over there," she said, nodding toward several volumes stacked in a chair. "If you would carry them to my room, I'd be mighty grateful."

Winston met Lacey at the top of the staircase and followed her into her room.

"Just put them anywhere." She dropped the clothing onto the floor. "I'll sort everything tomorrow. Tonight, I want to sleep."

"I will take my leave, Miss Kendall." He stacked the books into one of two available chairs. "We can talk more at breakfast. Goodnight." He closed her door then reopened it a crack and pointed to the knob. "Don't forget to lock the door," he said.

Lacey shook her head and walked to lock the door behind him. She pulled off her soiled, smoke-smelling dress and poured water from a pitcher on the dressing table into a large washbowl. She cleansed the bulk of dirt and grime from her face and arms before collapsing on top of the bedcovers.

Brandon washed away the soot, but nothing washed the anger from his heart. Lacey seemed so desolate. He yearned to take her in his arms and hold her forever. However, the words of Winston Beaumont lingered heavily on his mind. Mace and Lacey were the same person? He worked side by side with her and she'd put on an act, and a mighty convincing one at that. The toe of his boot made solid contact with the thick wall of his kitchen. *Dang her.*

He reached for a clean slate-blue shirt hanging from the back of a chair. And not only did she portray herself as a boy and work side by side with him and Adam, but also her deception involved tricking him into marriage for a piece of land, no less. He lifted his Stetson from a hook by the front door and rode Thunder into town.

Lacey awoke to the sound of pounding on her door. She crawled out of bed and decided to be firmer with Winston Beaumont. Just because they stayed at the same hotel, it didn't give him the privilege to disturb her whenever he pleased. And why was he knocking so loud, for criminy sake?

"Mr. Beaumont," she said with her hand on the knob and enough fury to wake the entire hallway of guests. She startled when, as the door opened, Brandon stood on the other side wearing the same fiery expression Lacey imagined mirrored her own. She clamped her lips together. A lady didn't say the kind of words swirling around in her mouth and pressing against clenched teeth.

"You were expecting Beaumont?"

"I have nothing to say to you, Mr. Chandler," Lacey said, gearing to give the door a good slamming.

Brandon halted the swinging door with his boot. "This is not a social visit. Quite the contrary. I assume since your charade has been exposed, you will be leaving town, and I owe you wages for your last week of work at the Burkes." He reached into his pocket. "That is, of course, unless you find another man to fall for your deception."

"What? What are you talking about? What deception?"

"What deception? You make a pretty liar, but a liar none-theless." He shook his head with a faux chuckle. "You can look me right in the eye and let deceit flow from your lips like you're saying a prayer."

She stared blankly. "I don't know what you're talking about."

"Let me remind you then, Miss Forgetful. I had a long chat with Beaumont. You do remember Winston Beaumont, don't you?"

She set her mouth and glared at him like a warning cloud coming from the southwest. She couldn't believe what he was saying.

"Well, it seems the man knows a lot about your situation. He informed me of your aunt's will stipulation of being a married woman and of your deceptive nature, Lacey, err Mace, or whatever you're calling yourself today. And then your amorous change of attitude toward me became clear. Your final wages, Miss Kendall." He tossed the bills on the floor by her feet and turned to leave.

ust a gall darn minute, Chandler. I may have posed as a boy to find work, and yes, perhaps I wasn't totally honest with you, but to set fire to my cabin and burn me outta my home is —"

"Set fire to your cabin?" He interrupted her vehemently. "I may be angry with you, but I never stepped foot near your cabin, and I am not an arsonist."

"Then how did your gold shirt button find a home in my charred grass?" She flashed him a hostile glare. "Tell me that, Mr. Chandler."

Brandon's anger abated as his expression turned to confusion. "If one of my buttons, from one of my shirts, ended up in your grass, I swear by all that is holy, I don't have the foggiest idea how it got there." He hesitated and leaned toward Lacey. "And what gives you the notion that it's *my* button?"

Lacey reached to grab the seared object from the dressing table. She opened her hand and thrust the button forward. "Look familiar?"

Brandon looked at her outstretched palm. His jaw tensed as he reached for the button.

Lacey pulled her hand back. "Evidence."

"Evidence? Evidence, my ass," Brandon scolded harshly before storming back down the hallway.

Bright fingers of morning light streaked through the starched, white ruffled curtain in Lacey's room. She woke and shielded her eyes from the sunny intrusion. Not even a minute passed before tears rolled down her cheeks. She slammed her fist into the pillow. Dang that blasted no-good man. And, to think she'd fallen in love with the arsonist brute. Now, she had nothing left to her name except a few salvaged items from the cabin.

She glanced at the heap of clothing laying on the floor. Angrily, she snatched her overalls and tattered shirts and stuffed them into the waste can. "Good riddance, Mace," she said aloud, brushing his memory away with hand swipes. She hung the pretty dresses she'd saved and carefully folded her undergarments and lace gloves. Aunt Molly's ruffled ivory parasol found a home on a brass hook near the window.

She sat on the bed and contemplated her situation as she counted her wages. Heck, she didn't even have enough money to pay for the still warm bed where she'd just slept. Hating to admit it, she knew unless she found work, and fast, she'd be hightailing it back to Pa before the end of the week. She buried her head back in the pillow for a minute before having a fleeting thought. Standing, she paced in front of the window. No way would she allow the likes of Brandon Chandler to run her out of town no matter what criminal acts he pulled.

She stopped to drum her fingers on the windowsill. As she looked toward the end of the street, the doors on the Crystal Saloon swung back and forth. Busy place. She sighed. Busy place? Maybe she could get a job? She hurried to ready herself and ran zigzagged past buggies before dashing across the street.

She stopped when reaching the saloon and smoothed her dress, pulled her shoulders back, and walked through the swinging doors. A rumble of baritone laughter and loud voices spilled into the street. A woman in a dress of flouncy corn yellow ruffles sat on a round stool playing a lively ragtime tune on an upright piano. Her dress spilled around her to the floor. The saloon was a bit too dark for Lacey's liking and awful smoky. She waved her hand in front of her face and noticed a mishmash of chairs surrounded each table. Groups of men slapped cards down with a whooping and a'hollering.

"Where's the owner?" she asked a tall man behind the bar with a yellowish-brown residue in his mustache. "I be lookin' for a job."

He poured whiskey into five shot glasses all lined in a row atop the bar, snickered, and said to one of the stool warmers, "This here little lady, she *be lookin'* for a job." He threw his head back and joined the others in laughter.

Lacey frowned and walked toward a doorway covered by a long, tattered curtain. A woman with a lower-than-low-cut neckline came bustling through and nearly knocked Lacey over.

"That's a dangerous place to stand, sugar," she said, balancing a tray of empty glasses. "Are you looking for somebody?"

"The owner. I'm lookin' for, umm, looking for the owner. I need a job."

The woman frowned and shook her head before setting the tray on the bar. "I need another round, Rusty," she told the bartender, then placed her hands on her hips before reaching toward Lacey's chest.

Lacey took a quick backward step, her hand covering her bosom. "What are you doing?"

"Sugar, I'm seeing if you have the right merchandise to work here. Big Joe ain't going to hire you if you can't produce for him."

"Produce? Whaddya mean produce?" She maintained her distance.

"Make money for the saloon," she said. "If the men are happy with what they see, this place makes a heck of a lot more money, sugar-belle."

Lacey smelled whiskey on the woman's breath. "I don't think so," she said with an edge to her voice, and turned to leave.

"You can't beat the pay," the woman cooed and clicked her tongue.

Lacey stopped and muttered uneasily, "How much…pay?"

"Depends on what you're willing to sell," she answered. "I heard Big Joe talking about needing a pretty poker dealer. If you want, I'll go with you to speak to him."

"A poker dealer?" Lacey sure won her share of poker back home at the Cactus Rose.

"Vera," the woman called to a buxom redhead standing behind a customer with her arms draped seductively around his shoulders. "When Rusty gets my order poured"— she nodded toward the curtain —"take them in to the fellas."

"What's your name, sugar?"

"Lacey, Lacey Autumn Kendall."

"No, what's your real name?"

"That *is* my real name."

The woman placed her hand on the stair rail. "Well, Lacey Autumn Kendall, I'm Thelma. Follow me, I'll get you ready to meet the boss man."

Thelma tied Lacey into a tight, burnt-red corset with thin black ribbons and lace, making her look as if she had the waistline of a wasp. "I can hardly breathe in this thing," she managed to say before making a futile attempted to pull it away from her body.

"Don't have to breathe, sugar." Thelma laughed. "Just have to deal. Anyway, you won't care much about breathing when those fellas are handing you wads of money." She brought a dress from the closet and said, "Lift your arms." Black lace trimmed the crimson dress falling to the floor in narrow flounces.

"I can't wear this," Lacey said, gulping with wide eyes as she looked at her reflection in the mirror.

"Why not, sugar? You've got all the right equipment, that's for sure."

Lacey pulled and tugged at the neckline. "But you can see the tops of my, you know, titties."

"Breasts, honey, never be ashamed you're a woman." Thelma grasped the top of the plunged neckline and jerked it back in place. "Now, leave it alone, you look stunning."

If Lacey weren't hungry and desperate for money, she'd pour herself right back out of the sensual dress.

"Here," Thelma said. "Let's put a touch of this on your face." She took a small brush and colored Lacey's cheeks with a deep rose hue and her lips a sultry red. Her lashes appeared to lengthen tenfold with a touch of coal. "Baby girl, you are gorgeous," she said. "You ready to make some *real* money?"

Lacey attempted to take a deep breath in the tight dress. No success. "Yeah, I'm ready." She followed Thelma back down the steps and through the curtain. A heavyset man in a too-tight suit sat at a table with a group of men. He bellowed a loud laugh with a fat cigar hanging from the side of his meaty lips. Lacey decided she didn't care much for Big Joe.

The man looked at Thelma and nodded his head toward Lacey. "Who's that?"

Thelma shifted her weight. "This here's Lacey and she's looking for work."

"Is that so?" He stared at Lacey's cleavage with bloodshot eyes.

Thelma leaned in close. "Don't get excited, Big Joe. She's a card dealer."

"Oh." The man's features appeared to slacken and near burnt a hole staring at Lacey's curves. "Hired. Let her watch Bobbi Sue for a while and give her a table." He winked at Lacey and turned back to his conversation.

"C'mon, sugar," Thelma said and took Lacey's arm. "Let's go introduce you."

Bobbi Sue was a tall blonde with huge breasts threatening to fall from her dress when the woman breathed, giggled, wiggled, or coughed. Heaven forbid she sneeze.

"Sit here beside Bobbi Sue and watch her deal," Thelma said and pulled out a chair.

The woman dealt, but as the men rearranged the cards in their hand, she giggled, which caused her to jiggle, and all their eyes were on her bouncing breasts. Bobbi Sue held a second deck of cards on her lap. Lacey reckoned the men never noticed she had more cheat in her than fair. After each hand, Bobbi tucked the extra cards under the table and danced over to the winner for a kiss, and a tip that she tucked into her cleavage.

Lacey watched the action for a while and decided she'd seen enough. She stood to leave and at the same second, Brandon strode into the saloon. A hush fell over the patrons. This tall, handsome man commanded immediate respect and left no question in anyone's mind who he was, or what he stood for, and against. He was a man who had fought many battles on the right side of the law. He became immersed in conversation until he turned to assess the crowd. He glanced her way and then past her, but then jerked back toward her and focused his attention on her alone, with the scowling, wide-eyed expression of an obsessed madman.

Lacey blinked twice as Brandon took long, heavily planted strides to reach her side, ripping off his shirt as he walked, and sending buttons splaying across the floor. When he reached her, he threw it over her shoulders and pulled it closed across her breasts, then grasped her wrist with a solid grip and pulled her away from the table.

"What are you doing?" Lacey demanded, planting her feet on the floor, unable to keep herself from staring at his bare, washboard physique and muscular arms.

He leaned in nose-to-nose and said, "Trying to regain your decency. What the…what in the world are you doing?"

"I don't think my decency, or anything else about me is any of your business." She shrugged his hand from her wrist.

He ground the words between his teeth as he commanded, "Come. With. Me. NOW."

Lacey jerked his shirt from her shoulders, wadded it, and threw it at his boots. "Put a hand on me again, I'll go to the sheriff and have you arrested. What I do, what I wear, nothing 'bout me is any of your dang business. Nothing." She rubbed her palms together. "Now, leave me be, I have a game to deal."

He eyed her while strolling to an empty table. She grabbed a deck of cards, broke it into two stacks, and shuffled. Nearby tables emptied as men crowded to fill the chairs around her. From the corner of her eye, she watched Brandon return to the bar. Within seconds, his hand wrapped around a fresh drink from Rusty, and he turned his seat around for a clear view of her table.

After her five-card deal, she waited for the men to ask for replacement cards and recalled the night of the barn dance, when she and Brandon embraced as they lay in the soft grass, and how she had returned his kisses like two flames burning out of control. His hands, she recalled the sweet memory of his hands, gently stroking her cheek and neck, trailing down her arms, and wrapping around her fingers. *Was he recalling the same vivid memories?*

When the men with losing hands threw their cards down, she bent over the table to gather the discards and exposed a fair amount of her breasts to the leering eyes of her tablemates. When one man reached his hand toward her, Brandon nearly spit out his drink. He slammed his whiskey glass on the bar top causing many to flinch as the loud, sharp, shattering of glass sprayed across the bar and onto the floor.

Six heavy-booted strides and Brandon stood across the poker table from Lacey with eyes so deep and dark it made her wonder if his vision were fueled by embers. He continued to stare at her, his lips becoming thinner and growing tighter before her eyes. He placed his hand on an occupied chair. The man who inhabited the seat glanced at the intruder and without a second of hesitation, abandoned his seat. Brandon yanked the chair out a little further and claimed it, then bent and brought his fist down hard on the table as he demanded, "Deal me in."

Lacey shrugged her shoulders and attempted to replace her anger with the appearance of indifference. She took pleasure in performing a perfect one-handed shuffle before announcing, "Deuces and one-eyed Jacks wild." As she dealt the cards, she noticed a small muscle flinch in Brandon's jaw as each card hit the table. "Gentlemen, place your bets."

When it came time for Brandon to bet, he laid his cards face down on the table and stared blue eyes to violet. "I bet *you*, Lacey."

Her nostrils flared as the men around the table chuckled at his ribbing. "I don't know what you're talking 'bout. Why don't you go get yourself another drink? I don't think you're drunk enough."

"I'm more than sober. I'm more sober than anyone else in this saloon. Like I said, I bet *you*."

"You bet me? What are you talking 'bout?"

"I bet if my hand beats yours, you walk out of this saloon with me and never come back. That's my bet."

"You're on, cowboy." She dealt herself a hand and lifted the cards to her chest. Gently, with no damage to the cards, she bent the corner of each one back a little, to assess her odds. She held two kings and three tens. She eyed Brandon under her coal-enhanced lashes. "And iffin' I win, you walk away and mind your own business?"

"If that's what you want," he said in his deep, calm voice.

His confidence caused an annoying tremble all the way to her guts.

"Yes, I will walk away."

"And mind your own business?"

"And mind my own business," he answered.

Lacey looked from one player to the other. "Any more bets?"

The rest of the table folded. Lacey made a grand show of fanning her winning full house onto the table.

Brandon leaned back in his chair and shook his head in mock resignation. He stared into her eyes for a few seconds before a smile formed on his lips and he showed the table his four ten spots.

Lacey's eyes grew wide as she took a quick intake of air. Not wanting to believe what she saw, she proclaimed loudly, "Brandon Chandler, you cheated. You must have cards hidden under the table like Bobbi Sue."

Suddenly, the room turned ghostly quiet and a dull roar akin to thunder rolled through the saloon. Brandon grabbed Lacey's hand and the two hustled through the swinging doors as a chair crashed through the window, causing jagged slivers of glass to shatter at their feet.

"Cheating? Not a good thing to holler in a saloon full of drinking gamblers." Brandon whisked her down the walkway.

Lacey stopped to face him, her breasts rising and falling with every breath, but she maintained her composure. "You got what you wanted, and now I don't have a job. No job means no money. Go on and leave me be." She scurried down the walkway.

"We all say things in anger we regret," Brandon said reaching her side. "Please, let me —"

Lacey raised her hand to stop further comment. *How can he appear so sincere, yet attempt to destroy everything I own?* "Leave me alone, Brandon." She rushed down the boardwalk, crossed the street, and when she entered Miss Helfrich's, she took the steps to her room two at a time. The revealing saloon dress and all thoughts of Brandon were tossed on the floor. She figured there would be plenty of time to think about it later. Sitting on her bed, it took every bit of restraint to control the tears pooling behind her eyelids. Retrieving her pocketbook, she reckoned there was enough money to pay her bill for a week. That is, if she didn't eat much.

She prayed:

"Dear God, please help me find a job tomorrow.

And, while you're at it, can you make it pay good?

Amen."

She lay her head on a pillow so starched it crackled. In seconds, she fell asleep.

After breakfast, Lacey walked toward the Stardust Eatery as Horace left the telegraph office, sauntered down the boardwalk, and stepped into the General Mercantile. *Heck, iffin' Horace can be a telegraph officer, certainly I can, too.* She hurried down the walkway and stepped inside the telegraph office. Someone sneezed from behind a glass enclosed office to her right, where a stout man sat at a massive desk surrounded by glass walls. He repeatedly licked his index finger as he turned sheets of paper from one stack and put them into another. Every third paper or so, he'd reach to tap a typewriter key. *One of those newfangled typewriters.* Lacey remembered seeing a picture of it, or one like it, in a magazine article. A large picture window awarded him a clear view of the street.

She walked to knock on the glass. "Good morning," she called. Not sure if the man could hear through the glass, she rapped harder.

The man answered with a sharp edge to his crotchety voice. He didn't bother to look from the keys. "What can I do for you, little lady?"

Lacey pointed at his typing machine. "You're jabbing at them keys like a chicken pecking feed corn."

He took his fingers off the keys and let his arms hang like limp dishrags at his sides. "Is there something I can do for you, miss?" He looked at her over the top of his bifocals.

She squared her shoulders. "I'm here for a job."

"A job?" He eyed her warily and resumed his slow, purposeful key pecking. "And what is it you can do, young lady?"

"Just 'bout anything," Lacey retorted and noticed his head bobbed with each pecked keystroke.

The man sighed heavily, pulled the paper from the carriage, and dropped his hands to his lap. "I don't need another telegraph officer," he said. "I got Horace and he does an outstanding job." He placed a new piece of paper in the typewriter and returned to pecking one key after the other with plenty of pausing between keystrokes.

"Hey, mister," she said. "I'll bet these fingers"— she held them upward and wiggled each digit —"could type whatever you're working on there…just like"— she snapped her fingers —"that."

After a few more pecks, his face turned beet red. "I have this newfangled typing machine," he said wiping sweat from his brow. "A friend of mine is trying new designs, and asked if I'd use this for a year or so and then answer questions about it. It's called a Densmore and that's all I know except it sure is a smooth, and I mean smooth, typing machine." He shrugged. "And I'll tell you something else, I bet it's going to cost a bundle. She's got a fully removable cartridge and look at this…ball bearing bars. And do you know what else, little lady?"

"No, I reckon not." She tried to appear interested. *A paying job means I get to eat dinner.*

"I'll tell you what else," he said, jerking another flawed paper from the machine. "It doesn't make a hill of beans how much you spend on a fancy typewriting machine like this, if an old-school fella has yet to master a two-cent typewriter first." He eyed her warily. "You say you know how to type? You type good, do you?"

"I sure do. I type about every other day." She stretched the truth a little. A lot. She *had* read about the machine in the newspaper. "Here." She swung a short set of swinging doors that separated the customer side from the office counter and made her way to the door entering his office. She opened it and approached his desk. "Move over and let me show you how to make this Densmore sing." The man vacated the chair and she sat and placed her hands on the keys.

"Mr.? What's your name, Mr.?"

"Jim, umm James Tierney, but everyone calls me Jimbo."

"Well then, Jimbo, this typewriter is a lot different from the one I'm used to. Why don't you go on"— she shooed him away with a wave of her hand —"and let me practice for a bit."

"You sure you know how to use one of these?" he asked, handing her a clean sheet of paper, then reconsidered and pulled it back. He reached over her shoulder and removed the loaded piece from the paper feed.

A soft gasp escaped Lacey's lips as she fluttered her hands, attempting to halt the paper from being whisked away.

"I figure if you're experienced on a typewriter," he said with a wry smile, "you don't need anyone to load it with paper for you."

She waited until Jimbo's footsteps sounded distant, grabbed a sheet of clean paper, and attempted to insert it into the place Jimbo pulled out the other. *Surely, I can figure this stupid thing out.* She grasped both edges of the paper and willed it to go in, but it wouldn't budge, just sat, and looked at her. *C'mon please paper, please, please.* She peeked over her shoulder to guarantee no one watched, then tried to force it into the feeder, but it wrinkled something fierce.

After wadding the paper and throwing it into the trash can, she reached for another. Putting the bottom edge of the paper on top of the black roll and quickly spinning the knob on the side of the machine, she hoped it would grab the paper and carry it around the cartridge. *No, of course not. Why should anything be easy?* She tried to mash the paper into the machine but only ended up with a wad of mashed paper.

When the bell above the entrance door tinkled, Lacey leaned back in Jimbo's chair to see who entered.

"Good morning, Miss Lacey," Horace said, wrinkling his brow as he walked through the door and into Jimbo's office.

"What are you doing here?" Horace pointed to the typewriter. "Are you working for Mr. Tierney?"

Lacey pretended to be preoccupied dusting the tops of the keys. They reminded her of short pads on the ends of spider legs. She handed him a clean sheet of paper. "Well, maybe I will be getting hired on here. I'd be as happy as a hog-in-a-holler, but I can't seem to get this paper to go 'round this here roll."

Horace took the sheet and inserted it for her. "There you go, Miss Lacey." He spun the sheet into place on the reel.

"In answer to your question," she said, "I hope to work here. Jimbo seems to want a typist, and I admit to needing a little, a lot of practice on this contraption."

"You take all the time you need," he said. "I won't bother you none, no, not at all. I have a lot of important work to do." He pulled an envelope from the desk drawer and continued, "I sure do hope you get a job here. If I got to see a pretty lady like you every day, I would be one happy O-fficial telegraph officer. Yes, ma'am, I would."

Lacey attempted to tune Horace out as she practiced pecking at the keys. She tried several hand positions before getting the notion to look for a manual. Right away, she found it under a file on Jimbo's desk and positioned her hands like it showed on page four.

"Horace!" called Jimbo. "Did you get those telegrams transposed for me?"

Lacey jumped at the sudden intrusion. She'd been so focused on her typewriting practice, she wondered how much time had passed. When he finished talking with Horace, she called him over. "Jimbo?"

"Yeah, what do you have there?"

She stood with a big smile and zipped the typed paper off the reel. She danced toward the man. "Look here." She held the sheet of paper full of random words so he could see her typing skills. "See how well I can type. Will you hire me? How much money will you pay me? Can I start tomorrow? What about today?"

Lacey had typed her name, Pa's name, and anybody else's name she could think of and proudly handed her masterpiece to Jimbo.

"This is fine and dandy, young lady, but anyone can type names in a row." He handed her treasure back. "I need someone who can type sentences quickly and efficiently."

"Quickly?" It had taken the entire morning to get one piece of paper with a few random names and no mistakes.

Jimbo chuckled and said, "I'll tell you what. You stay here and practice typing. At closing time, we'll see how much you've improved, and I'll make a decision."

"The boss must like you, Miss Lacey," Horace whispered as he lumbered into the office. He walked to her right side and opened the window shade. "Mr. Tierney never once mentioned he needed a typist. And look at you typing words like you've been schooled all your life."

Lacey stomach growled so loud it caused Horace to check the time.

"My goodness. It's time for a break," he said. "Past time, really. Miss Lacey, would you give me the pleasure of buying your lunch at the Stardust Eatery?"

She was certainly hungry, and for all of Horace's shortcomings, he seemed nice enough. She stood and smoothed her dress. "I'll take you up on that. My guts is groaning something fierce." Horace walked nearly sideways all the way to the cafe. With every comment, his arms flapped like a mother hen and his flabby lips bounced like two thick pieces of fatty bacon. Lacey couldn't help but find the man comical.

"You sure 'nuff are a pretty little filly," Horace said after they took their place at a window table. "Heck, I could sit and look at you all day. All day and all night if you want to know the truth."

"That's a fine compliment, Horace," Lacey managed and quickly added, "What are you gonna order?"

"I don't need to look at the menu," he said. "I always get the lunch special, and I've never been disappointed." He gazed into her eyes with a big, toothy horse grin.

Lacey ordered vegetable soup. Horace devoured a plate of flour-breaded and fried liver and onions, along with a big ear of corn on the cob soaked in butter, and a heaping helping of applesauce.

She glanced to see Winston Beaumont seated by himself at a nearby table. *How dare that poor excuse for a man reveal her plight to Brandon.*

"Hello," Winston mouthed as he nodded, then rose and approached their table. "Fancy meeting you here." He extended his hand to Horace. "Winston Beaumont the Third," he said. "I believe I made your acquaintance at the recent barn dance."

Horace wiped his mouth on a square of folded linen and as he began to stand, returned a hearty handshake. "Horace Sparker," he said. "And, yes sir, I do remember meeting you there."

Winston glanced at the black band on Horace's white shirt. "I see you work for the telegraph company?"

"Yes sir, I sure do," Horace replied. "And Miss Lacey started working for Mr. Tierney"— he pointed his index finger to the floor —"this very day."

Lacey cleared her throat and glanced at her dining partner. "Well, I'm not sure I have a job yet, Horace. My typing has to improve before he makes a final decision."

"How lovely, Miss Kendall," Winston purred. "You must keep me informed of your progress. Moreover, there is an issue I would like to speak about. Rest assured, only out of my deepest respect and admiration for your Aunt Molly did I feel compelled to reveal your dire work situation to Brandon Chandler. I had no idea what a scoundrel the man would prove of himself. Please, forgive me for my foolishness?"

Lacey stopped rearranging the vegetables in her soup bowl, met his eyes for a brief second, and returned her attention to the diced carrot and green bean smidgen on her spoon. She could say she forgave him, but in her heart, she'd been betrayed and lost her home because of his flapping jaw. *He doesn't deserve my forgiveness, and he ain't never gonna get it.*

Winston hesitated for an uncomfortable moment before nodding at the two and saying, "Good day, then," and strolling back toward his table. Rather than order, he left the restaurant.

Horace scrunched his eyebrows. "I don't mean to interfere, but —"

"Then don't," Lacey said and dipped her spoon for another bite.

As the two were returning to the telegraph office after lunch, Horace stopped and blocked Lacey's path.

"May I…." His voice trembled. "Miss Lacey." He cleared his throat. "May I have the pleasure of cour…courting you?"

Lacey noticed Horace had three straight hairs sprouting from his left ear. She blinked the image away. "I don't want anyone to court me, Horace," she said gently. "Brandon and I were in love, I thought. Now, I need to get my thoughts together." She took a quick sidestep around him to halt further conversation.

The bell hanging over the doorway as customers entered the telegraph office stayed silent the rest of the afternoon, so when it rang, Lacey startled and glanced to find Brandon standing in the entry. He stepped to the counter and he and Horace began talking. She remained quiet in the hopes of eavesdropping. After Brandon said he needed a telegram sent right away, voices changed pitch and she could not distinguish individual words.

She moved her fingertips on the typewriter keys quicker than buttered lightning, tip-tap-tapping as fast as her fingers could strike random letters. Brandon probably thought her only skills consisted of farmhand chores, and perhaps, after the saloon incident, an exhibitionist. *I'll show him.* She typed impressively faster, a mishmash of letters falling like a shower of spring raindrops upon the white paper. A swift movement from the corner of her eye startled her, and she looked to see Brandon walking toward her…closer…closer…. She stopped typing and hurried to pull the paper riddled with scrambled nonsense from the typewriter cartridge.

Brandon put his hand over hers the instant before setting the paper free and held it with a gentle squeeze while he inched his hip onto the corner of her desk. "It appears you have quite a talent for typing," he said, and plucked the paper from the cartridge.

Lacey's eyes grew wide as she stood and reached to snatch it from his hands. *Too late.* She glared at the man, her lips becoming thin and tight as he scanned the mess of gibberish.

He halted and released a hearty chuckle, turning the paper for her to see the mess he witnessed.

Feeling intense fury and humiliation, she grasped the knob on the end of the typewriter carriage to slide it into the rightful position. With the added momentum of rage, she gave it a massive heave-ho and shot the carriage straight across the platen and crashing through the opposite knob…and, right through the massive plate glass window. Outside foot traffic halted to the sound of a tremendous shattering of glass. The startled passersby dodged the carriage toppling end over end with a combination of multi-sized, jagged pieces of window for several feet.

Lacey shrieked and covered her mouth with both hands as she stumbled to the broken window to ask if those on the boardwalk were all right. She gasped at the shards covering the walkway and inching into the street. Folks with shocked faces stared back, some shaking their heads in disbelief. Worst of all, a heavy sigh heaved behind her — Mr. Tierney. She didn't figure she'd be calling him Jimbo no more. She turned, hands on hips and declared, "Well, ain't that dandy? You oughta write that typewriter friend a letter and demand he send a new machine for you to test and to pay for all that," she said pointing outside, "big ole mess."

Jimbo stepped to the window which was intact mere seconds before. The expensive typewriter carriage now lay outside among thousands of jagged pieces of glass. "Bring me a broom," he yelled to no one in particular.

Lacey bent forward for a better look at the boardwalk and soon felt a two-fingered tap land on her shoulder. She turned to see Mr. Tierney, face redder than a sugar beet and glasses fully steamed, holding a broom in his outstretched arm.

He thrust the broom in her direction. "Sweep that mess, every last piece, and then get out of my sight."

"Miss Lacey," said Horace with a quiver in his voice. He sprinted to her side. "Don't you worry none, you hear. It was an accident." He flashed a deep scowl at Jimbo and emphasized his words. "Axe-i-dent."

Brandon's tone sounded apologetic as he reached for Lacey's trembling hands. "I'm sorry. If I had known this was going to happen —"

"Apology not accepted." She dashed from the telegraph office.

*L*acey sidestepped the broken glass of the telegraph office. She held her chin high and made a purposeful dash into the alley and away from the growing crowd. Once out of sight, she covered her face with her palms and let the tears flow. When had she ever been so humiliated, not to mention embarrassed, and angry? Naturally, the incident happened in front of Brandon, of all people. Each time she recalled the heavy cartridge flying through the window and landing outside among a thousand pieces of shattered glass, she cried harder. Lacey decided no man ever made her as angry as Brandon Chandler. She closed her eyes, took a deep breath, and slowly exhaled. She needed to think, but she knew one thing for certain; Lacey Autumn Kendall was no quitter.

She reached into the pocket of her dress and pulled out an object dangling from a thin silver chain — her mother's crucifix — the one piece of jewelry her mother had owned. She had asked Pa to buy it for her in place of a wedding ring. Every evening, Ma had taken it from the pocket of her stained and floured apron and prayed over it. The next morning, she'd drop it into the pocket of a clean apron. Sunday church, she wore it 'round her neck and Pa would make a show of seeing it and smiling right square into Ma's violet eyes, like she was the most beautiful woman this side of Hog Holler. Ma would blush and cover her mouth with a hand, then come the next Sunday, the same thing would happen again.

Lacey opened her hand to reveal the necklace, the once shiny cross made dull from years of reaching into her pocket when she needed to feel closer to God, or if she'd swayed from him. She walked down the street and pulled the heavy door open. Seeing no one around, she stepped into the church. If Lacey needed to think with a clear mind, she knew nothing more powerful existed in her world than a faithful prayer. Pa reminded her many times that her ma used to hold this cross and pray at least once every day, some days all day if there was sickness in the house or something else bad happening. Pa had said, "When things was going right, she'd thank the good Lord for that, too. She'd say, 'A person shant only be fixin' to pray when they be a'wantin' somethin'. Yunce gotta pray when ya'll receivin' a blessin' from the Lord, too.'"

Lacey prayed with all her heart as she fingered the cross and whispered in the silence of the chapel. When finished, she walked down the front steps and glanced kitty-corner as a sunshine-yellow sign swinging above the building caught her attention. The weather-beaten letters spelled out *Clemmie's Café*.

She fingered a stray wisp of hair from the loose bun on top of her head. *So what if I can't cook?* She twirled the strand of hair around her finger. *Cooking can't be all that hard.* She returned the cross to her pocket.

Lacey opened the café door and stood in amazement. Rather than square tables like at the Stardust Eatery, there were long benches lined one after the other as tightly spaced as rows of sweet corn.

"We're closed for lunch," hollered a plump woman from across the room. "And we ain't gonna open till the big sausage breakfast in the morning." She wiped her hands over a deeply stained apron.

Lacey smoothed the front of her cotton dress before answering. "I'm not here to eat, ma'am. I'm lookin' for work."

The woman reached for a frayed blue and white striped cloth draped over her shoulder and approached Lacey. "You say you're looking to work here?" she said, wiping her hands briskly onto the tattered material.

"Yes, ma'am, I sure am," Lacey said eagerly. "And I can start right away."

"You know how to cook, do you?"

Lacey tried to sound convincing. "Yep, I sure do. Heck, I cooked all the time for my pa and brothers. I —"

"Girl, this is your lucky day," the woman interrupted with a grin. "Grab an apron, you can start right now, right this very minute."

"Now? Really? I can work here. Thank you so much, and you won't regret it!"

"Follow me," the woman said as she hustled away. "By the way, what's your name? I've never seen you around here before."

"I'm fairly new to town," Lacey answered. "Lacey Kendall."

"You can call me Miss Clemmie," she said before tossing her a white apron with red hearts sewn this way and that. "Put this on so you don't smear your dress."

Lacey took the patched apron and tied it around her neck and waist.

"Tomorrow is the café's biggest eating day of the year," Miss Clemmie said. "I cook a sausage, gravy, and biscuit breakfast and the entire town and folks near and far come to eat. The profits are donated to an orphanage not too far away. That's why the tables are in long rows," she said, waving her hand. "Come back into the kitchen, honey, we have a lot of work to do."

Thankfully, Lacey's first job became frying and crumbling massive skillets of pork sausage. She reckoned if she stirred the pans and didn't let anything burn, she couldn't ruin things too awful bad. After frying one skillet after another of the crumbled meat, she decided it would be a long time before she'd crave sausage again. When she finished the chore, Miss Clemmie used the skillets to cook a big ole mess of gravy. Lacey helped the woman pour the thick, white substance into four large crocks. The two added the fried sausage and stirred the mixture with long slotted spoons.

"Let's carry the crocks to the cellar for the night," Miss Clemmie said as she lifted a crock and motioned for Lacey to take another.

They carried the last crock to the cellar, and Miss Clemmie looked so tired Lacey feared she'd drop dead right there in the kitchen.

"Thank you for your help today, dear. I guess I'm getting old. I never remember being this tired the night before the big town breakfast." Miss Clemmie wiped the tail of her apron across her face. "I sure don't know what I'd have done without you. Tomorrow morning, we'll clean the kitchen mess and roll out the baking powder biscuits. For now, we need to go home and get some sleep."

Lacey untied her apron and Miss Clemmie mumbled she had one more thing she needed to do.

"What is it?" Lacey asked.

"I need to take the lids to the cellar. Those crocks must have a cover over them." Miss Clemmie yawned as she gathered the lids.

"You go on home and let me finish." Lacey insisted and placed her hand gently on the woman's arm. "I'll cover the sausage and gravy and see you bright and early in the morning."

Lacey smiled and watched Miss Clemmie leave the café and close the door behind her. The woman seemed so nice and sure saved Lacey a lot of grief by hiring her. She looked at the skillets dripping with thick globs of dried gravy and decided to do Miss Clemmie a favor. She took the wash pan to the pump and filled it with water, then scrubbed the skillets, pots, pans, cups, and utensils. She barely remembered crawling into bed near dawn.

Lacey awoke to a commotion outside her window. She parted the curtain to see a bunch of folks gathered outside Clemmie's Café. She hurried to dress, excited at such a large turnout.

"Morning, Miss Clemmie," Lacey said after entering the café and locking the door behind her.

"Morning, Lacey," Miss Clemmie said in a sing-song voice as she bustled around the long tables setting out baskets of forks and napkins. "I see we have quite a crowd this morning."

"Yes, ma'am," Lacey said, unable to contain her excitement. "And they look mighty hungry, too."

"You are a godsend, girl," the woman said as she placed hands on Lacey's shoulders and gave her a gentle squeeze. "I came in this morning fixing to be greeted with a greasy kitchen mess, and by darn if you hadn't already gone and cleaned it."

Lacey smiled at the woman's gentle face and thought about her prayers. *A Godsend?* "I wanted to show my thanks for hiring me, Miss Clemmie. Now, what can I do to help?"

"Go out to the cellar, dear, and carry the crocks inside." She motioned toward the dining room. "You'll see where I left room on the serving table. You do that, and I'll take the next batch of biscuits out of the cookstove.

Lacey swallowed hard and stared straight ahead. *Jumpin' Jehoshaphat, the lids!*

"Shoo now, girl," Miss Clemmie said and hustled toward the kitchen. "We have a swarm of hungry folks outside itching to eat."

Lacey forced her feet to follow her body. She trudged through the kitchen and out the back door to the cellar in a trance. *How could I forget to cover the crocks?* She'd been so intent on scrubbing the dirty pans, she forgot all about the lids. She opened the cellar door and stood on the top step. The delicious aroma of the gravy emphasized how dreadful it was she hadn't followed Miss Clemmie's instructions. She walked to the nearest crock and peeked inside. It sure *looked* all right. She needed to taste it and glanced around for something to dip inside but couldn't find a thing.

She ran back to the café and opened the kitchen door, trying to not make a sound. Peeking inside, she noted Miss Clemmie was nowhere in sight, so after scurrying across the kitchen floor, she grabbed a ladle, and ran back to the cellar. After dipping deep into the thick substance, she said a silent prayer and brought the ladle to her lips. It sure *tasted* all right.

Lacey thrust the ladle into the next crock and gave it a quick stir. Something odd bumped against the dipper as she pulled it from the thick goo. Dipping the ladle a second time, she quickly stirred the mixture and once again the heaviness of an odd presence pushed against the spoon. After several attempts, she managed to get the foreign object into the dipper of the ladle, and carefully lifted it out of the gravy. She squealed as the excess gravy dripped, revealing the form of a drowned baby bat.

"Are you coming, Lacey?" Miss Clemmie called from the cellar steps.

Lacey jumped and flicked the ladle, throwing the drowned creature into a corner. She turned as the woman stepped onto the cellar floor.

"What's taking you so long, Lacey? We have mouths to feed."

She faced the woman, her mouth moved, but no words came. Miss Clemmie lifted a crock and hurried up the cellar steps.

Lacey numbly followed her to the dining room and made two more trips to the cellar. *I must tell Miss Clemmie.* Every time she uttered a syllable, Miss Clemmie scurried away, bringing just one more thing to the tables at the front of the room nearest the kitchen door.

"Go tell the folks to come in," Miss Clemmie said, clapping her hands together. "They're a hungry bunch, and we're ready."

Lacey opened the door to the café and stood aside as customers entered, all seeming to talk at once. She headed for the serving table.

Folks waiting in line with empty plates and silverware in hand snapped Lacey to her senses. *I need to tell Miss Clemmie, and fast!*

Miss Clemmie was busy pouring an overloaded ladle of sausage and gravy on top of piping hot biscuits. "As soon as everyone gets dipped up," she hollered, "Reverend Thomas will say grace and we can eat."

Lacey's stomach churned as if hot, greasy butter raced through her body instead of blood.

Miss Clemmie called to the crowd. "Thank you all for coming this morning. I must say, this is the best turnout ever." She lifted her apron and wiped a tear with the edge. "I've prepared my mother's recipe for sausage and gravy, like I do every year." She chuckled and said, "Mom called this dish, excuse my language Reverend Thomas, she called it, 'Shit on a shingle.'" The patrons laughed on cue. "And with this joyful crowd, we're going to need every single drop this morning."

Lacey's palms dampened and her legs wobbled like a boiled noodle. "Miss Clemmie," she managed to say. "I must talk to you."

"In a minute, dear." Miss Clemmie continued topping biscuits until each plate heaped full and three crocks sat empty. Finally, when everyone had a heaping serving on their plate, she clapped her hands together to quiet the rising voices in the room. "Everyone, quiet now, please. Reverend Thomas is about to speak."

Lacey needed time to think and willed the preacher to pray the entire bible. She cast quick glances at the tables of hungry folks and knew when the prayer ended, they would dive into Miss Clemmie's breakfast. Way too soon, in Lacey's opinion, the preacher said a hearty amen and everyone respectfully waited for Reverend Thomas to sit and take the first bite. Lacey stared, wide-eyed and bone-dry mouthed as the preacher reached for his fork.

Lacey panicked and ran toward the front of the room, shouting, "STOP, STOP! Wait. Everyone, please WAIT!"

Lacey cast quick glances at the startled faces of the crowd, most of them holding forks, ready to stab the tasty feast on their plates. "Umm," she hollered. Her heart raced and zigzagged through her chest. Thought she might puke — yep, pretty sure she would. "Before you eat, I would also like to say a prayer." The hungry crowd snickered and groaned. She didn't have a clue what to say, but she best say something, and fast:

"Lord, please bless this meal
And I beg forgiveness for the shock,
But I forgot to place the lids last night
And found a dead bat in the crock."

Her prayer met with a dull silence from the crowd followed by shrieks as the patrons realized what Lacey's words meant.

Miss Clemmie thrust her finger toward the door and forcefully demanded Lacey leave her café. Immediately! Lacey burst into tears and ran out the door and back to her room where she threw herself on the bed. She'd stay there, she reckoned, until time for the next stagecoach out of town. That blasted Brandon Chandler, not to mention everyone else in town, had to drop in for the sausage breakfast and see the whole humiliating scene. She quieted her sobs after hearing a knock on the door.

"Miss Kendall," Beaumont said. "Please, let me in. I would like a word with you."

Lacey blew her nose. "Go away, I don't wanna see anyone right now." Beaumont was the last person on God's green earth she wanted to lay eyes on. She thought of Brandon. *Almost the last person.*

"Miss Kendall," Beaumont continued. "I witnessed the travesty bestowed upon you at the café, and I would like to offer you a proposition."

Figuring the man would pester her until he said his peace, she rose and opened the door. "Whaddya mean, a proposition?"

He peered over her shoulder. "May I step in for a moment to speak with you?" He glanced down the hall. "This is of a personal nature. Please, I believe you'll want to hear what I have to say."

Lacey hesitated, released an audible breath, and said, "I suppose." She stepped aside and closed the door behind him. After pointing to the nearest chair, she took the other for herself.

Leaning forward, Beaumont didn't waste any time getting to the point of his visit. "How would you feel about beginning our tutoring sessions again? If that would please you, I have a grand idea."

"*Grand* idea? What kind of *grand* idea?"

"Remember when we spoke at the Stardust Eatery of your Aunt Molly's desire to open a lady's school right here in New Harmony?"

"Yes." She eyed him questioningly. "But what does that hafta do with me?"

"I intend on opening that school," he said, quick to add, "in your aunt's memory, of course. I will need qualified instructors." He cleared his throat. "So, now that brings me to the reason I asked to speak with you, Miss Kendall. I would like to recruit you as a student and prepare you as Head Mistress of the Winston Beaumont School for Proper Ladies."

"A lady school? Really? Head Mistress?"

"Really, Miss Kendall. It's going to take a lot of work on your part, but yes —"

"Me, the Head Mistress? I don't know much 'bout being a lady, much less a teacher, and nothing about no, what'd you say, Head Mistress?"

Beaumont chuckled. "I must admit we have much work to do in preparation, but I am willing to exert the time and energy, if you are?"

"Yes, of course I am. I mean, this must be my lucky-star day," Lacey said before her expression turned sullen. This meant she wouldn't have to crawl back to Pa, but how would she live without a job, and money?

Winston studied her expression. "Why the sad face?"

Lacey stood and paced in the small room. "I was thinking, umm, Miss Clemmie fired me this morning after my mishap with the sausage gravy and"— she fanned her hand around the room —"and to pay for this room, much less have something to eat, I need to find another job."

"I realize that will be a primary concern. There are a multitude of subjects in which to tutor you, and I must confess to selfishness on my part. I demand you devote a vast amount of time to tutoring and study time."

Lacey stopped pacing. "But Mr. Beaumont —"

"Winston. Please call me Winston."

"Umm, Winston." The name stuck in her throat like gooey molasses. "It's really perty simple, iffin' I don't work, I don't eat."

"Let me continue my proposition, Miss Kendall. I will pay for your room and board and —"

"Mr. Beaumont, I mean W…Winston, I can't be beholden to you like that."

"I have not finished speaking. After I open the school, I will withdraw funds from your wages until your debt to me is repaid."

"You would do that for me, Winston?" His name rolled off her tongue a little easier now.

"It will be my pleasure, dear." He stood and placed his hand on the doorknob. "It is settled, then. I will see you after dinner to discuss a schedule for lessons."

When the door closed, Lacey sat on the bed. Maybe she and Beaumont got off to a poor start. He might be a snake in the grass, but at least this meant she didn't have to go home, not just yet.

She intended to close her eyes for a few minutes but woke to find it nearing twilight. She threw the covers back and hurried down the stairs, her stomach growling like a tormented grizzly as she raced into the dining room.

"I hope I'm not late," she called toward the kitchen where Miss Veronica Helfrich, the owner of the boardinghouse, made sounds like vittles getting scraped from skillets into serving bowls. Lacey slid into an empty chair at the long, narrow dining table.

Ten houseguests were seated with their lips still and backs straight against their chairs like they'd been cast in plaster or maybe some green-horned monster would eat them if they moved or spoke. Miss Veronica entered the dining room balancing two platters on her thick, stocky forearms, her ample bodice straining at the seams of her flour and grease splattered apron.

The matronly woman stopped to glare at Lacey. Her lids squinted until the teensiest bit of her eyeballs showed.

I just met the green-horned monster.

Speaking in a thick German accent she said, "Just about too late, missy. I'll let you in on a little secret." Her index finger poked out from beneath one of the platters to point at the new arrival. "You come to my table late again and you can forget about eating. Do you understand?"

"Umm, yes, ma'am. I mean, Miss Veronica," Lacey replied. She wondered why Miss Veronica moved so close behind her chair. The woman handed a platter to the guest on her right side, barking at him to take his share and pass it along.

The stout woman's warm breath tickled at the base of her neck.

"What did you call me, missy?"

Lacey turned her head and did a quick jump as Miss Veronica's flared nostrils, each adequate to house a buggy, were mere inches from her face. She smelled like old sweat, and garlic.

"If you ever address me as anything except Miss Fronie, you will eat the slop I normally throw to the hogs. Do I make myself clear, missy?"

"Yessum, Miss Fronie," Lacey said and reached to take the platter from the woman's hefty grip.

Miss Fronie jerked the platter back and kicked one leg of Lacey's chair with the gusto of a goosed bull.

Lacey bounced clear off her seat and onto the floor, the chair landing sideways in her lap. She stared wide-eyed into the face of a she-devil. It would be impossible not to call her Sour Fronie.

A booming voice landed inches from Lacey's eardrums. "Were you raised in a pig sty without a set of manners? If you ever, ever go reaching for one of my dishes again it will find a home on top of your head. Do we understand each other?"

"Yessum, err yes, Miss Fronie. I understand." She looked to the other diners for support but found them all staring into their laps, stiff as dead folk.

"Did barnyard beasts teach you how to speak?"

"Yessum. I mean no."

"Yessum is not proper talk. Next time I best hear you say, yes, Miss Fronie. Is that clear?"

"Yes, Miss Fronie." Lacey pinched her lips shut. She sure didn't want another whack from Sour Fronie. She picked herself off the floor and righted her chair before sitting and positioning her shoulders and back straight as a soldier.

When the robust woman retreated to the kitchen, Lacey let out a held breath and said, "Somebody tell me what brave soul rammed a skunk up *her* backside?" Lacey snickered and glanced around the table at the other patrons and said, "She ain't no Miss Fronie, I got a new name for her…Sour Fronie." Lacey's shoulders shook as she chuckled, but stopped dead when mashed potatoes landed on top of her head like a steaming cow patty. She jumped from her chair, slinging away the hot eats as globs ran down the side of her face and fell from her nose. "I don't believe you did that!" she screamed at the woman.

Miss Fronie poured a pitcher of water over Lacey's head, then placed her thick palms atop her shoulders and pushed her back into the chair. "Don't you think for a second I won't do that again. Do you reckon I was born lacking ears, missy? Now, you eat what I put on your plate, and you best not leave a nibble. Not *one* nibble." She stomped back to the kitchen.

A scrawny man with more of a squeak than a voice broke the silence. He stood halfway and said, "Could you please pass the mashed potatoes?"

Lacey wanted to deck him.

"And I'll tell you another thing," Sour Fronie said when she returned with a fresh pitcher of water. "If you so much as come to my table late again, you can fuss, whine, and moan all you want telling me how gawd-awful hungry you are, and that you are going to die if you don't eat, and it will go on deaf ears. Do you understand?"

Lacey glanced around the table at the other patrons and settled her gaze on Winston, who settled his gaze directly on the plate in front of him. No one wanted to make eye contact with "Lacey the Troublemaker" except for the serious stare she received from Sour Fronie.

"Now, that's a fine policy you have there, Miss Fronie," Lacey said. "I declare, how anyone could be so rude as to arrive late for eats, and then expect a hot meal." She shook her head as if it were the craziest thing she'd ever heard.

Sour Fronie eyed her curiously for a minute before placing steaming bowls of vegetables and hot rolls on the table. "Breakfast is at six o'clock sharp, dinner at eleven, and supper at five." She strolled around the table. "If that does not suit you, that is too bad. Do you understand?"

"Yes, Miss Fronie," Lacey said. She reckoned Sour Fronie must have got ahold of a cayenne corncob in the outhouse to give her such a hostile disposition.

Lacey waited for Sour Fronie to leave the room before asking, "What time would you like to meet tomorrow, Mr. Beaumont?" The room turned midnight-at-the-cemetery quiet as all eyes looked in her direction. Lacey cleared her throat. "Mr. Beaumont has kindly offered to teach me how to be —"

"A teacher," Beaumont said quickly. "I have offered to tutor Miss Kendall on some of the finer points of higher education."

Lacey wondered why Mr. Beaumont seemed so jittery. It wasn't like they intended on holding lessons behind closed doors or anything improper like that. What would be wrong with telling them the truth — that she wanted to become a proper lady and head mistress?

"Immediately following dinner shall suit me fine, Miss Kendall. We may start our lessons this evening if you like."

"That will suit me fine, too, Mr. Beaumont," she said, as a dollop of creamed peas rolled off her spoon and landed on the table. "Oops," she said, and scooped them with her finger. She tossed them in her mouth. "No sense letting the 'lil boogers go to waste."

THWACK! Her head slammed forward like she'd been walloped with a sack of sweet taters.

"Is that the proper way for a young lady to speak?" Miss Fronie shouted as she lifted her arm to whack her again. "Were you raised by hounds?"

"No, Miss Fronie, umm, it ain't, and I weren't."

"For all my life, I never heard a girl with such poor vocabulary. I am sure Mr. Beaumont is a qualified teacher, but he is no miracle worker."

Lacey noticed Beaumont's shoulders did a quick shiver motion.

None of the patrons talked much during dinner. Lacey tired of trying to make conversation and finally finished her meal in silence before returning to her room and gathering Aunt Molly's lady books. She hurried to meet Winston in the sitting room.

"I'm ready for my lessons, Mr. Beaumont." She whispered in his ear, "I didn't think it proper to call you Winston in front of them other folks. I sure don't want anyone gittin' the wrong idea."

Winston appeared to force a smile. "I understand."

"I'm ready to get down to business," Lacey said as she plopped into a plush chair. "What are you gonna teach me first? Have you thought of something?"

Winston stared at her for a full half minute before he finally said, "No more gits and gonna's."

"Whaddya mean?"

"Or whaddyas, Miss Kendall."

"Iffin' you gonna do nothing 'cept hoop 'n holler, I ain't gonna sit here and listen." She stood to leave.

"Miss Kendall, please." He motioned for her to sit. "What I am trying to tell you, and I apologize for my frustration, but let us please begin again. Git is get…and gonna is going to."

"Gonna what?"

He shook his head for several seconds. "Let us save that lesson for another day. The first section you will be instructing at the school deals with facts concerning a lady's toilette etiquette. Without question, we have details to discuss."

"Toilette etiquette?" Lacey straightened in her chair and tilted her brow. "Everybody knows 'bout the three dubbyas… wipin', washin', and wearin' clean clothes."

"No, I am talking about proper grooming in relation to hair and perfume."

"Perfume etiquette? You're gonna tell me there's such a thing as perfume etiquette? That sounds like ole Miss Potts from back home," Lacey said. "I'm thinking she only took a bath nearing Christmas time. She'd get all scaly and itchy and start stinking like a sow after rolling in —"

"Miss Kendall, please. Stop!" Winston interrupted and straightened in his chair. "Close your mouth, open your ears, and listen to me." He sighed before continuing, "One evening, I attended a play. There aside of me sat a ghastly woman who wore upon herself a saturated bouquet of perfume that sent my senses into utter havoc. So, in principle, Miss Kendall, all strong odors are in poor taste. Always remember a perfume is to enhance the senses, not to cover odor or overwhelm those in your presence."

"I understand, Mr. B. Hey, I like that. Can I call you Mr. B?"

"Absolutely not. You may call me Winston."

Lacey rolled her eyes. "Then, drop the Miss Kendall and call me Lacey. I'll make a lesson note 'bout that perfume. How much is too much?"

Winston stroked one of his long fingers. "Pinch a quantity of scented powder —"

"A quantity of what?" Lacey couldn't reckon what Winston yapped about now.

"You lay the scented powder in a drawer in which you have placed gloves, handkerchiefs, and the like. The items will draw in the fragrance and smell quite lovely. Exquisitely pleasant to the olfactory."

"Pleasing to the what factory?"

"The olfactory. The sense of smell."

Lacey's voice took on an edge of frustration. "Then why didn't you say so, Winston?" She rolled her eyes skyward. "I guess I don't see why ladies need to go putting on all these airs. So, I am to teach the ladies that unless they put on smelly goods, they're gonna stink?"

Winston took a deep breath and attempted to smile. "Lacey, you are to instruct them on the finer delicate practices of being a lady. You will teach them not only the proper toilette, but some facts behind it also."

"Facts such as —"

"Such as," Winston stood and paced in front of her. "The fact that extracts of certain scents such as roses, violets, and lavender make the best perfumes. And hair," Winston said, "The longer the hair, the more appealing."

"Heck, I remember the time I took big ole sheers to Matthew's hair and —"

"Are you listening to me?" Winston interrupted through a tightly held jaw.

"Yes, of course," she said too quickly.

Winston sighed. "Too frequent shampooing of the hair is unnecessary. Instruct the ladies to use a mild soap due to the possibility of fading. Also, advise the ladies to wash their hair no more than once or twice a month."

"Once a month?" Lacey reckoned perhaps this is the reason Winston had a slick, grease-plastered look to his hair.

Lacey wrote a few added notes and stood to leave.

"Where are you going?"

She fluttered her hand and eased over to the staircase. "'Nuff lessons for one evening. All your talk of perfume and shampoo makes my head spin, and besides," she said yawning, "I have reading to do before I fall asleep."

Winston stood and brought forth a pipe from his pocket. Soon, gray smoke encircled his head as he said, "May I ask what you are reading?"

"A short story by Mrs. Thomas Frank Weber I found in a magazine," Lacey answered. "Trials and Tribulations of a Young Bride."

"I see," Winston said. "Enjoy your reading I will see you at breakfast." As an afterthought, he called, "And Lacey —"

Lacey turned on the step and frowned, her fingers clutching the banister. *Now what?*

"I almost forgot to mention that you should never wash your hairbrush. It will soften and spoil the bristles." He waved her adieu. "That is all."

She made a dash for her room, and once inside with the door locked, poured a glass of water, and snatched the magazine next to her bed. She sat in a chair, lit the lantern, and flipped through the pages to where she'd bookmarked with a yellow hair ribbon.

A forceful knocking on the door startled her. "Who is it?"

"It's Brandon. I need to have a word with you."

She looked from her reading and hollered, "Go away," and nestled further into the soft chair.

The pounding on the door became more forceful as Brandon's voice thundered through the barrier. "Open the door, Lacey."

She glanced over her shoulder and lined her voice with sarcasm. "What, Brandon, open the door or else big, bad Brandon Chandler will bust it from its hinges? Or will you burn down the Boardinghouse to get what you want?"

"Lacey, I don't know why you insist I started the fire at your cabin, but…open the blasted door!"

"I'm busy reading."

Brandon's voice became soft, yet firm. "Please open the door."

"Go away and don't come back," she said, loud enough for him to hear. She turned the lantern down, bathing the room in semi-darkness and walked toward his deep timbered voice. She brought the palm of her hand forward and laid it on the door, resting her left cheek atop her hand. The tears trailing down her cheeks turned to sobs when the thunder of his boot steps echoed down the staircase.

Brandon slammed the front door of Miss Fronie's and unhitched Thunder. If he couldn't get Lacey to talk to him, how could he convince her of his innocence? Furthermore, how could his button not only have fallen off — and he checked for certain one of his buttons was indeed missing from his black shirt — but have been pulled with such force to tear the material? How it appeared at Lacey's cabin, he didn't have a clue. "Wait a minute. Beaumont, that's how." His hands became white fists. *He stole the button right out from under my nose the night he dropped by to give me news of Lacey's deceptive ways.* Brandon glanced at the window in Winston's room, the lights blazing, and made a pledge to find the underlying cause of the story behind the sinister Winston Beaumont the Third.

Brandon dismounted Thunder and tossed the reins over the horse's back before storming into the boardinghouse. He'd watched the place for over a week and knew that sleazy Beaumont was up to no good. All attempts to speak with Lacey had been futile; she wouldn't give him the time of day. But she made time to spend with Beaumont. Miss Fronie informed him Lacey took book lessons from him every evening after dinner.

Brandon slipped upstairs and ducked into an empty room. He didn't have to wait long before Beaumont stepped into the hallway and closed his door. Brandon expected the man to continue to the staircase. Instead, he stopped and tapped on Lacey's door. Brandon's face heated with rage as the two descended the steps together. The scent of her perfume wafting under his nose caused an immediate manly reaction.

After a few minutes, when her scent cleared, he inched his way down the hall and turned the knob on Beaumont's door. *Idiot left the door unlocked. Can't blame the imbecile, probably assaulted with Lacey's intoxicating, rose petal perfume.* Discovering

Beaumont was a complete and utter slob was his second surprise. He stared in disbelief. Miss Fronie had informed Brandon she'd received strict instructions that no one enter his room for any reason, not even to clean. For such a prim acting son-of-a-gun concerned with privacy, he couldn't fathom him leaving the door unlocked. The bed covers were torn apart, dirty clothes hung over every available spot, and a stench mixed with the smell of coal tar filled the air. Three leather-bound books lay on a table near the bed, and two more lay on the floor in disarray. Brandon flipped through the pages, found nothing of interest, and replaced them. He noticed a pair of boots near the door as he turned to leave. He stepped into the hallway and started to shut the door but glanced back at the boots. *Why do I smell coal tar?* The answer dawned on him in a vivid recollection.

Lacey and Winston settled right into lessons after dinner. Lacey eased herself into a chair, crossed her legs, and reached for the gloves he held out for her.

"After marriage, Lacey, it will be expected that you furnish your home and entertain guests," Winston said as he paced. "What furnishings do you feel are necessary items?"

"Well, Pa always said all honest country folk need is a bed, a chair, a chest, a looking glass for cutting whiskers, and a table for vittles."

He sighed. "There are a few more furnishings you will need to acquire."

"Like wallpaper curtains? I saw some of those hanging in a train station window during a rest stop."

"No, not like wallpaper curtains. I am referring to —" He shook his head. "Never you mind. And as a table for *vittles*," he spat the word, "were you referring to a masculine table in the hallway?"

"I was referrin' to an eatin' grub table in the kitchen."

He ignored her remark and resumed pacing. "A hallway is also a respectable place for the storage of one's umbrella."

Lacey looked to the ceiling. "And now you're gonna tell me there's a special stick of furniture for a stinking umbrella?"

Winston grimaced and dug something invisible out of his ear. "Now we shall discuss the what-not."

"The who not?"

"The what-not. It is a range of shelves, also known as —"

"Enough."

"We are almost finished. We have two more rooms to cover."

"Two more rooms? Heck, that's bigger'n my whole cabin." She looked intently at Winston. His mouth wasn't moving. Had her wish come true? Had Winston finally stopped yacking? She hurried to grab her gloves. "I'm finished for the evening."

"We are almost finished. I want to review one more lesson."

Lacey plopped back into her chair. "And what might that be?"

"What do you remember about the movements of the fan?"

"That's easy. I studied hard and we already reviewed this." She pulled a peach fan from her pocket and let it rest on her right cheek. She sighed. "This means yes." She drew it lazily across her left cheek. "And this means no."

Winston approached her chair. "What does it mean to hold the handle against your lips?"

"That would mean I wanted you to kiss me. That's what it means."

"To do what, Lacey?" He leaned closer than necessary.

She rolled her eyes and huffed. "To kiss me, Winston. It would suggest I was agreeable to a kiss."

Winston lunged forward and kissed her square on the lips.

Lacey pushed his shoulders away and shot out of the chair, the gloves fluttering to her feet. The room silenced except for the sound of thundering boot steps across the wood floor. She gasped as Brandon took long strides toward Winston, his fists clenched so tight his knuckles showed white.

She didn't know which man to chastise first. Winston for kissing her, or Brandon for witnessing it. She took care of the matter in one swift motion by slapping Winston hard on his left cheek and burying the toe of her boot into Brandon's shin. She hurried from the room, her heart echoing in her temples as she ran up the steps.

"Lacey?" Brandon called when she slammed her door with a resounding bang.

She stood with her back pressed against it, catching her breath. Her pounding heartbeat echoed inside her ears. She mumbled to herself. *Stupid, stupid, stupid, how could I be so stupid to let Winston trick me like that?*

Brandon beat his fist against the barrier like a man who had lost his senses. "I have to talk to you right now, Lacey."

"I have nothing to say to you. Nothing at all." She hustled to grab the porcelain water pitcher and threw it at the door. It shattered on impact.

"Lacey, what are you doing? This is important, you *must* listen to me. Five minutes. Give me five minutes, and then if you want, I will leave. Please, what I must tell you is more important than your being angry with me."

She bit her lip. "What could possibly be of such importance you hafta talk to me right now? I can't think of a thing we need to discuss except the fact you owe me a place to live."

"That's exactly what I want to talk to you about. I know who set fire to your cabin, and I can *prove* it."

Lacey inched her way around the broken shards and cracked the door. One look at the sincerity of Brandon's eyes and she knew his words were true. Her voice was soft as a whisper. "Come in. Watch out for the glass."

He stopped in the door frame and pushed the larger broken pieces to the side with his boot. "I'm not going anywhere until I've said my peace, so you may as well take a seat." He closed the door and held a pair of filthy boots in front of him like a trophy.

"What's that?"

He dropped them onto the floor.

"What are you doing? You're making a mess on the floor." She grimaced and stepped back from the foul-smelling lump at her feet.

"Evidence. Remember the night of the fire when I spread coal tar on the smokehouse floor? Remember?" He tucked his fingers into the top of one boot, turned it over, and watched her expression.

"So, you got coal tar on your boots." Lacey shrugged. "That don't prove nothin." She stepped back and pointed at the hardened muck. "This is supposed to convince me you are innocent?"

"These aren't *my* boots."

Lacey opened her mouth to speak and eyed the boots. "What are you trying to prove? Whose boots are they?

Brandon lined the words with thorns as he said, "Winston Beaumont the Third. In fact, the sheriff is with him right now. He has a few important questions to answer about his whereabouts the night your cabin burned."

"Winston?" Lacey sat on the bed and stared at the tar-laden boots. "Winston set the fire?"

"When I discovered Winston stole the gold button from my shirt, I knew he started the fire. He wanted to frame me, and he almost succeeded.

"When Beaumont came inside my cabin the evening of the fire, he stood next to where I had placed a stack of clothes. I poured two shots of whiskey, with my back turned, mind you. Winston must have seen my black shirt and jerked a button free. It accounts for the loose threads on my shirt, too. He must have tucked the button into his pocket, for I never saw it again."

"I don't understand. Why would he want to burn my cabin?" Her muscles weakened, a numbness settling into her body. "What did I — what would make him want to hurt me?"

"I don't have the answer to that." Brandon's voice softened. "I guess you'll have to ask him yourself."

Lacey stormed down the hallway toward Winston's room.

Winston smirked at Lacey's confused expression. "It appears we've had our final lesson, Miss Kendall," Winston said with cool reserve. "Might I add, you have been a horrendous student."

The sheriff prepared to lead Winston from the room, but Lacey blocked the door. "Tell me why you did it? What did you possibly have to gain?"

"Gold. A man will do many things for riches." He nodded at Brandon standing in the doorway. "Ask your friend there, he knows about the prospects for that land. I have no doubt the cad will marry you to get his hands on its riches."

Lacey's insides boiled, her palms were moist, and her head pounded like it was going to explode. She looked at Brandon. "You *did* know about the gold, didn't you? I know you did 'cause of a —" She caught herself before betraying Horace's confidential words about Brandon's telegram. "You may not have set the fire, but you most certainly had your reasons for courting me."

"Wait a minute." Brandon walked toward Lacey. "Yes, I knew about the gold, I'm not going to lie, but you hear me, and you hear me good. That knowledge has no bearing on the way I feel about you."

Lacey walked in a daze toward her room, Brandon at her side. "You knew about the will, too. You knew I had to marry to inherit Aunt Molly's land. So, you courted me."

Brandon's voice became a gentle whisper. "Months ago, that land meant something to me. I wanted to buy the property and mine for gold. But not now. The only thing important to me now, is you." He touched Lacey's arm and turned her to face him. "I fell in love with *you*, my dear lady, not a potential gold mine. You are the only gold mine I will ever want or need. I am in love with you, Lacey Kendall."

Lacey's heartbeat quickened as his words registered. "You're what?"

Brandon stepped closer and took her hands in his. His smile filled the room. "I fell in love with you, Lacey, and I will say it as many times as you need to hear it."

Lacey searched Brandon's face, full of heartfelt honesty, love, and sincerity. "I…Brandon, I don't know what to say. Yesterday,

I was angrier at you than a rattlesnake with a broken rattle, and today, well, I can't…I can't stand here and tell you what you want to hear." Her voice quivered and she dropped her arms to her sides. "I felt such an attraction, I suppose I would have done anything to stay in Montana to see if we'd develop into something, even if it meant pretending I was a boy. But, I felt you tried to destroy me. Tried to take everything that ever meant anything away from me. Right now, today? I don't feel it. "I'm so sorry."

As Brandon placed his palm on her cheek to wipe away her tears, his eyes flooded with moisture. He turned to walk down the hallway. Lacey's shoulder shook as her tears flowed. She willed him to stop. Not until his footfalls landed on the stairway did her pain reach an intensity that would haunt the rest of her life if she allowed it. His touch had filled Lacey with the knowledge her body and soul needed to accept Brandon's eternal love.

"Brandon. Brandon?" She cleared her throat and attempted to call his name. "Brandon?" Her whispered voice sounded as though she woke from a dream and her words were without sound.

She ran down the hallway. and as she reached the fourth step down, his hand was on the doorknob. "Brandon, NO! Don't leave me. D-d-don't go." Her legs lost all strength and she lowered herself to the step, buried her face in her palms, and wept like a young girl. In a heartbeat, Brandon was on the step below taking her hands in his. He touched his cheek to hers and their tears melded as one. Nothing would ever sever the intensity of their love for one another.

"I am sorry, so sorry. I said such hurtful things to you. I —"

"You don't have to explain, Lacey, I —"

"I got scared. Ma died when I was so young. I never had anyone to show me how to be a girl, and certainly not how to be a lady, wife, or mother. One day, I want children, lots of children. I found you and know you genuinely love me. But, if not for Pa sending me here thinking I'd be learning from Aunt Molly, I'd still be pitching in with farm work back home wearing stinking overalls and never, probly ever, wear a dress or meet the most wonderful man and fall in love."

He gathered her in his arms and held her close. "You will be the most loved and cherished wife any husband could dream of, and the most loving mother any child could pray for. There isn't a doubt in my mind."

A soft curve to her lips became a bright, beautiful smile. Brandon looked into her eyes, then focused on her lips as the lovers shared a kiss only a couple with true passion experiences. When Brandon's lips eased from hers, she drew her body closer and initiated a kiss that if visible, would glow like an ember throughout eternity.

"You're going to drive me insane, aren't you?"

"I'd say rather than a possibility, it's a fact, my love." The two stood and Brandon escorted his lady to her room.

After crossing the threshold, Lacey took a step back. The expression on Brandon's face was one of pure mischief. "What?" she asked. "What are you thinking?"

His blue eyes twinkled as he touched the tip of her nose with his finger.

"There's something I want to do."

"Okay, what?"

"Where's my gold button?"

Lacey pointed to the lace covered table beside the chair. The charred button lay next to her open book. She scooped it into her hand and tossed it to him.

He held it for a moment, rolling it in his palm and headed for the door. "Stay right here," he pleaded. "Don't go anywhere. I'll be back within the hour." He ran back to kiss her before rushing downstairs and out the door.

Lacey stared down the hallway for a full minute before shaking her head. *I wonder what that's all about?* She sat in her chair, closed her eyes, and couldn't stop smiling, nor did she want to. The clock ticked away the minutes and finally boot steps dashed toward her door. She hurried to open the barrier and fell into Brandon's waiting embrace.

He held her in a bear hug. "Lacey, I cannot fathom loving you more than I do this second." He stepped back and took her hands in his, then looked into her eyes.

The dark lashes shadowing Lacey's cheeks flew wide as she searched Brandon's face. She took a quick breath and wondered if Brandon intended to do what it sure looked like he intended to do. *Shit fire and save matches. Is Brandon going to —* A kaleidoscope of butterflies took giddy flight in her stomach, and so in love, she couldn't hold still.

Brandon reached into his pocket, never taking his eyes from hers, and as he withdrew a meticulously drilled and filed gold ring, he bent to one knee.

Her stomach groaned and tried to convince her a hornet's nest had ruptured and that was what all the buzzing inside her stomach meant. She was sure, any second now, she'd throw up on her shoes.

This man kneeling before her was about to propose marriage.

Her bouncing got a little out of hand and she wished her body would calm down.

He took Lacey's hand and gently kissed her ring finger, his lips remaining on her skin a full sensuous moment before asking, "Lacey Autumn Kendall, I shall never love another as I love you. I promise to love you until I die, and if there is a life after that, I will love you then. Please, share my life. Lacey, will you marry me?"

Lacey stood mesmerized as she listened to him speak ever-lasting words of love. She could have said the exact words to him, she loved him so. She bent to wrap Brandon in her loving embrace and gazed into his bluer than blue eyes. "I love you with all my heart, Brandon…Chandler. Hey, wait a minute. I don't recall you ever telling me your middle name?"

"I don't recall you ever asking," he said with a teasing smile. "Lee, Brandon Lee. So now the deep, dark mystery is solved."

"Well, Brandon Lee Chandler, I love you with all of my heart." Joyful tears trickled down Lacey's cheeks as she both laughed and cried the words, "Yes, I will marry you."

21

Lacey and Rachael scoured through stacks of material in the General Mercantile and both gasped when they came across the perfect white fabric for a wedding gown. "I love it," Lacey exclaimed as she held the soft fabric to her cheek. "Oh, my goodness, feel how soft." She rubbed a corner of the material against Rachael's face.

"I would say that feels angel soft," Rachael said and put the material aside. "Now, what about the style? What are you envisioning?"

"I'd like the sleeves fitted," Lacey said. "With a line of round, covered buttons on the cuffs and down the back. That's the kind of dress Miss Aimee, from back home, put me in the first time I wore a dress. I want that magical feeling to happen again. Well, there was some magic but a lot more shock."

"Then, that's what I'll make," Rachael said clapping her hands together. "Let's find a pretty lace for the overlay and a piece of point lace to trim the sleeves."

Rachael took Lacey's measurements, then pulled out a chair from behind her desk and sat. She retrieved a pad of paper and a pencil. "I will design you the most beautiful dress you have ever imagined," she said and began to sketch. Within minutes, she motioned for her future sister-in-law to come to see her design.

Lacey walked around the corner of Rachael's desk. She covered her mouth with her palm and pointed at the sketch. "You can make that?"

"I can, and I will," Rachael said with a bright smile. "Come back at the end of the week for a fitting." She shooed Lacey out the door. "I am so excited for you and Brandon. I can hardly stand it."

Lacey returned on Friday and Rachael led her into the back room. Standing upright in the center of the room was a dress form. A beautiful white gown with fancy faux pearls sewn into the lace sparkled like white diamonds. Ribbon lined the sweetheart-shaped neckline and delicate French lace hung in scalloped folds to the floor. A fitted waistline opened into a full skirt bordered by several more rows of satin ribbon and French lace. The sleeves narrowed to the wrists, fastened by a long row of round, fabric-covered buttons. Duplicate buttons fastened down the back.

Lacey touched the lovely creation with her fingertips. "Rachael, this is the most beautiful dress I have ever seen. How can I ever thank you?"

"Lacey, the look of happiness on Brandon's face when he sees you walk down the aisle is all the thanks I will ever need."

"Anyone home?" The two women hurried from the back room at the sound of Brandon's voice. "What are you ladies doing back there?" he asked.

"None of your concern," Lacey said as she stood on her tiptoes to wrap her arms around him and plant kisses on his cheeks. "Rachael is sewing my wedding dress and she let me have a glimpse."

"Is that so?" Brandon wrapped his betrothed in a bear hug and rocked her back and forth, kissing the top of her head. "Do I get to take a peek?" He nuzzled her neck and tucked a few stray hairs behind her ears, then nibbled her lobes.

"Stop, that tickles. Brandon, aack." She scrunched her shoulders and turned her head side to side trying to avoid his tickling lips. "Brand…s-s-stop it." She tried to sound serious, but his wispy neck kisses tickled her to the core and words became mishmash.

Breaking free of his sweet tickle-torture, she said, "No, you don't get to peek. Ew." She blotted her neck with a fabric swatch. "You got spit on my neck."

He threw his head back for a belly laugh.

"You'll see my dress soon enough." She gazed at his handsome, rugged face, wrapped her arms around him and whispered, "I've decided if you behave and don't try and get a look-see at my wedding dress, I have a surprise for you on our wedding night."

"You have a surprise for me? Guess what, I have a surprise for you, too."

They embraced, laughing, and Brandon raised his voice so Rachael could hear. "How about I take my two favorite ladies to lunch?"

Rachael joined them from the back and picked up a roll of white satin ribbon. "Thanks, not today, I'm anxious to get back to my sewing." She winked at Lacey. "Ask me another day."

"I'll see you tomorrow, Rachael," Lacey called over her shoulder as she looped her arm in the crook of Brandon's. "Thank you again, the dress is lovely."

The couple walked to the Stardust Eatery and both ordered a cup of coffee and the pork roast lunch special with all the trimmings. "Do you have a particular design in mind for our home?" Brandon said after taking a drink of coffee.

"I've been thinking about that. I would like it built with a loft in case we would need extra room one day."

"You mean for all those kids we're going to make…err have. Of course, I meant have," he said with a sly grin.

"Yes, you're reading my mind. I want *lots* and *lots* of kids." She loved that they enjoyed such simple fun together. "Unfold your napkin, honey, here comes lunch."

Brandon reached to take his plate from the waitress. "A loft sounds like a great idea."

"I would also like to have a large front porch. And I would love for it to wrap around the front and both sides."

"We can do that. I've been drawing some ideas on paper. Let's look at them together when you get a minute."

"Perfect. I can't wait to see your ideas. Oh, I meant to tell you, I received a letter from Pa. Jeremiah won the pie eating contest at the county fair." She frowned. "But Matthew had sprinkled bitters on the filling and Pa said poor Jeremiah's been sicker'n a mule in a field of daffodils."

"From what you've told me about your brothers, it doesn't surprise me."

"Not to be outdone," she said with a chuckle, "Jeremiah took Matthew's blue-ribbon cow on a date to Big Jake's pasture. He's the meanest, ugliest bull in the county. Matthew is so mad Pa says he could split rocks with his teeth." She smiled and became quiet for a bit, memories of happy times with Pa and her brothers streaming in her mind.

Brandon waved his fork in the air between them. "What are you thinking about?"

"I guess I'm a bit homesick. Imagine that. I miss the daylights outta Pa and my brothers, and Pa says they're all having a hard time finding work. I'm terrible worried."

"You may have told me, and if so, I apologize, but how old are your brothers?"

"I don't think I've ever mentioned their ages. Luke is twenty-four, Matthew is twenty-three, and Jeremiah is twenty-one. Why do you ask?"

"We have plenty of work. Ask your Pa if he and your brothers would like to come and help build our home. I could use the extra hands. Our wedding is what, fourteen weeks from now?" He reached across the table and placed his warm hands over her fingers. "I want to carry you over the threshold of our new home after the ceremony," he said. "I'll make an honest woman out of you," he added with a wink. "The more help we have, the faster it will be finished."

Lacey threw her hands in the air. "Settled. I'll send Pa a tele-gram right away. He won't be able to wait to tell my brothers. Thank you, I've been missing my family more than I ever thought possible. In fact, I never woulda thought I'd miss my brothers at all." Lacey quieted again and picked at her napkin. "Brandon, what if there *is* gold on the property?"

"Then, so be it. *You* are my precious commodity. Gold or no gold, making you happy is my lifelong dream. And, my love, this is one dream I promise will come true."

Lacey bit her lip and looked into his eyes. "I truly believe you love me, Brandon, and I love you with all my heart." She hesitated. "I've been thinking —"

"What? What's on your mind?" He laid his fork on the table and leaned forward. "If there's something you want to talk about, I'm all ears. I know you've been trying to become more… ladylike, but you need to understand something, Lacey. I love you the way you are and you must never change the way you speak, dress, or talk. Do you understand? I love you exactly the way you are."

"I understand, thank you. However, I want to hire a digging crew, so we know for sure…about the gold."

"Well, don't I look like an ass." He laughed. "Here I am going on about your deep country ways. Why didn't you stop me?" He placed the soiled napkin on his empty plate and moved it to the side. "Lacey, as you well know, at one time I felt gung-ho about acquiring that piece of property and having it mined." Brandon leaned forward in his chair. "I had a gut feeling about the quartz area near South Sunday Creek. Now I have more important things on my mind." He winked. "Like making you the happiest woman in the world."

"Brandon, you do make me happy," Lacey said. "But I want to do this."

"I'll tell you what, we'll mine the property under one condition."

"Condition?"

"Yes. If gold is found," Brandon said, "no matter if it's before the wedding, or after, any profits are to be in your name only. I want you to realize how much I love you, only you, and not the prospect of a fortune. Deal?"

"Deal," Lacey answered with a quick nod of her head. "Brandon?"

He looked at her, eyebrows raised in anticipation of her question. "Yes?"

"Have I told you lately how much you mean to me? And that my heart"— she placed her hand over her heart —"aches for you?"

"Before I answer, do you feel the love I have for you? If so, you know exactly what it feels like to be loved and know it is a forever, until death do we part, love."

"I feel it."

"Exactly," he said and reached for her hands. "I feel it, too."

"Where is that stagecoach?" Lacey said days later as she paced up and down the walkway. "They should have been here twenty minutes ago."

"It isn't unusual for it to run late," Brandon said.

"I know. I'm anxious to see everyone, that's all. It's been months, and I miss 'em so much. Luke is courting Emma Stellar, the new teacher in town, so Pa wasn't sure if he'll make the trip or not." Lacey turned to the sound of distant horses. "Brandon, here they come."

Rueben stepped from the coach ahead of the boys and embraced his daughter. "My, oh my, look at you. Heavens, girl, what a fine lady you've become. Boys, get out here and take a gander at your perty sister."

Luke assisted a young lady from the coach. Her long hair, the color of butterscotch, reminded Lacey of the wrapped candies at Miss Aimee's Hotel. It fell straight as an "in the ditch" quilt stitch to her narrow hips. "Emma, this is my sister, Lacey."

"How nice to meet you, Emma." Lacey said as she embraced the newcomer.

"The pleasure is all mine," she responded in a crisp, English accent.

"Emma and I are getting married, Lacey," Luke said. "We reckoned why not get married where there's work to be found."

"Wonderful," Lacey said, reaching to hug her brother. "Have you decided on a date?"

"Not yet," Emma said. "We need to save money, and I must procure a teaching job."

"Where did you study?"

"I attended a private school in London named the *Ladies of Royalty Proper*," Emma answered. "Since traveling to America, the employment position for such a teaching job is a scarcity."

Pa placed his hands atop Lacey's shoulders and shook his head. "Who would have reckoned my Lacey girl would turn out to be such a lovely lady. I sure am proud of you."

"Thank you, Pa," she said and kissed his cheek. She wore her prettiest dress for the occasion, along with her favorite lace gloves and parasol, like the lady she'd become. She had never been so happy.

She introduced Brandon and waited for the men to shake hands before speaking. "Miss Fronie has your rooms ready at the boardinghouse," Lacey said. "It's late, and I know you'll want to get settled in."

Lacey and Brandon escorted the group to Miss Fronie's who met them at the door. After an introduction by Lacey, Miss Fronie took a long, hard look at the brothers and planted her hands on her hips. "You eat a lot, don't you." It was a statement not a question.

Jeremiah and Matthew exchanged glances. "Yeah, I…we do," Matthew said, knocking his shoulder into Jeremiah who, in turn, said, "He eats more'n I do."

Miss Fronie twitched her raised finger between the two boys. "I'm going to give you the rules like I do everybody else, and I mean for you to follow them. I'm not about to cook up a mess of food and watch it get cold and rot, you hear?"

Both boys hesitated until Pa swatted them upside the head. "Yes, ma'am," they answered in unison.

"And, another thing," Miss Fronie warned. "I better not see any girls sneaking into your rooms." She pointed a finger directly in Matthew's face. "If I do, there is going to be," she said pointing to herself, "Miss Fronie aiming the bottom side of her cast iron skillet between your ears. Do you understand?"

"Sure," Matthew said, his eyes wide.

She pointed across the street. "I don't know what goes on over there at the Crystal Saloon in the wee hours, and I don't want to know, but it is *not* happening here. Not once, not ever."

Lacey noticed a gleam in Jeremiah's eye as he glanced toward the saloon. *Pa best talk to that boy.*

"Now, one more thing," Miss Fronie said, "and this may be the most important piece of information you hear today. Do you know why?"

The boys looked at one another and suppressed chuckles.

"Why's that?" Luke braved to ask.

Matthew and Jeremiah started a giggling fit and Miss Fronie took a few steps toward them. "Something must be awful funny over here. Do you boys have your," she said, grabbing the tops of their ears, "listening ears on?"

"OW, yikes, ouch, please let go."

"Do you?"

"Yes, yes," the boys said at once. "We's listenin.'"

"Then hear me good. You will address me as Miss Fronie. No other way. Call me something else and you miss dinner for two days. Understood?"

She let go of their ears and as the boys rubbed the sides of their heads, they both agreed several times to call her only Miss Fronie."

"Come hither, young lady," Miss Fronie motioned to Emma. "Let's get you settled in and then"— she motioned to Pa and the boys —"I'll show the rest of you to your rooms."

Luke took Emma's flowered carpetbag and followed the women to the upper floor. The men decided on a time to meet at the building site, and Brandon accompanied Lacey to her room.

"I'm so excited. I never thought I'd miss Pa and my brothers this much." She noticed Brandon peering at her, the lines in his forehead more prominent. "What?"

Brandon smiled. "I'm thinking how lucky I am to have met you, Lacey Autumn Kendall. You are a ray of sunshine." He opened his arms wide and summoned her with his curled index finger. "Come here a minute."

Lacey lowered her eyes and sashayed toward him, swinging her hips in an accentuated sway before wrapping her arms around Brandon's neck. They gazed into each other's eyes. "Who is the lucky one, my love?" she said before their lips met in a hungry kiss.

Brandon had framed the cabin and figured the five men could finish in six weeks of solid work. That is, until he worked with Matthew and Jeremiah.

"Lacey," he asked while eating lunch at Clemmie's Café one afternoon, "has your Pa ever considered taking a switch to those boys? I swear if —"

"I told you," Lacey interrupted. "Didn't I tell you those two are a couple of scoundrels? What did they do this time?"

"*Do* this time? How about *didn't* do? Those two can think of more ways to get out of work." The more Brandon spoke, the more his temper flared. "I sent them off in the wagon for supplies, and your Pa and me waited over two hours for them to return. They still hadn't shown at the building site when I left to meet you for lunch."

Lacey almost feared asking, "Our cabin will be ready before the wedding…won't it?"

"If I have to work day and night to finish, I will," Brandon said as he stabbed three green beans with his fork, rose, and jerked the window curtain aside.

"What are you looking at?" Lacey asked as she bent next to Brandon to peer out. Her eyes widened as Matthew and Jeremiah staggered through the swinging doors of the Crystal Saloon.

Brandon stormed from the café.

"Oh my," Lacey whispered as Brandon's hands clenched and released several times while he charged across the road like a raging bull. When he reached the two, his hands made erratic gestures then pointed his index finger touching Jeremiah's nose. Lacey could only guess at the conversation. She closed the curtain and finished her lunch before Brandon bolted back into the seat across from her.

"Drunker'n skunks," he said. "And they smell like a bottle of cheap toilette water. I told them to sleep it off for a couple of hours and meet me back at the building site." Brandon cut a slice of pork chop and dipped the meat into a mound of mashed potatoes and white gravy. He pointed his fork at Lacey while he talked. "Those boys need to learn a good lesson, and I mean to do just that."

Lacey patted the side of her mouth with a napkin. "What are you gonna do?"

"I don't know yet, but I'll think of something to teach them a lesson, a darn good lesson."

They finished the last of their meal and Brandon escorted Lacey to the boardinghouse. "I'll see you at dinner," he said, and pulled her close for a kiss.

Brandon waited for the boys to show at the building site. Rueben and Luke were aware of Brandon's plan for paying the boys back and anticipated the fallout almost as much as he did.

The wagon with Matthew and Jeremiah came rolling onto the property. Brandon quit hammering and waited for the wheels to stop. He crossed his arms over his chest and shook his head. The boys jumped off the seat and sauntered over to him.

"Well," Brandon said and exhaled a long, audible breath. "I guess you two have gone and done it this time."

"Huh?" they replied and looked at one another.

Rueben rounded the corner and plodded over to his sons. He held out his hand. "Congratulations, boys. Dagnabbit, I reckoned Luke would be hitched long before the two of you."

"Huh?" Jeremiah repeated.

Pa poked the boys playfully in the ribs. "Yes, sir. You best be settin' a meetin' with the preacher man and"— he scratched his fingers over salt and pepper whiskers —"it'll probly save you two some money to go on and get hitched in a double weddin'."

"Hitched? Double weddin'?" Matthew's eyebrows shot to a painful height. He stared wide-eyed at his brother.

Jeremiah's skin had turned a pasty pale and beads of sweat peppered his face. He gnawed on his bottom lip, his eyes seeking an escape route.

Brandon pointed toward the meadow. "Those women you spent the better part of the afternoon with, they showed up here looking for you two boys."

"Here? They did?" Matthew said. "How's come for?"

"Whaddya mean how's come for?" Pa chimed in. "You did spend *time* with them two women, didn't you?"

"Well, yessir, we did," Jeremiah said, shuffling his feet. "But they is ugly and fat and smell like left-over pork bellies. I ain't marryin' either one of 'em."

Brandon shook his head and frowned. "Boys, in these parts if you spend *time* with a woman, you're expected to marry her. Heck, they're planning your weddings right now."

Matthew's skin went white as flour, resembling his brother's, and pools of sweat ran from his forehead, past his temples, and slowed a bit over his cheeks before dripping off his jawbone. He held his hands out incredulously. "But, Pa, they's *saloon* girls."

"Don't matter, fellas," Brandon said holding back laughter as he stretched his arms over his head and yawned. "That's the way it works 'round here."

"You gotta hide us," Matthew said in a rush of words as he glanced over his shoulder. "I swear, Brandon, they got possum faces."

"Pa, do somethin'." Jeremiah's swallow was audible. "We can't marry 'em. You gotta help us. Think how ugly your grandkids'll be. Imagine 'lil possum-faced youngin's runnin' and dartin' through the house, diggin' up the yard, and stinkin' the place up."

"Now, Jeremiah, they ain't gonna dig up the yard." Pa sighed. "You can fence 'em in."

"I suppose," Brandon said after a moment's silence. "No, that would be too much to ask."

"What would be too much to ask?" Jeremiah said hurriedly. "What, Brandon?"

"Well, this is if your Pa agrees." He tipped his head toward the construction. "I need this place finished and ready to move into, at least Lacey and my essentials, in a couple two or three days. That gives us just enough time before the wedding. There's still plenty of work needs done, and, like I said, Rueben, you'll have to sign off on this. I'm thinking you boys could sleep on the floor of the cabin, work sunup to sundown, and if those women come around, I'll convince them you are both idiots and unable to legally marry."

"Pa, will you grab our clothes from Miss Fronie's?" Jeremiah asked, the tension in his voice at frantic proportions.

"We can trap and hunt for our eats," Matthew added. "I'll eat roasted rat if I have to, Pa. Please say yes. Don't ruin our lives. Say yes."

"All right. I'll agree since you'll be helping Brandon and your sister get their home built. If I catch you playing around, one time not working when you're supposed to, I'll haul your carcasses into town and personally deliver you to the preacher. You hear me?"

"Loud and clear, Pa. We'll work hard, real hard. Promise."

Jeremiah whole-heartedly agreed and the two took off to set traps for dinner.

Brandon's smile turned into a belly laugh as he faced Rueben and said, "Roasted rat?"

22

acey glanced at the clock and wondered what in the world was keeping Brandon. Pa knocked on her door almost an hour ago and told her Brandon wanted to go to dinner. Miss Fronie sure wouldn't cook anything up for them at this hour, and Clemmie's Café and the Stardust Eatery were already closed for the day.

Finally, there was a knock on the door.

When she opened the barrier, Brandon stood in the hallway bathed and changed out of his work clothes. He held a bouquet of fresh wildflowers in his hand.

"Beautiful flowers for a beautiful lady, my dear." He handed Lacey the bouquet with a slight bend at the waist.

"Thank you, my dear," she said and wrapped her arms around his neck for a long, sensuous kiss. She placed the flowers in her water pitcher. "I don't think we're gonna find Miss Clemmie's open for dinner."

"No worry, my sweet." He tapped a finger on the tip of her nose. "C'mon, let's go." He escorted her to his buggy and assisted her onto the seat.

"Where in tarnation are you taking me?" she asked as they rode out of town.

"You'll see." He winked and lightly slapped the reins over the horse's back.

"Did you cook dinner for us?" she asked when it seemed they were headed toward Brandon's home.

"You don't think I can cook? Listen here, you are not aware of my many positive attributes." He flashed her a devilish "just you wait" grin. When they reached his cabin, Brandon sprang from his seat and rushed to assist Lacey. His hands encircled her waist and he placed her boots on the grass as gentle as a fallen leaf touching ground.

Lacey released a blissful moan as Brandon placed his large palms on the sides of her face and kissed her with the passion of a man in love. She ran her fingers through his hair and drew him closer, returning the heat of his kiss with her own desire.

Brandon gazed into her eyes with lids half-closed. "I love you with everything I am, Lacey Kendall," he whispered.

Tears welled in her eyes. "I couldn't love you more, or be happier, if I tried."

Brandon took a deep breath and placed a quick kiss on her lips before making a giant sweep of his arm. "This way, my dear."

She walked inside the cabin and smiled brightly. "Brandon, how beautiful." White linen covered the dining table and two red tapered candles stood tall in glass holders.

Brandon lit the candles and the flames danced in the air to cast a waltz-like pattern onto the linen tablecloth.

"Thank you, sweetheart. You made everything so nice."

"Well," he whispered in her ear. "Don't thank me too much until you've tasted my cooking."

Lacey decided the vittles tasted worse than awful. She did her best to nibble an iron-hard chicken thigh without Brandon realizing she couldn't possibly chew it. She sawed her way through under-cooked carrots quite ladylike with a knife. "Everything tasted delicious," she said when the meal finished. She rose and hurried to hide her plate with half-eaten food under his empty one.

Brandon followed her to the sink and wrapped his arms around her waist. He tucked his forehead into the back of her neck and inhaled her sweet scent. After unclipping her hair, he ran his fingers tenderly through her tresses before laying it over one shoulder and kissing her bare neck, then the sensitive area behind each ear. He savored the nape of her neck before turning her to face him and tasting her lips. "I love you, sweetheart," Brandon said and placed feather-light kisses on Lacey's lips before hungrily gathering her in his arms.

Lacey's knees weakened and she returned his fevered kisses. Her pulse quickened as Brandon's hands traveled from the neckline of her dress to rest on the sides of her breasts. His lips brushed from hers to nibble an earlobe, causing her to moan and turn her head, exposing the flesh of her neck. Warm lips on her exposed skin sent a smoldering heat throughout her body.

Brandon gently caressed her cheek with small kisses. "I have never felt a love so deep, and I never want to live a day without you."

"To know you will soon be my husband," she said, rubbing her arms, "gives me chills. I am the luckiest woman in the world." She melted into his strong, capable arms.

23

mma and Lacey left after breakfast the next morning. Lacey hoisted a lunch basket Miss Fronie prepared for them and a quilt into the buggy. She looked curiously at a small book Emma carried in her hand. The cover splashed with water paint read, *Wild Flowers, 1872.*

"I thought since we were taking a ride it would be the perfect day to start a flower book," Emma said as she handed it to Lacey. "Mother and I keep one each year, and I would like to share some of Montana's foliage the next time I see her."

Lacey turned it over to admire the dainty deep-rose colored ribbons that secured the pages from the backside.

"It is actually an autograph album deprived of its covers," Emma said as Lacey flipped the pages. "And inserted between blotting paper."

"What a lovely idea."

"And it is such a folly to make," Emma added as they lifted themselves into the buggy seat. "I fasten the various flowers I gather at different places of interest, and on each page below the flower I write the date, place of gathering, and little incidents of the day that may be interesting to read in days to come."

"Now, how did you get so clever?" Lacey teased as she led the horse and buggy out of town and onto a side trail that would take them near the grasslands and South Sunday Creek. "And how do you keep the flowers nice over a long period of time?"

"Before fastening bits of flowers or shrub," Emma said as she tightened the ribbon on the back of the book, "you press them between sheets of blotting paper until they are perfectly dry."

Emma hesitated as the wheels of the buggy hit a large rut. "If you turn each piece over and brush it carefully with the white of an egg — or thin mucilage would work — and spread the mixture upon the page with the aid of a large pin, they will keep nicely."

"I'll have to start a flower book of my own," Lacey said excitedly.

"That plant has a pretty leaf," Emma said pointing to a plant with a long circular stalk growing out of the center.

"That's called mullein and they get as big as seven feet tall," Lacey said and halted the buggy so Emma could step down and pick a leaf. "Don't those 'lil hairs feel like velvet?"

A small patch of bright yellow flowers caught their attention next. "Snapdragon," Lacey informed Emma. "Or better known to these parts as butter and eggs."

Lacey was excited to find a patch of wild roses. "These make sinfully good jelly," she said and again stopped for Emma to pick blooms as well as purple lupine, prairie coneflowers, and bitterroot. Lacey led the horse toward the tree line.

"The greatest number of plants seem to be here at the edge of the trees and down by the creek," Lacey said as the buggy bumped down the slope. "Let's walk a ways and see what we can find."

"Heavens, look at that," Emma exclaimed, pointing at a cluster of Calypso orchids.

"Aren't they pretty," Lacey said. "They are also known as fairy slippers. Doesn't it look like a delicate fairy ballerina might wear one of these petals to a spring dance?"

Emma laughed as she picked one of the lovely pink "slippers."

"This is our lucky-star day, Emma," Lacey said when she spotted a large bunch of mountain Lady's Slippers. "This has to be one of Montana's most beautiful flowers. My favorite has a slight twist and deep purple petals."

"I simply cannot believe it," Emma said when Lacey pointed out a patch of daylillies. "I actually found a flower I am slightly familiar with. I saw these once during a visit to Scotland, but they called them Witch's Thimble," she said and picked one for each of their flower books.

"If only I could keep all this beauty year around." Lacey sighed as she gazed across the meadow.

"I suppose in a way you can, Lacey. You know there are endless ways of keeping summer all the year."

Lacey glanced at Emma with one eyebrow raised. "Like how? What do you mean?"

"Mother used to take bittersweet berries and preserve them in a rain shower. No matter how dusty and dry and past the point of reviving they may have looked, a gentle shower always freshens them nicely, as if newly picked."

"I didn't know that, but I do know how to preserve cattails," Lacey said remembering how she and her brothers used to fish at the pond and bring bundles of cattails home in their arms. "As soon as you pick them, or within a few days after, dip them in a weak mix of gum arabic and water to keep the outside from popping open."

Emma pointed toward a small mountain range. "One day we'll take an afternoon and see what we can find."

"It's still early," Lacey said. "Let's at least go as far as the edge of the bluff. We can stop and eat our lunch, and look for foliage."

They stopped near the gently flowing South Sunday Creek and hopped out of the buggy. Lacey took the basket of eats and handed Emma the quilt.

"This looks like a dandy place to lay our blanket," Emma said, pointing to a smooth spot overlooking the creek.

They straightened the edges of the quilt and dug into the basket hungrily. "So how did you and Luke meet?" Lacey said before taking a bite of fried chicken.

"It is rather comical, actually," Emma said after wiping her mouth. "I closed the schoolhouse for the day, and when I turned to make my way down the steps, the tail of my dress caught in the door."

Lacey threw her head back and laughed. "Let's hope you realized it before you made your way down the steps!"

"Yes," Emma chuckled. "I noticed a gentle tug, and when I reached to pull the skirt free, it would not budge. Luke happened to notice my predicament from his position across the street and came to my assistance. The rest is history, so they say." She brushed crumbs from her bodice and said, "He is such a kind and gentle man, Lacey. And I absolutely love him."

Lacey smiled and lay back on the quilt. "I know exactly how you feel, Emma. I love Brandon with all my heart and feel as if there is an angel on my shoulder that led me to him."

Emma sighed as she said, "It is amazing what love does to the soul. The birds sing sweeter, the aroma of the flowers is more succulent, everyday trials do not seem so overwhelming."

Lacey and Emma relaxed on the quilt, each lost in thought before Lacey sat upright. "How adventurous do you feel, Emma?" She stood and pointed to a small cave dug into the side of the mountain.

"You're not thinking of going inside that cave, are you?" Emma asked warily as Lacey took off in the direction of the steep and rocky pathway leading to the top of the bluff.

"Sure, I am," she hollered over her shoulder as she raised her skirt and started to climb. The rumble of thunder sounded in the distance.

Most of the rocks were embedded deeply in the soil and helped them to climb, but smaller pebbles gave way under their shoes and threatened to send them sliding back down.

"I don't know if this is such a good idea," Emma said as she slipped on a rock and grasped a small branch to keep from falling.

"We're almost there." Lacey hauled herself to the top and bent to help Emma take a final step. The two brushed their hands together to rid them of rock dust and dirt before approaching the entrance to the cave. They held hands and took a few unsettling steps inside.

"It's too dark to see anything," Emma said with disappointment. "Even my own hand." They heard thunder and returned to peer at the sky. "It's getting dark early."

"And I don't like the sound of the thunder. It seems awful close."

"Perhaps we should head back to town," Emma said, already moving away from the cave.

Both jumped as a large thunder boom echoed through the sky.

Dark, angry clouds gathered overhead. "Heavens, please don't let it rain," Emma said as she turned to climb down the slope.

A bolt of lightning flashed overhead and splintered into six squiggly lines of yellow gold. A large drop of rain hit Lacey's forehead as she looked at the sky, and then the rain fell in torrents.

"Be careful, it's getting slippery," Emma called as Lacey walked to the edge of the bluff and turned to climb down. In an instant, her boot slipped on the wet gravel and she slid, grasping at a large rock, missing, and tumbling down the slope. Her dress caught on a branch and jolted her body to a dead stop.

Emma threw her hands against the sides of her face and screamed, "Lacey." She grabbed ahold of an imbedded rock and attempted to climb toward her, but the blowing sheets of rain and rapidly darkening sky made it impossible to grip her hands on even the largest rocks. A trail of blood ran down the side of Lacey's head, the rain washing it down the rocks and creating a winding pink trail. "Lacey, please wake up," she said to unhearing ears. She gasped when the rain stopped for a second and revealed Lacey's right ankle swelling with fluid.

A sharp crack of lightning caused Brandon to stop cutting the end of a treated log. He looked skyward. "We're going to get a helluva storm," he hollered in Rueben's direction.

The developing wind nearly blew Rueben's hat off as he reached to steady it. "Boys," he hollered. "Scout around…gather the tools and toss them into the smokehouse." He climbed down from the roof.

They gathered anything that could blow away or ruin by water and Brandon, Luke, and Rueben climbed into the wagon.

"Run me over to my place," Brandon said to Rueben. "I'll ride Thunder into town and see if I can get him shoed while we eat dinner."

Matthew and Jeremiah ran into the smokehouse for shelter while everyone else headed toward Brandon's cabin.

Brandon expected to see his buggy sitting outside of the boarding-house. His pulse raced when he realized it was nowhere in sight.

"I'll bet Emma and Lacey got caught in this storm," Luke hollered to Brandon as he jumped off the wagon seat and into a mud hole. "I sure hope they found some shelter."

Brandon glanced skyward as dark billowing clouds rolled overhead. "This storm sure doesn't look like it's going to pass any time soon," he said in a quiet, troubled voice. He planted himself in the doorway to Miss Fronie's, his eyes narrowing as he stared down the street.

Emma sat on the ground, grasped Lacey under her arms, and inched up the slope and inside the cave's protective walls. She hurried to clear gravel and rocks with her hands before sitting and easing Lacey's head into her lap. She ripped a large swath of material near the hem of her dress and pressed it against the side of Lacey's head. The material rapidly became soaked with blood. She tore another piece and held it tightly to Lacey's wound before wrapping a thinner piece and tying the ends to hold it in place.

"I have to leave you, dear," Emma's voice shook as she whispered in Lacey's ear. "But I promise, I'll be back with help …as soon as I can…I promise." Emma stood and ran to gather the sparse dry leaves blown into and around the cave opening before the rain and tucked them around Lacey's drenched and shivering body. She stood on the edge of the bluff and shielded her eyes from the torrents of rain for a second before climbing down and running to the buggy.

*L*acey woke to the sound of wolves howling. Her body prickled as if it were covered with pins and needles. Her breaths came in short gasps and soon her entire body shook. A hot sweat broke out on her forehead about the same time her stomach clenched in fear. *Where…?*

She brought her hand to the side of her aching head to a thick gel-like clump of sticky warmth. *Blood.*

"Emma!" she called as her heart beat like the pounding of a heavy drum inside her temples. Lacey wondered when she had ever hurt so bad or been this cold. Her head buzzed before a dark curtain at the edges of her vision became a black cloud and consumed her consciousness.

Emma could barely see where to lead the horse through the thick sheets of pelting rain. She wished for a path to follow. The tracks she and Lacey had made earlier were now deep, mud-soaked ruts. Attempting to keep her nerves in control, she sang softly to herself. It seemed to take hours to reach Miss Fronie's.

When she halted the buggy, Brandon and Luke ran toward her from the covered doorway. Luke held out his hands to assist her and Brandon peered into the buggy.

"Emma," Brandon shouted. "Where's Lacey?"

"Brandon, she's hurt…her head…bleeding." Emma, near out of breath, forced her voice louder than the intense, swirling rain and gusts of wind. "We climbed a bluff to investigate…a cave and…Lacey slipped down a rocky bluff and…I had to leave her." Tears streamed down Emma's face. "She's bleeding and I fear her right ankle is swelling…and I feel so fretfully bad for her."

"Where is she?" Brandon shouted to be heard over the thunderous storm.

"A cave. It overlooks a creek at the top of a short bluff. I will step inside and procure blankets from Miss Fronie." Emma hurried into Miss Fronie's, her hands shielding the cold, howling wind from her ears.

Brandon untied Thunder and swung his leg across the horse's broad back as Emma came running with a stack of blankets and a lantern. He stuffed the blankets into a saddlebag and the lantern on a loop. He rode off toward South Sunday Creek, knowing the approximate location of the cave entrance. With the fierce winds and sheets of rain it would take him a good forty minutes to reach Lacey.

The rocky bluffs and cave he had passed many times before on property assessments came into view. *Please, let her be inside.* Brandon dismounted, threw the reins over a tree branch, and grabbed the lantern. He ran through mud-drenched gravel, clawed his way up the bluff with his free hand, and then ran inside the entrance.

Empty.

Spiraling black spots clouded his vision and a buzzing sensation filled his head. He dropped hands to knees to catch his breath. Nausea consumed him as he attempted to slow his racing heart. He touched the wall — damp — and a musty odor hung heavy in the air. He stood still to listen to deafening silence.

Lord, strike me dead if it means Lacey lives.

When his eyes adjusted to the darkness, a potato sack against the far wall became clear. On closer inspection, he ran and dropped to his knees. "Lacey." He shook her shoulder and bent to hold her chilled body against his warmth.

Her clothing, sodden with rainwater, was pasted to her skin. When he touched her face, he withdrew his hand, startled by the cool chill of her flesh.

"Lacey," he said and shook her shoulders. "Wake up. Open your eyes and look at me," he pleaded. "Wake up, sweetheart, and open your eyes for me." Nothing. "Can you hear me? Open your eyes." He couldn't see her wound in the small amount of remaining light, so he took care to scoop her gently into his arms and carried her to the entrance. He had never seen a living person so pale or lips the shade of blue he equated with death.

Emma was correct, Lacey's right ankle was swollen, and she had a three-inch gash above her temple. He returned to the cave and laid her down as gentle as an angel's breath before hurrying to retrieve his saddlebags filled with blankets and a full canteen of water. He rushed back to her side.

"Lacey," he called again and shook her shoulders. "Lacey, please, honey, wake up." The only sounds she emitted were ones denoting pain. Brandon couldn't stand the helpless feeling of hearing the love of his life hurting, suffering, and in sheer agony. Her teeth chattering, he untied the bodice of her wet dress and pulled it down from her shoulders and unfastened the delicate ties of her chemise. He put his arm behind her back and set her forward to pull the wet clothing from her shoulders and down her back. After turning sideways to grab a blanket with his free hand, he tossed it on the ground, smoothed it the best he could, and laid her back down. When he lifted her hips to pull the clothes from her body, she cried out, but fell quiet again. Her rain-soaked shoes fought to stay on her feet. Brandon hesitated before reaching for her delicate lace-edged garters. He took a deep breath, and after removing her intimate clothing and stockings, he covered her in the two extra blankets and tucked them around her body. He silently thanked Emma for sending them and rubbed his hands briskly over Lacey's chilled shoulders and arms. When the shivering stopped, he brushed aside gravel and laid beside her.

"I love you, Lacey," he whispered in her ear, and swallowed hard.

Lacey rolled her head to the side and opened her eyes to see Brandon lying next to her, his warmth shielding her from the cool, damp air.

"Hello, angel," Brandon whispered as he reached to touch her cheek. His eyebrows became close together and his forehead wrinkled. "You have a fever, sweetheart. Your face is flushed and"— he brushed a few stray hairs from her forehead —"you feel warm."

She rolled to her side to face him but cried out in pain when attempting to shift her right leg. There wasn't a place on her body that didn't hurt.

Brandon sat and reached for the chemise he had tossed aside. He ripped it into strips and wet them with water from his canteen. "I'd like to get this fever down," he muttered and dabbed her face and neck.

Lacey leaned into the coolness against her hot skin but didn't have the energy to keep her eyes open or protest. She attempted to ask for a drink of water, but all she managed was a coarse whisper.

Brandon understood and supported her head while she drank. "Slow down, honey. Not so fast. You don't want it to make you sick." Before he finished speaking, she fell back into a restless sleep.

Lacey opened her eyes to the flickering light of Brandon's lantern throwing shadows on the cave's walls. She patted her body beneath the covers and verified — she was naked as a newborn under the stack of blankets. Pulling the edges to her chin, she glared at Brandon with as much fury as she could muster even before noticing the torn fabric of her chemise lying in a pile near where Brandon slept. "How dare you…where the hell are my clothes?"

"Whoa, Lacey," Brandon startled to her voice as he held his hands in the air. "Before you go throwing a crazed fit, do you remember what happened to you?"

Lacey fought through flashes of foggy cobwebs to get her thoughts in order. "Emma, is Emma all right?"

"Emma is fine. I found you soaking wet and chilled to the bone on the floor of this cave," Brandon said as he reached for a strip of the fabric, folded it in fours, and pressed it against the side of her head. "And, you have one nasty cut here."

Lacey did remember being cold and every piece of her body aching and sore. "But," she said and pointed under the blanket. A warmth penetrated the skin of her face and she glowered at Brandon.

"No need to fret, Lacey," Brandon said with a trusting smile. "I was a perfect gentleman. I only removed your wet clothes and wrapped you in a blanket."

Lacey pointed to the object and demanded, "Why is my chemise torn?"

"You were burning with fever, doll." He cleared his throat. "I used the strips of cloth to sponge your body."

Lacey's eyes grew round as hotcakes as she took a quick intake of breath.

Brandon winked, rose in one fluid motion, and strolled out of the cave, leaving Lacey to stare wide-eyed at his backside.

randon returned to find Lacey trying to button the sleeves of her wet dress. The rest of her garments remained in a heap where he'd left them. She held a strip of the chemise against the side of her head.

"I think we'd best get you to town and let Doc Petitjean sew that cut and set your leg," Brandon said as he squatted beside her. "I imagine your pa and Luke are half-crazy with worry about now."

"Has the storm eased?" Her left leg lay weak as rope licorice and her right leg proved completely useless.

Brandon glanced toward the entrance to the cave. "Yes, the rain has eased quite a bit, but the bluff is slippery. I'm not worried about getting you down the bluff and saddled on Thunder if you're feeling well enough to go."

"I can make it," Lacey said as she steadied herself by holding Brandon's arm.

"I can carry you."

"No, let's try it this way first."

Brandon wrapped his arm around Lacey's waist and inched the two of them down the slope of the bluff. When they reached flat ground, he scooped Lacey in his arms and lifted her onto Thunder's back before settling in behind her. "Lay your head on my chest, doll," he said, and they rode toward New Harmony.

Emma had informed Miss Fronie of Lacey's predicament and Doc Petitjean waited with her and a group of folks for their arrival.

Doc Petitjean quickly set his coffee cup down when Brandon walked through the door carrying Lacey in his arms. He grabbed his black leather bag and followed Brandon to her room.

Brandon layed her on the bed and Miss Fronie came bursting inside. "Out of here while I get those wet clothes from that poor girl's body," she said with a grand shooing motion of her arms.

Brandon and Doc Petitjean stepped into the hall and waited until Miss Fronie gave them permission to enter Lacey's room.

Lacey wore a white cotton nightdress, and Miss Fronie had piled a bundle of fresh blankets on top of her. Brandon sat on the edge of the bed and held Lacey's hand while the doctor busied himself on the opposite side.

The doctor cleansed her wounds and splinted her leg, then pulled the thick blankets back under her chin.

"She sustained quite a jolt in her fall. That's why she is so sleepy," he said to Brandon.

"But she's going to be all right, isn't she?" he said, as if Lacey weren't also in the room.

She didn't have the strength to argue.

"Lacey will be like new in no time, however she needs a few days of rest." He patted Brandon's shoulder and clasped the handle of his doctoring bag. "Let me know if you need anything," he said and turned the doorknob. Almost as an afterthought, he turned to Lacey and said with a wink, "I'll be over to check on you tomorrow."

Brandon mumbled a thank you and held Lacey's hand until she fell asleep.

Lacey awoke in the morning to a fitfully hungry stomach. She touched the wad of padding on her head and had a hazy recollection of Doc Petitjean standing over her. She jerked the covers back to see her splinted right leg and couldn't help chuckling as she imagined herself crawling down the steps and hoisting herself to the dining room table. Miss Fronie would most likely holler at her for stirring dust bunnies as she dragged her helpless body across the floor.

She pulled the covers back under her chin and startled to see Miss Fronie come bustling through the door carrying a tray of breakfast eats.

"Good morning, Lacey dear," she sang with a merry tune.

Oh Mercy, I've died and gone to Fronie-hell.

The woman held a plate of warm flapjacks dripping with butter and syrup nestled aside two pieces of sausage.

Lacey looked skyward and mouthed, "Thank you."

"Let me help you sit a little higher in bed, honey," Miss Fronie said as she took her pillow, gave it a big fluffing, and repositioned it so Lacey could eat. "Now, sugar plum, you rest, and let me take care of you."

Lacey wondered if the eats were poisoned. She flaked the top flapjack with her fork, hesitant to take a bite.

Brandon knocked on the open door and stepped inside. "Good morning, Lacey." He reached her bedside and leaned to kiss her forehead. "How are you feeling today?"

"Well," Lacey said a bit hesitantly. "I thought I was feeling fine until a few moments ago." She pushed the tray of eats aside and Brandon tore off a piece of flapjack and chewed it before she could warn him. She watched intently for signs of gasping, or spasms, maybe even foaming at the mouth. Seeing none, she pulled the tray back in reach and ate hungrily. "Just a passing wooziness, I guess," she said between mouthfuls.

"I'll be back to check on you in a little while, dear," Miss Fronie sang gaily. "Take this bell," she said, handing Lacey an oversized cow bell. "And if you need me for anything, you just ring-a-ding-a-ling this here bell, you hear?"

Lacey slowly nodded her head "yes" as the woman hustled through the doorway.

"What in Sam's tarnation is goin' on with that woman?" she asked Brandon. "That's not the miserable Miss Fronie"— she lowered her voice —"Miss Sour Fronie, I've come to know and dislike."

Brandon laughed heartily and sat on the side of the bed. "I just found out myself from Emma as I walked through the lobby." He leaned close and whispered, "Your Sour Fronie is in love."

"No, you're teasing."

He shook his head. "No, I'm not teasing, and if you think that's a surprise, wait until I tell you who's sparking her."

"Tell me. Tell me right now." Lacey hoisted herself further up in bed.

They both turned as Rueben gave her doorframe two quick knocks and stepped inside. Brandon shot Lacey a dramatic wink.

"No," she whispered and nearly choked on a bite of sausage.

"How are you this morning?" Brandon said, standing to shake the man's hand.

"Good, I'm really good." Rueben sauntered to Lacey's bedside. "How's my girl?"

"Much better. In fact, I feel like gittin' outta bed today. I wanna walk around a bit."

Rueben patted Lacey's hand and cleared his throat. "Well,

I best get down to breakfast, darlin'." He stood and spit into his hands before running them through the thinning hair on top of his head. "Wouldn't want to get Fronie's feathers in a ruffle waiting on me."

"I don't believe it," Lacey said after hearing his footfalls on the steps. "Pa and Sour Fronie?"

"Believe it, dear. Rachael mentioned she saw Fronie digging through material over at her store, and it certainly looked like she was planning to sew a fancy dress."

Lacey could barely contain herself. Miss Fronie's sudden change of personality was almost more amusing than anything she could dream on her own.

Brandon returned at nightfall to join Lacey for dinner. He carried a tray of steaming vittles and two cups of coffee.

"How sweet of you," Lacey said as she took a cup of the brew. "What's the occasion?"

"There doesn't have to be an occasion to sit and have coffee with the one you love."

Lacey took a sip of the hot liquid.

"I have to travel for a few days. Horace brought me a telegram and it seems the digging crew I contacted a few months back is billing me an insane amount for — what did they call it?"

Lacey waited patiently while he dug in his pocket.

Brandon produced a folded paper. "For consulting time," he said and shook his head. "I need to straighten this mess out and your pa offered to go with me."

"Pa always said he reckoned he'd be buried seeing no more'n his own backyard," Lacey said and took a sip of her coffee. "I bet he volunteered straight away."

"You're right. He was more than willing to accept my offer."

"When will you leave?" Lacey asked.

"The first light of morning we'll be heading to the railway station, but the timing isn't good," he added. "I hate to leave when you're not well."

"Don't be silly, Brandon. I have Emma and Miss Fronie here to take care of me. Heck, it'll give me time to recuperate while you're away."

Brandon kissed her forehead. "Miss Fronie was excited at the prospect of coddling you a bit," he said with a wink. "After the harsh way she's treated you lately, and now your pa's courting her. I'll bet she'd do about anything to get on your good side."

Lacey rolled her eyes. "I still can't believe it," she said with a chuckle that jiggled a few drops of coffee from her cup.

"I'm going to head on home and let you go to sleep now," Brandon said as he sat on the bed and took Lacey in his arms. They embraced in a meeting of lips. Meant for one another and each prolonged the moments of tenderness. As the kiss ended, he lifted her left hand and touched his lips to the place she would wear their symbol of eternal love. "I'll be here at your side the second I get back to town."

"Have a safe trip," Lacey said, holding back tears. "I love you."

"I love you too, darling," Brandon said and closed the door behind him.

*L*acey awoke hours later to a sound that sent instant shivers down her spine. She swore the door to her room made a creaking sound, but as she stared into the darkness, nothing looked out of place. She took a deep breath and brought the covers back under her chin, but her heart still beat like a scared rabbit as she tried to cozy her head back into the pillow. She decided the noise must have been part of a dream and closed her eyes.

In the next instant, a moist palm clamped over her mouth and the pillow was jerked from behind her head and pressed into her face as a male voice told her to remain quiet.

Lacey attempted to scream and bite the fleshy hand, but her actions caused more pressure to be placed on the pillow.

She squirmed and kicked with her left leg but found herself swept from the bed and eased onto the floor where her intruder knelt beside her. He tossed the pillow aside and replaced it with a thick material he wrapped over her mouth and around the back of her head. He tied it way too tight. She screamed as loud as the air in her lungs would allow, but the gag muffled her voice to a whisper.

"Be quiet," the man said, sounding like his teeth were gritted. "If you don't want to get hurt, you better listen to me."

The room turned black. For a second, Lacey thought she had fainted, but she took a couple of whiffs through her nose and recognized rank, rancid sweat. Whatever this monster put over her head, he needed to take it off. Right now! She twisted and tried to remove the hood by tilting her head and rubbing her shoulders in an upward shrug, but it didn't budge. He must have been watching her for he pulled on a couple of hanging cords and tightened the hood.

He sat her up before lifting her from the floor, and propped her over his right shoulder. He carried her down the steps and out the door. Outside, her hands were tied behind her back with a thick, scratchy rope, and she was lifted and placed into a wagon, the hard wood pressing into her back.

She squirmed and attempted to free her hands, but they were bound so tight she couldn't get them loose. The gag made her feel like she was suffocating and the stench from the hood gave her dry heaves. If not for calming herself with thoughts of Brandon, she would surely lose her sanity. Brandon would rescue her from this snake in the grass.

The wagon bumped along the road for what seemed like an eternity. Finally, it came to a stop and she was pulled across the hard surface and lifted over someone's shoulder. She smelled old bacon grease and dirty socks as the man opened a squeaky door and stepped inside before plopping her onto a mattress.

."You can holler as loud as you want, Miss Lacey," he said, and untied the bag. He brought it over her head, then removed the gag. "Get it all out of your system, and you'll feel a whole lot better."

Lacey stared straight into the face of Horace Sparker, Official telegraph officer.

Her words spit like flaming arrows. "What in tarnation do you think you're doing, Horace?"

"Oh gee, gosh, I'm sorry, Miss Lacey," he said. "When I heard you were gonna marry that Chandler fella"— he spun around, and his lower lip fanned out like a fattened worm —"I couldn't let it happen."

"No, I did not just hear what you said. That would be impossible. Why? Because that's the most idiotic, stupid thing I have ever heard from a creature who was supposed to get in the brain line but was taking a dump. So, excuse me, I want to make sure I got this right." She pointed to herself. "I fell in love with a man I will love until my last dying breath. And this: He fell in love with me and feels the same way. But, Horace Sparker, the O-fficial telegraph officer decides to steal me away from the man I love, and you think I'm gonna sit here like a cross-eyed hen and suddenly realize I've made a mistake, and I don't love Brandon. That I love Horace and want to marry him instead? Are you moonshine drunk stupid?"

"I love you, Miss Lacey," Horace said as he knelt on one knee in front of her. "And, you'll come to love me, too. I promise to take real good care of you, you'll see."

Lacey's voice rose an octave and her teeth clenched so tight it hurt. "Do you have any idea how dead you're gonna be when Brandon finds out you nabbed me outta my bed and brought me here to your...disgusting rat hole?" He's gonna turn you into buzzard bait. She was fueled with the fire of ten angry women as she demanded, "Horace, you take me back this instant!"

Horace stood and paced in front of her. "I'm sorry, but I can't do that, Miss Lacey. I gotta show you how much I love you, then you'll see the proper man you need to be hitching up with." He stopped pacing and untied the rope that held her hands. "Anyhow," he added, "that man you think you're in love with. He won't be looking for you anytime soon."

Lacey squinted her eyes as her nostrils flared. Her voice, lined with disgust, dropped three octaves. "And, why might that be, Horace?"

The man bent and slapped his thigh. "I transcribed a telegram this evening and presented it to Brandon. He leaves outta town in the morning, right?" His eyebrows arched. "If I'm not mistaken, he has a bill to dispute?"

"Horace, don't you dare let harm come to Brandon." Her throat burned and she held back tears. "I mean it, I love him with all my heart. I swear, I'd die if anything happened to him. Whatever you did to cause Brandon to leave town was a miserable, rotten thing for you to do. If you think taking me against my will and keeping me here with you is gonna make me fall in love with you, you got another thing coming."

"We'll have to see about that, Miss Lacey," he said with an easy smile as he finished untying her hands.

Lacey looked at her splinted leg. *How in tarnation am I gonna get outta here? I must find a way to warn Brandon.* Her eyes flashed wide as Horace cut the rope around her wrists, pulled her arm to the bedpost, and started tying her again. "Wha…what the hell are you doing? So help me, Horace, you even think about what you're thinking about and I swear, I'll kill you. I'll kill you dead so fast you won't even know you're dead till the devil tells you to stop stinking up the place."

"Miss Lacey, I wouldn't hurt you for nothing. Don't you worry. But I wouldn't want you to try to leave and end up hurting yourself. This will keep those dangerous thoughts from getting into your pretty little head."

"Listen, Horace, I wouldn't *dream* of trying to get away on my own. Heck, with this broken leg and all, it would be senseless for me to even think about it."

"No." He reached over Lacey's head to grab her other arm. "I'm not taking any chances, not until you show me I can trust you." He tied the other wrist to the bedpost and bent back into Lacey's face. "You rest now, honey. I'll cook you a nice meal in the morning."

Lacey flung every dirty word she knew at Horace's back. "You rotten, miserable two-bit-fly-by —"

The door shut as she jerked, tugged, and pulled the ropes binding her hands.

She tossed and turned the entire night. Visions of Horace Sparker hanging from the nearest tree danced in her head. She wondered how long it would take Brandon to get to his destination and realize he'd been tricked. And what torturous death would he choose for Mr. O-fficial telegraph officer?

After the morning sun began shining into her window, Horace clattered around in the kitchen. Her insides went wild with anger.

"I fixed you up some breakfast vittles, Miss Lacey," Horace said as he walked into the room carrying a plate of eats.

"I'm not hungry," she said and narrowed her eyes at the man.

"You gotta eat and get your strength up." He placed the plate on the floor and untied her wrists.

Lacey released a painful moan when her stiff hands were set free. She brought her arms forward and rubbed the red, indented lines on her sore wrists where the rope dug into her flesh but fortunately didn't open her skin.

"Look at my arms, Horace. Look at this." She thrust her hands in his face. "Is this how to treat a lady you claim to love?"

"Sorry about that, Miss Lacey," Horace said casually as he put his arms around her waist and heaved her up in bed. "Sorry if those ropes hurt and all, but it can't be helped right now." He placed the plate in her lap.

"Take me back to Miss Fronie's this instant!" Lacey shouted and threw the plate on the floor. She stared directly into Horace's eyes.

"I'm sorry, Miss Lacey, I can't do that," he said and glanced at the mess on the floor. He shook his head and retied her wrists before walking away and closing the door behind him.

Emma paced in the long upstairs hallway until the front door slammed. She ran down the steps. "Sheriff Kahler," she said. "Thank goodness you've arrived."

"Did you hear anything last night, Miss Stellar?"

"Not a sound."

Miss Fronie came bounding through the entrance to the kitchen. Her eyes were red-rimmed and she held a handkerchief in her fist. "I went to take Lacey her breakfast plate this morning," she said. "And, when I walked into her room, I saw she was gone. I didn't hear a peep all night."

"Where's Brandon and Rueben?" the sheriff asked as he turned for the door.

"They headed out this morning and we don't expect them back for at least a week," Emma said.

"I can't imagine who would nab the poor girl," said Miss Fronie holding the apron's hem to her moist eyes.

The sheriff simply nodded and took a few notes on a piece of paper. "If Miss Kendall doesn't turn up by nightfall, I'll go out looking for her."

"By nightfall?" Emma said. "Sheriff, you don't understand —"

"By nightfall, ladies," the sheriff said as he tipped his hat and sauntered to the door.

"I brought you something, Miss Lacey," Horace said as he opened the bedroom door and swiveled to grab an object from the entry. He brought a chamber pot to the side of the bed and pushed it against the wall with his foot.

"If you need to use this, you let me know and I'll untie those hands for you."

Lacey bit her lip. Surely Horace would give her privacy to pee. *Maybe this would be her chance for escape.*

"Actually," she said before Horace left the room, "I could use it right now."

"Miss Lacey, you have to promise you won't try anything sneaky." Horace untied her hands and paced in front of the bed. I'm going to stand right outside that door," he said thrusting his finger toward the door, "and, if I hear footsteps on the floor, I'm coming in."

"Hobble is a better word, Horace," Lacey said pointing at her leg splint.

"All right, Miss Lacey," he said. After shuffling his feet in place a dozen times, he stepped from the room and closed the door. "I'm standing right out here with my hand on the doorknob and I ain't going anywhere, Miss Lacey. You best hurry."

Lacey glanced around the room. How in tarnation was she going to get out of this mess? Even if she could make it across the room without alerting Horace, she knew it was pointless to think she could pull herself through the window with her leg in a splint. She used the chamber pot and sat on the bed to think. She had an idea and hollered, "Horace, I'm all —"

The door sprang open before she could finish her sentence and Horace bounded into the room. Right away, he went to tie her wrists, but when he reached for her arm, she bit him as hard as her teeth could chomp, right on the side of his thumb.

"Ouch!" he screamed in pain and jumped back. "Miss Lacey," he said and shook his hand east, south, north, and west about fifty times, jumping around like he'd been bit by a grizzly and stung by a hornet's nest. "Why did you go and do that?" He shoved his pulsating thumb inside his mouth.

"Oh, you think that hurt, Horace? You ain't seen hurting yet." She lunged to grab his oversized ears.

They both fell tumbling and Lacey shrieked in pain when her leg contacted the hard floor.

She pinched his ears with all her might, kicked her good knee into his groin, and poked him in the eyes with her index fingers.

"Gall darn it, knock it off! Miss Lacey, let go of my ears right cotton picking now!" Horace screamed as a whirlwind of fury jabbed, bit, and pinched every inch of vulnerable skin she got her hands on.

Lacey hunched over like a cat after a juicy mouse and twitched her bottom, prepared to lunge at Horace's first wrong move. Her nostrils flared with fury. "You ain't gonna tie me up again, Horace, and don't you dare even try."

She let her lips pull back to show him her teeth and snarled like a bear bit in the behind by a rattesnake.

He looked at her, his ears as flaming red as the bottom of a hot pan on the cookstove. He wiped blood and snot from his nose as he attempted to see through swelling eyes that watered his cheeks and dripped off his pointed chin. "All right, all right," he said, the pain evident in his cracking voice. "Just keep that mouth full of teeth to yourself, and I promise not to tie you."

"That's better." Lacey relaxed her shoulders. "Anyway,"— she pointed at her ankle and rolled her eyes — "can't go far."

"I said I won't tie you," he said as fluid continued to seep from the corners of his eyes. "But if you try to get away, I mean it, Miss Lacey, I'll be really, really mad at you."

"No, Horace." Lacey stared daggers into Horace's eyes. "You even think of tying me up again, and you'll be the sorry son of a snake who'll pay hell for it! And you better bet I mean what I say."

Horace stood and reached to help Lacey from the floor.

"Don't even think about it," she spat and twisted her body to stand on her good leg.

Horace hung his head like a fight weary hound dog. He left her room and pulled the door closed with a childish slam.

Emma and Miss Fronie pounded on the door to the jailhouse and finally the lock turned on the other side. The women stepped back as the door opened.

"Sheriff, it's nightfall," Fronie said with her arms crossed over her chest. "And there hasn't been one sign of our Lacey."

"Yes, ma'am," he drawled and spit a wad of tobacco, missing Emma's foot by inches.

"Well, you gather a bunch of men and go looking for her," Fronie demanded.

"First light of day, I'll scout around for her and ask some questions," he said and took a long swig of whiskey. "I'm calling it a night here real soon."

"First light of day?" Emma said. "But sheriff, you promised if Lacey did not show by nightfall, you would go looking for her."

"What do you think I'm going to see in the dark?" He exhaled a long, whiskey-reeking breath. "What I meant was that"— hiccup —"if the girl didn't show by"— hiccup-hiccup —"nightfall, then I'd go back to bed. Err, think about looking for"— hic —"her."

"Think about looking for her?" Miss Fronie's voice boomed through the small doorway. "Just what do you mean by that remark?" Fronie stepped nose to nose with the sheriff. "If I don't see you high-tailing out of town at the crack of the rooster call, I am personally going to come over here and —"

"I would suggest you take two"— hic—"steps back, Fronie." Sheriff Kuhler looked into the woman's face. "I'm still the"— hiccup-hic—"the law in this here town, and if I told you I'd" — hiccup-hiccup —"look for Miss Kendall in the morning, then I will!"

"Come now, Miss Fronie," Emma said taking the woman's hand and leading her away. "First thing in the morning, we shall go to the telegraph office and send a telegram to Rueben and Brandon advising them to return home immediately."

"When they get back, and Brandon gets his hands on that no-good drunken lawman," Miss Fronie said over her shoulder, "that scalawag sheriff will have to stand on his head to take a sh —"

"Come now, Miss Fronie," Emma interrupted with finesse and led the woman back to the boardinghouse.

*L*acey woke the next morning to Horace hovering over her bed holding a dry biscuit for her breakfast. She devoured it as soon as he retreated. Moments later, banging and tapping noises outside made her wonder if he was nailing her window shut. She didn't wonder long, for soon after, clopping hooves and a squeaky wagon told her he had left for work and would be gone at least until lunchtime. *Come hell or high water, I'm gittin' outta here.*

She tossed the covers aside and hobbled to the bedroom door. It wouldn't budge. Same thing with the window. He had boarded it up so tight, she couldn't get it to move, not even an inch. When she peered out, she realized it wouldn't do her any good to break the window. He'd nailed cross boards to prevent her from crawling through. *Reckon he ain't as dumb as he acts. No, he's dumb.*

She sat on the edge of the bed to ponder her situation and a thought passed through her mind. She'd make Horace so miserable, so insanely miserable, he'd jump barbwire fences to take her back to town.

Where's Horace with my food? He sure knew how to make her angry and the closer it got to lunch, the angrier she became. *Does that no-good skunk think he ain't gonna feed me?* She punched a fist to her palm.

Winston Beaumont stood and clasped the cold metal bars at the sound of gunfire outside of his jail cell. When two familiar faces walked through the archway and into his cellblock, his mind raced through possible scenarios.

The taller of the two men peered intently at Winston. The stub of a sodden cigar hung from the side of a crooked smile missing all but three teeth. The man cocked his head, nodded in Winston's direction, and sauntered to his cell. "What you think, Simon, you think today is payday?"

Winston raised his hands in defense. "Percy, you must allow me more time. How do you think I can obtain the money you requested when," he shook the bars, "when I am inside of a locked jail cell?"

"Listen, mate," Percy said. "You swore you'd have the money directly after arriving in Montana." He reached into his pocket and pulled out a gun. "And, from what we hear, you were a free man for quite a while before ending up in jail."

Winston scurried to his thin mattress and lifted the edge. "Yes," he said, "but I have something guaranteed to interest you. Would you like to see?"

When he didn't receive an answer, he slid a hand under the mattress and swept back and forth before retrieving a pouch. He dangled the cord that secured it shut as he walked to the bars and stood in front of the cigar smoker. "See, Percy," he said pulling a gold nugget from inside the pouch. He held the treasure in his sweaty palms. "Gold — just as I told you."

Percy tilted his head back and eyed the nugget. "Fool's gold, you mean."

"Not on your life," Winston said. "This is the genuine article."

"You mean on *your* life," Percy said with a sly grin. "Because if you're trying to pull one over on us, Beaumont, you're going to be nothing more than a stiff corpse in a wrinkled suit." He reached for the nugget and studied it as he rolled the heavy object in and out between nicotine-stained fingers. "Where did you get this?"

Winston attempted to calm his voice as he tapped his finger in the direction of the nugget. "The schoolteacher I told you about, Molly Kendall, she showed me this stone one day. She referred to it as a good luck charm she picked up near her creek bed back home. Said she had a ton of it sitting there bathed in milky quartz and just waiting to be mined."

"Maybe this is only a worthless rock, Beaumont, and you're taking me and Simon for a ride."

"No," Winston blurted as he eyed the gun in Percy's hand. "I offered to have it placed into a setting for Molly. I took it to a chemist and learned it is pure gold. Pure gold, my friend."

"You owe us a lot of money, Beaumont. If this is true, if what you're telling me is true, why weren't you on her property with a shovel?"

"A slight glitch to my plans," Winston explained. "I knew Molly Kendall had died, and I anticipated slipping onto her land to make a claim, but it seems her niece had arrived with the intention of making *her* claim on the property."

"The deputy out there at the desk, he said you landed in the slammer after catching fire to somebody's homestead."

"I needed to chase her niece, Lacey Kendall, away before she married this Brandon Chandler fellow. According to Molly's will, the niece and legal husband own the land fair and square.

"Then what are we waiting for, mate. We got us a wedding to attend."

Near dark, Lacey heard the crunching of gravel as the buggy wheels neared the cabin. She hobbled to the door and pressed her ear as close as possible. Sounds of shuffling and scraping came from the kitchen and soon the aroma of cooked eats caused her stomach to growl so loud Horace had to hear it.

When the sound of his footsteps approached the door, Lacey sat on her bed, crossed her arms over her chest, scowled, and glared at him when he entered. The second the door swung open, she demanded, "Why in tarnation didn't you bring me any lunch?"

Horace looked at her as if she had grown green horns and a yellow-forked tail. He placed the plate of food well out of Lacey's reach. "Well, Miss Lacey," he mumbled. "I'm rightfully sorry you went and tossed your nice breakfast on the floor yesterday morning, but if you've got a mind to eat while I'm at work all day"—he nodded toward the plate of food, "you best eat the vittles I bring you, and not waste them. You would have got more than a biscuit this morning had I not been angry with you."

"Just hand me that plate and shut your trap."

He set it down and snatched his fingers back.

She grabbed a warm biscuit dripping with apple butter off the plate and shoved it into her mouth. After several hurried chews, she brushed a hand over her clothing to rid the crumbs. "I suppose you expect me to wear a dirty nightdress all day, too?"

"I reckon I could rinse that one out for you, if you think it needs it," he said, biting his bottom lip.

"Iffin' I think it needs it, Horace? What kinda stupid remark is that?" She pulled roughly on the tail of the nightdress. "Look how filthy I am after being dragged around in the back of your smelly wagon!"

Horace puckered his meaty lips and looked everywhere except at Lacey.

"I want new clothes, Horace." Lacey slammed her fists onto the mattress causing Horace to jump. "And I want them NOW!"

Horace took a quick step backward and reached for the plate of eats. "I'll go to the dress shop tomorrow, Miss Lacey, and buy you something real pretty. How will that be?"

Lacey eyed him warily. "Make sure you tell Rachael you want something with fitted sleeves and tiny 'lil covered buttons on the cuffs." Lacey looked toward the heavens, hoping her request would ring a bell with Rachael.

"And I want a rope of licorice and a handful of candy." She thought for a minute. "And a surprise."

"A surprise, Miss Lacey? What do you mean by a surprise?"

"Just what I said," she answered briskly. "Iffin' I told you what to buy, it wouldn't be much of a surprise, now would it? So, bring me a surprise, and make sure it's something I will like." She grabbed the plate of eats and shooed him away with a wave of her hand. "Now go and leave me alone."

Horace walked clear around the entire General Mercantile the next afternoon, eyeing all the assorted merchandise and avoiding Rachael's inquisitive looks. After spending all except a few minutes of allotted lunchtime, he approached the counter and cleared his throat. "I'd like a rope of licorice, please," he said, "And a nickel worth of rock candy."

"Got a sweet tooth today, Horace?" Rachael teased as she scooped the candy and let it trickle into a small brown bag. "Just one rope of licorice?"

"Make it two, Miss Rachael." Now all he needed was a dress for Lacey and he'd be on his way. "And I'll be needing a dre, that is, a dre, a dreadful amount of navy beans."

"Navy beans?"

"Yes, ma'am, just fill a sack for me, and that'll do it for today."

Horace took the sacks of licorice, rock candy, and navy beans and headed home. He inhaled a deep breath as he stood outside her locked door. He sure hoped Miss Lacey was in a better disposition today.

The key turned in her door lock and when Horace stepped inside, she peered at the two small sacks in his hand. She sat up in bed. "Whaddya have there?" she asked, knowing full well there weren't no dress inside either one of them little brown bags.

Horace's step quickened as he approached. "I got your licorice ropes and some real nice rock candy." He left the sack of beans by the door. "And some navy beans for dinner."

"And my dress?" She folded her arms over her chest. "Where, pray tell, is my dress?"

Horace placed the bags of treats on the table by the bed. "Miss Lacey —"

"Don't you tell me you didn't buy a dress. This evening ain't gonna go well for you iffin' there ain't a dress all folded up nice'n tight in one of them there 'lil bags."

He shuffled his feet. "Try some of this candy, it's tasty and sweet, and look at all the pretty colors —"

"Horace, I'm fearing for you." Lacey pursed her lips and pointed her finger like a gun. "Did I, or did I not tell you to buy me a dress? Whoa, and wait a gall darn minute. What about my surprise?"

"I forgot all about your surprise, Miss Lacey. I can get you one later, but about that dress —"

"Tomorrow. You either bring me a dress with fitted sleeves and tiny 'lil buttons on the cuffs or…or else."

"Miss Lacey," he hung his head and paced. "I can't walk into the Mercantile and say I want a dress. Heck, I ain't never bought a dress before." He shifted his weight from one foot to the other. "And what if somebody hears me or asks a question?"

"Let them ask, that's what. March right up to Rachael and tell her whatcha want. She won't think a thing about it." She took the bag of rock candy from the table. "Now go on and make my supper. I'm hungry."

Horace nodded and shut the door.

"Horace," she hollered at the top of her lungs.

He opened the door a crack and peered inside.

"I'd like pie for dessert this evening."

"All…all right, Miss Lacey." He nearly closed the door.

"And Horace, make it taste good." She shooed him away. "That's all."

By the time Horace appeared with Lacey's supper tray, she was fit to be tied. "What the heck took you so long?" She picked up a spoon to knock around a few navy beans floating in a bowl of murky water doused with pepper flakes. "What in tarnation is this?"

"This here is navy bean soup. I'm not much on cooking vittles," he said. "But since we can't very well go eat at Miss Clemmie's, I'm doing the best I know how."

"Go fix me something else, Horace," she said and handed him the bowl. "Bean soup makes me fart."

Horace took a step back. "Gives you gas?"

"No, it makes me fart."

He scratched his head.

"What are you looking so stupid for, Horace?"

"I guess, I reckoned ladies didn't fart."

Lacey stared at Horace for a full minute without speaking, hardly believing how serious he looked. "Just give me the soup," she said reaching for the bowl.

"Good day, Mr. Sparker," Emma said as she strolled into the telegraph office the next morning.

Horace stumbled over his feet as he turned from the file cabinet to where Emma stood on the other side of the counter.

"Good day, Miss Stellar," he offered, his hands trembling as he placed his paperwork down and adjusted the arm band on his white shirt.

"I need to send an urgent telegram to Brandon," she said.

Horace reached for a piece of paper and jotted her information. He watched as she left the office and entered the General Mercantile across the street. He glanced over his shoulder before shredding the telegram, then hid it deep within the wadded papers in the trash can.

When lunchtime rolled around, he was too rattled to consider buying Lacey a dress, but she sure would be mad as a mule chewing on bumblebees. Horace fretted so much the rest of the afternoon his hands sweated like soggy milk toast as he locked up for the day and headed home.

He decided Miss Lacey sure was getting awful cantankerous. He didn't like her attitude one bit. He'd tell her this evening she was acting a bit too big for her britches.

Lacey's angry voice boomed in his ears the instant he opened the door to his cabin, causing his legs to wobble like boiled noodles as he crossed the room. He sure hoped Miss Lacey wasn't going to holler at him again.

"Horace Sparker, you get your fantail in here this instant!"

He unlocked the door and when he stepped inside, Lacey slammed the backside of her dinner plate right square dab into his face. He hollered and clasped his nose with both hands.

"I'm bored." Lacey hoisted the plate for another blow. "And I want out of here." She reared her arm back for another whack.

Horace straight away lifted an arm as a shield and attempted to grab the plate. The other hand remained secured to his nose.

"You boarded up the windows, you nincompoop, so I can't even raise 'em for fresh air." She pointed toward the now open bedroom door. "And, you've got me locked in, so I can't leave this stinkin' room all blasted day."

"I'm sorry, Miss Lacey," he said as he patted the knot appearing on the bridge of his nose. "But I can't have you taking off on me while I'm at work."

"Iffin' you're concerned 'bout that, Horace, then put a lock on the main door going outside, but I wanna leave this stuffy room during the day, and I mean it!"

"I suppose I could do that." He kept one eye on the plate she white-knuckle gripped in her hand.

"Now fetch my supper. I'm half starved." She eyed him with renewed vigor. "You did buy me a dress today, didn't you?"

Horace shuffled back and forth and adjusted his arm band. "I have an idea, Miss Lacey. I'll give you some of my old clothes and you can rip out the seams and make yourself something real pretty from them."

"What?" she screamed. "You come on over here a little closer. I'm gonna fix your face. C'mon, get your face over here!"

"Miss Lacey, I'm not going into the store and asking for a dress, and that's final." He straightened his shoulders. "I'm sorry, but it's either you get imaginative with a needle and thread, or …or do without." He snatched the plate from her hands and returned to the kitchen.

Lacey hobbled back to bed and plopped down on the mattress. Horace destroyed her hope of Rachael catching on to his request for a dress with fitted sleeves and tiny buttoned cuffs. She fingered the dirty tail of her night dress and rolled her eyes skyward. Well, if she had to go and make herself a dress, at least it would give her something to do during the day. She was sick and tired of staring at four walls. Her stomach roiled like a remnant of bean soup rattled around in the empty pit of her belly. *Maybe tomorrow, I'll scrounge up something to cook for supper.*

Emma and Miss Fronie hurried to stand when the front door opened. "Sheriff?" Emma called. "Please tell us you found Lacey."

"Not hide nor hair of her," he said with a shake of his head. "I've been all over the county asking questions and nobody has seen or heard anything out of the ordinary."

"That's not good enough," Miss Fronie began. "You hightail it back out there and find her and don't show your face until you do."

"I'm doing the best I can, Fronie," the man drawled. "Tomorrow, I'm getting a group together to scout the woods, but other than that, there isn't a whole lot I can do. Good day, ladies."

"I feel so helpless," Emma said after the sheriff took his leave. "It could be days before Brandon gets back, and I cannot bear to think, what poor Lacey could be going through. It breaks my heart."

Lacey, quiet as a hobbled church mouse and thankful he left her door open, snuck up behind Horace with the dirty skillet from the kitchen table and whacked him a good one in the back of the head.

"OW-ow-ow-OUCH! What did you do that for?" Horace hollered, as he dropped the ladle he'd been stirring beans with and grabbed the back of his head. "You scared the dickens out of me, and doggone it, that hurts."

"Is that bean soup you got cooking there?"

"Yes, this here is bean soup." He picked the ladle off the floor and stirred the pot of bubbling liquid.

"Oh, fire and tarnation," she said dropping into a chair. "Don't you know how to cook anything besides bean soup?"

"Not really, Miss Lacey." He shrugged. "I told you, I mostly eat Miss Clemmie's cooking over at the café."

Lacey put her face in her hands, her stomach rolling. The thought of Miss Clemmie's cooking caused her mouth to water. "Tomorrow, I'll see if I can cook something up for us," she said as she lay her head on the table and wished for a plate of Pa's beef and gravy.

"I laid out a pair of tan trousers and a couple of shirts for you." Horace pointed toward the stack of clothing. "I bet you can sew up something real pretty for yourself."

She frowned and reached across the table, dragging the trousers and two white shirts he must have worn to work and spilled some of Miss Clemmie's lunch down the front. She'd rip out the leg seams and cut the waistband. Maybe she could make something with a heaping dose of imagination.

"What kinda eats you got for when I get hungry?"

"I've got some dried pork and a bit of beef in the cellar I could bring up for you, and there's plenty of flour, sugar and the like on the shelf," he said motioning his head toward a set of shelves hanging on the wall.

"Horace," Lacey raised her head and looked directly into his eyes. "You're gonna take me to Miss Fronie's in the morning. You made a big mistake bringing me here, and you need to make it right 'fore it goes on one more day."

Horace took a deep breath and pulled the remaining chair from under the table. He sat and took her hands in his. "Do you still love that Chandler fella, Miss Lacey, or are you now seeing what a good husband I'd make?"

Lacey sighed. "Horace, I'm sorry, but I could never love you. My heart belongs to Brandon, and I'm gonna marry him." She lowered her voice to a mere whisper. "You need to take me back 'fore he comes to kill you."

"Can't take you back, Miss Lacey," he said and returned to the stove. He stood with his back to her. "You'll come around."

"I'm not gonna come around, Horace. I'm never gonna be in love with you. Heck, I don't even like you right now." She stood and braced herself against the table before screaming, "Take me back!"

Horace startled but ignored her outburst and gave the soup a final stir before scooping a ladle full into a bowl and setting it on the table.

With a sweep of Lacey's hand, the bowl promptly sailed off the table and across the floor. As Horace turned to clean the mess, she hobbled back to the bedroom.

Lacey inched her way out of the bedroom the next morning and attempted to open the cabin's front door. Pointless. She eyed the clothing Horace left on the table. Anything would be better than lying in bed and staring at four walls all day. After ripping out the stitching, she tore off the waistband and laid the remaining fabric on the table. She measured and stitched, measured some more, ripped a few stitches, cursed, and finally held up something resembling a dress.

After easing into the garment, she took a gander in the mirror. She'd show Horace what a fine wife and seamstress his Mrs. Horace Sparker would make. "Perhaps with a few alterations," she mumbled to the reflection and admired her work from side to side. After slipping the garment over her head and adding a few more pins here and there, she giggled before returning to the table to finish her sewing creation. Glancing at the time, she moved the needle swiftly through the fabric since she still had supper to cook.

Horace returned from work, opened the cabin door, and froze. He sniffed the air. What was that aroma? His mouth watered as he envisioned a home-cooked meal served by a pretty lady. He hurried to the kitchen. Lacey stood wearing some sort of… dress? She had stitched strips of the two materials he'd left for her onto a hoop she'd lifted over her head. It hung like a circus tent. Cuffs made from the waistband of his trousers sealed her wrists and multi-colored threads held buttons in various zigzagging locations.

He inched closer to the cookstove. "What is that?" he asked hesitantly. The strength of the brew caused his eyes to water and his nasal passages to burn.

"Fried wild onion and popcorn soup," Lacey said and opened the oven door. "Oops, the flour biscuits are burning," she said waving her hand into a puff of gray smoke. "I sure hope you don't mind I used all your popcorn, but I reckoned they'd make the soup look real perty. And, Horace, we have sugar pie for dessert!"

"Sugar pie?"

"Yep," she said hoisting the pan from the sidewall. A thick and sticky goo with a sprinkle of sugar on top greeted his eyes. "All for you. I already had my supper, so I'm going to bed now. Enjoy!"

Brandon stormed out of the offices of Smith & McKane, curses flying from his mouth with every step. He met with Rueben in the hotel lobby. "Let's get our bags." His lips were thin with anger. "We're going home."

Rueben glanced around the lobby. "We just got here." He shrugged. "Whaddya mean we're going home?"

"Just what I said. There was no telegram sent to me from the mining company," he answered, shaking his head vehemently as he headed toward the front desk. He paid the bill and turned to Rueben. "Something smells damn fishy and it smells a whole lot like Horace Sparker."

The two men rushed up the stairway toward their rooms.

"You think Horace gave you a fake telegram to send you out of town?" Rueben asked after he threw a pile of clothes into his worn carpetbag and joined Brandon.

"For whatever reason, yes. I'm going to find out why and tie that scrawny no-good liar to the nearest tree." Brandon glanced around his room, satisfied he had his belongings, and the men headed out of the hotel.

$\heartsuit \heartsuit \heartsuit$

"Miss Lacey, wake up."

Lacey rolled in bed and stared into a face lit eerily by a candle. She screamed and pulled the covers to her chin. "What in Sam's tarnation are you doing, Horace?" Her heart beat like a rabbit flushed out by a 'coon.

"Miss Lacey," Horace said, and hung his head pitifully. "I feel so gall darn bad about what I've done. I'm so sorry, and I don't know what to do to make it right."

"Horace?" Lacey asked sitting up in bed. "You mean you're going to take me back to Miss Fronie's?"

Horace nodded his head. "I am, but I know Brandon is going to kill me real slow and painful when he gets back and finds out what I've done."

"Listen to me," Lacey said with sincerity. "Iffin' you take me back this instant, I promise to convince Brandon not to kill you. Or, at least not to kill you slow."

He bit his quivering lip. "Do you have to tell him it was me who swiped you?"

"I have to tell him the truth. But I'll try to ease things over for you." She looked directly into his eyes. "Take me home. It's whatcha gotta do." She threw the sheet aside. "And you gotta do it right now."

"I'll get the buggy."

Lacey stood outside the cabin door and took a deep breath of fresh air as she waited for Horace to bring the buggy around. She decided rather than try and get comfortable on the buggy seat wearing a barrel hoop, she'd have Horace take her back to town in her dirty nightgown.

The wheels turned a cloud of dust as he brought the horse to a halt and jumped from the buggy. "Watch your step," he said in Lacey's ear as he helped her onto the seat. She shook her head at the irony of his concern.

Horace let the reins fall over the horse's back and after a click of his tongue and a loud giddyap, the horse started down the path toward town.

Hearing gunfire, Lacey let out a blood curdling scream and shot out of the seat to a standing position. She twisted sideways as Horace tumbled over the side of the buggy and landed in a heap on the ground. She grabbed the reins and stopped the buggy, terror gripping her chest when three riders emerged from the trees and headed straight for the buggy. She slapped the reins across the horse's back and shouted, "GIDDYAP!"

The frightened horse took off like a bolt and she held on for dear life, looking over her shoulder as she screamed at the horse to run faster. Ruts in the ground made the buggy sway back and forth as if it could tip at any second. One of the riders was closing in on her, getting closer and closer. She slapped the reins harder. The rider gained on her, and a black-gloved hand reached to grab the buggy's left side. He missed. Lacey turned to see him lean forward on his mount and soon his horse was neck to neck with Horace's. He managed to get a fingerhold on the reins and brought the buggy to a stop.

Lacey attempted to scramble from the the seat, but before her legs touched the ground, the rider dismounted and grabbed her.

She screamed in terror, "Help, help me, somebody help me!"

Jeremiah looked up from digging worms and asked Matthew, "Did you hear a gunshot?"

"Sure sounded like it. Reckon somebody got 'em a deer, or a squirrel, or possum, maybe."

"Reckon so." Jeremiah pulled a plump night crawler from the ground and added it to his bucket. "This here's plenty'a bait to get us started. Let's go see iffin' there's some good eatin' in that crick over yonder."

The boys saddled their horses and headed off through the woods. They dismounted, walked toward the brush, and tied their horses to a tree limb.

"Don't forget your bucket, stupid," Matthew said, pointing at the wiggling mass inside.

"Don't call me stupid."

"Stupid."

Lacey's expression changed from one of terror to shock when Winston rode toward her on horseback. An unfamiliar man rode alongside him. "What in Sam's tarnation do you think you're doing?" she asked with an angry glare as Beaumont dismounted and approached her.

"Here, Winston," Simon said without emotion as he tossed him a short piece of rope.

Winston knelt behind Lacey, jerked her arms behind her back, and tied her wrists together.

"Get it good and tight," Percy said as he puffed deeply on the stub of a cigar.

Lacey looked over her shoulder. "You're nothing but a miserable, rotten, stinking, snake-in-the-grass who's crazier'n a mess of loco-weed."

"Shut up," Winston said, shifting his position behind her.

"Excuse me?"

"I said shut up, you stupid hillbilly, and keep your hands still." He jerked the rope tight. "I am sick of playing games with you, and it is about time you repaid me for all the hours I wasted with your ignorance."

"Why, you miserable rotten —"

"That's right, Miss Kendall." He leaned close and whispered in her ear. "You have not had the privilege of seeing the best of me yet, madam. When we get to the next town, the two of us are going to be married."

"Married? I wouldn't marry the likes of you, even if I was dead," Lacey declared.

"True, absolutely true. But your body will not be dead until *after* the ceremony." He put his face against hers and rubbed his slick mustache hair against her cheek. "That way, I will inherit your aunt's property fair and square." He laughed. "And the best part? It is all legal. Except the killing, of course."

Lacey jerked her head to the side. Her anger could have sparked a fire bolt to shoot from her eyes. "Allow me to let you in on a 'lil secret, Winston. Never, mark my words, never will I marry you. You'd have to kill me and prop my dead body upright to make me your wife."

"You will marry me, Lacey." He emitted a forced laugh. "Like I told you a moment ago, you will, in fact, marry me tomorrow." He leaned in and whispered in her ear. "I am looking forward to our honeymoon almost as much as you."

Her stomach boiled with anger. She jerked her hands against the rope, but the sick, twisted man tied them far too tight for her to do any good. It wouldn't budge.

"Let's go, my dear." He jerked her hands upright. "We have a wedding to attend, and we are the guests of honor."

Percy untied the horse from Horace's buggy and held the animal still while Winston lifted Lacey into the saddle.

The men remounted and Winston grabbed the reins of Lacey's horse. They headed toward the northeast.

Jeremiah brushed back a thicket of weeds and startled when he peered into the face of Horace Sparker. "Whatcha doing out here in the middle of nowhere, Horace?" he said before noticing the seepage of blood on the man's shirt sleeve. He took a step back. "What in tarnation happened to you?"

"I was ambushed, yes sir, that's what happened. Lacey and I, we was ambushed by a mob of murderous thieves."

"Lacey?" Matthew perked. "You mean to tell us you found our sister?"

"Uh, yeah. I reckon I did," Horace said and lowered his eyes.

"Well, where is she?" Jeremiah said as he looked around.

"The men who ambushed us, and shot me…can't you boys see I've been shot?"

"Yeah, Horace, quite a bit of blood there," Jeremiah said as he leaned in closer for a look. "So, where's Lacey?"

"They took her with them, I reckon. The last I heard after rolling plum off the wagon was Lacey taking off in the buggy and screaming like her britches were on fire."

"Was they?"

"Was they what?"

"Was they on fire?"

"No, they wasn't on fire." Horace rolled his eyes. "She was screaming because the horse took off like lightening when he heard the gunfire."

"What did they look like? And how many was there?"

"I saw three, but I bet there was a whole mess of them hiding in the woods," Horace said as he eyed each one. "Big bunch of fellows they were. Ugly, too."

Matthew held out a hand to help Horace stand. "We'll get you to town so the doctor can take a gander at that gunshot wound, and we'll get the sheriff and some fellas together to search for Lacey."

Lacey sized up her abductors as they rode near her horse. With her sore leg, she didn't stand a chance against them if she attempted an escape.

Suddenly, the men stopped their horses and the larger of the two strangers dismounted.

"What are you doing?" she asked as he withdrew a vial of white powder from his pack and poured the contents into a near empty bottle of whiskey. He approached Lacey.

"What are you doing? What is that?" Lacey asked as the man dragged her off the horse and threw her on the ground.

"Drink it," he demanded as he knelt beside her.

"Drink it? You must be daft iffin' you think I'm gonna drink —"

"Shut up," Percy said as he grabbed her hair and arched her head back. He pulled her bottom lip down with his thumb and poured the bitter liquid into Lacey's mouth, keeping a tight hold on her hair until she swallowed.

"That bit of opium and whiskey should keep her cooperative until we get settled in for the night," Percy told the others as he walked to remount his steed.

Lacey coughed and sputtered as tears rolled down her cheeks. The bitter taste remained on her tongue long after the one called Percy poured it down her throat. Woozy, she wondered where the pretty, multi-colored lights came from. She reached to grab a twinkling orange prism and it emitted a faint, hysterical giggle. Lacey attempted to force her confused mind into order, smiled and made another attempt to catch the sparkling flutter. "Wheeee…."

The dull thunder of horse's hooves coming into town drew Miss Fronie to pull back the curtain to look outside. When Jeremiah and Matthew came to a stop, she ran outside with her hand over her heart, hoping to see Lacey.

"Howdy, Miss Fronie," Jeremiah said as he swung a leg over the horse's back and helped Horace dismount from his place in front of Matthew.

"I declare," Fronie began. "When I saw you and Jeremiah, I thought perhaps you had found our Lacey and were bringing her home."

Emma came running from inside. "Lacey? Do you have Lacey with you?" she asked as she searched for her dear friend.

"I've been shot, Miss Fronie," Horace said as he removed his hand to reveal his wounded arm.

"Well, I'll be," she said and glanced at the sleeve that had turned from bright red to brick. "Best you go on and see Doc Petitjean, Horace."

"Me and Matthew are on our way to the sheriff to get some fellers rounded up," Jeremiah said as he hitched his horse to a post. "We got some news about Lacey."

"What do you mean news of Lacey?" Fronie couldn't tumble the words off her tongue fast enough. "What news?"

"Well, ma'am," Matthew began. "When we ran across Horace —" He looked over his shoulder, but Horace took off down the planked walkway toward Doc Petitjean's. "Anyhow, Horace told us he was bringing Lacey to town in his buggy when he got shot by a band of outlaws. He reckoned they took Lacey with 'em."

Miss Fronie covered her mouth with her hands and stared wide-eyed into Emma's pale face. "Land sake's, poor Lacey accosted by near murderers?"

"We're heading to talk to the sheriff right now. We should have plenty of daylight left for a good search."

"I'm going with you to the sheriff," Fronie said. "If he doesn't get his tail moving right away, I'll move it for him."

Miss Fronie burst through the door of the jailhouse, her full skirt swishing all the way to the oversized oak desk. She placed her stocky hands on the top and leaned in, her large bosom taking up every bit of available space. Matthew and Jeremiah stood at her sides.

"Sheriff," she said. "We got proof that Lacey was accosted by a band of murdering thieves that shot Horace Sparker and took off with our girl to who knows where. We want you to get a posse together this instant and go looking for them."

Sheriff Kuhler stood and furrowed his brows. "Horace Sparker's been shot?"

"Yes, and the men who shot him have taken off with Lacey. How soon can you have a posse together?" Fronie left no question Sheriff Kuhler was about to feel real pain if he didn't comply, and fast.

"Matthew, go on over and ring the church bell. That'll signal we've got a big problem here and the townsfolk will gather. Go on now," he said and snugged his gun belt, "There ain't no time to waste."

Matthew bolted out the door with Jeremiah hot on his trail.

As soon as Lacey woke, she realized her hands were untied. She rubbed throbbing temples in gentle circles and moaned. When had her head ever hurt so bad? Never. Glancing around the room, she startled to see Beaumont and the two henchmen playing poker at a table by the window.

"I see my blushing bride-to-be is awake," Winston said. "I'm nowhere near as excited about our wedding as you are, I bet."

The burly one they called Percy added, "Fine day for a wedding, don't you think, boys?"

Their laughter turned her stomach. She honestly thought she would puke. She licked her teeth under closed lips. "I want to clean my teeth," she said, remembering the bitter tasting liquid she'd been forced to drink and concerned her tongue might stick permanently to the roof of her mouth.

"There's a wash pan right there." Winston pointed at a large bowl on a table by the bed. "Use that."

She splashed water on her face with cupped hands and glanced across the room. *I wonder if I could make it to the window and scream for help. Maybe someone would hear me.*

Percy removed a fat cigar from the side of his mouth. "What are you looking at?" He sat forward in his chair and tapped ashes on the floor before returning his attention to the cards in his hand.

"Jis' looking," Lacey said and dipped her hands back into the water.

"Don't get any fancy ideas, or you'll have two sore ankles instead of one."

Lacey held her words back by clamping her teeth shut and thinking of her future with Brandon. If she kept her mind on him, there wasn't a thing they could do to break her spirit. She inched her way back to sit on the bed.

Percy stood and poured whiskey into a glass, then pulled a vial from his pocket and added a small amount of the white powder.

"No, please…please don't make me drink that." Lacey pleaded. "I'll do anything you want, but don't make me drink that horrible stuff again."

"Sorry, we got too much ground to cover today, and we, little princess," Percy said as he approached her, "need you to cooperate."

Lacey threw her arms out to stop Percy from grabbing her, but he placed one knee on the bed and jerked her head back by her hair. He poured the bitter fluid down her throat.

Before noon, the front door of Miss Fronie's opened and slammed shut with a loud crack as Brandon entered and took the steps three at a time. He'd had many hours to think about why Horace would give him a bogus telegram and concluded Horace wanted him out of town for a reason, and every scenario led him to Lacey. He said a silent prayer as he knocked on her door and turned the knob.

Lacey's bed was empty and the room looked unoccupied. The anger within Brandon boiled up from his feet and surfaced out the strands of his hair. He thundered down the steps shouting for Miss Fronie.

"Oh, my goodness, Brandon," Fronie said as she threw down the armful of bed clothing she had taken off the clothesline. I am so glad you are back. Rueben!" She squealed and opened her arms for a hug as the gray-haired man came into the lobby holding two traveling bags.

"Where's Lacey?" Brandon demanded.

"My heaven's, everything has been awful since you two left."

"Fronie, where's Lacey?" he said and started for the door. "Where is she?"

Fronie tipped her chin downward. "We don't know, dear. Sit down and let me tell you what has happened."

Brandon rubbed his hands together as if to make fire. "You tell me what happened, and I'll stand right here."

"All we know right now…she disappeared. Horace Sparker found her and was bringing her back to town, and they were shot at by near-murderous bandits."

Brandon glared at Fronie. "What?"

"Who shot at my 'lil girl?" Rueben demanded.

Fronie took a nervous step back and told them the rest of the story. "Horace got shot in the arm and thinks the bandits took Lacey with them."

Shot by bandits? The words didn't want to register in Brandon's mind. His eyes turned to beads of fury as he grabbed Fronie's shoulders and demanded, "Is Lacey all right?"

Fronie rung her hands. "I don't know," she said glancing back and forth between the two men. Sheriff Kuhler got a posse together and they're searching —"

Brandon rushed across the street and into the jailhouse.

Sheriff Kuhler stood from his desk chair.

"I guarantee she's not inside your office, Kuhler."

The sheriff grabbed his hat and placed it on his head, all the while having a staring contest with Brandon. "I was just on my way out. I got a whole mess of men out there searching every inch of the county. We'll find her, Brandon, don't worry. I came back here to send out a telegram to the neighboring counties to keep a look out for a group of men riding with a young lady. I've been working my ass off on this disappearance, so just because I'm inside and not out searching for her, doesn't mean I'm 'sitting on my laurels. Got it?"

The thought of a telegram made Brandon think of Horace, and when he thought of Horace, his blood boiled with renewed vigor. "We have to find her. I'm sorry, I'm stressed and fearing for her…didn't mean to blow up, but she *must* be found, alive."

acey floated down the steps of the hotel. She decided her feet *did* touch the floor, but she reckoned if she took a mind to flying that would work out pretty well. She giggled and licked her lips as if they were covered with a delicious coat of honey. A female patron reading a book in the front room eyed her strangely, and Lacey cocked her head and asked, "Is this your wedding day, too?"

Winston squared his shoulders. "Miss Lacey and I are getting married today," he offered.

The woman shook her head and glanced at the two burly men walking close behind the couple, then returned to the book in her hands.

Simon and Percy led her outside while Winston paid the bill at the counter. Lacey's thoughts spun in more directions than a spiderweb, and she wished the obnoxious buzzing in her head would stop. She swatted at it, but it kept on buzzing.

"I'm hawngree," she announced as her feet stomped on the dusty road outside of the hotel. The hotel door closed behind her and Winston approached the group. "I'm hawwwngreee, Winston."

She swatted the air between them, pretended to catch a flying bug, and popped it into her mouth. "And I wanna eat right now."

"You are beyond disgusting," he said and straightened his jacket. He hooked his arm in hers. "We will eat after the wedding."

A little white church with a pointed steeple stood down the street where they were headed. "No." Lacey planted her feet. "I ain't getting married or doing nothing else till I've had me some eats. I'm hawngree."

Winton smiled at a small group of townsfolk walking nearby.

"Lacey, let's go," he said, tightening his hold on her arm.

"No. I said I'm hawngree, and I want something to eat *right now*. Stop digging your nails into my arm. You're hurting me, Winston. Stop it."

The group of townsfolk had heard the exchange of words and slowed their pace to eavesdrop. Some eyed Winston with frowns, squints, and lifted fists like he was a monster who refused to feed his soon-to-be bride.

"All right, dear," he said and ushered her back to the walkway. He forced a smile. "If you are hungry, of course, we will eat before we go to the church."

Percy and Simon growled as they followed the two inside the restaurant and pulled squeaky-legged chairs out from beneath one of the tables.

"It's no use searching the same places the others are looking," Brandon said over his shoulder to Sheriff Kuhler as they hit the main road out of town. "Let's ask questions at Millpond and Stringtown. We'll fan out from there."

Stringtown was a tiny town with a saloon on one end and a livery stable on the other. A person could see both buildings as they rode into town. The men dismounted in front of the saloon.

Sheriff Kuhler figured they'd find the lawman inside, and sure enough there he sat between two of the biggest, homeliest woman Brandon had ever laid eyes on.

"Hey, Buck." The sheriff greeted his friend with a handshake.

"Well, I'll be," said the man with a badge hanging crooked on the left side of his vest. "If it ain't Marty Kuhler. Have a seat there, boys," he said to the arrivals.

"Can't stay, Buck. Need to know if you've noticed some suspicious characters riding through. A small group of men, might have had a lady with them."

"Didn't come through here today," he said. "Hell, I've had my fat carcass parked on this here stool all day and you boys are the first riders I've heard in hours." He wiped his hand over a crop of burly whiskers. "Couple of stages went through earlier, but nope…no group of riders."

"Thanks, Buck, appreciate it," the sheriff said before the men saddled and rode toward Millpond.

"This won't be as easy as Stringtown," the sheriff said as they hitched their horses and headed to the Millpond Jailhouse. "Heck, you can spit from one end of Stringtown to the other."

Brandon followed Sheriff Kuhler inside the building.

Lacey wiped her mouth across her sleeve and belched. "That ain't bad manners, that's good eats!" she announced to the other customers before laughing and giving Winston a playful punch to his arm.

"Men," he announced, "it's time to leave." He shot Lacey a menacing scowl as he stood and grabbed her by the elbow.

"We're gonna go get hitched," Lacey said over her shoulder as the man led her through the door. "Me and ole tightwad Winston here is gonna get hitched," she said, slapping her thigh and letting out a peal of laughter. "Ain't that the craziest thang ya'll ever did hear? C'mon, tightwad."

Winston hurried, with Percy and Simon close on his heels, to get her across the street. They nearly dragged Lacey up the steps and into the church.

"Simon, go fetch the preacher," Percy said as they looked around the darkened interior. "Tell him to get over here right away."

Lacey swished her skirt and danced in circles toward one of the wooden pews. She plopped down and a strange feeling rumbled in her belly. She rubbed her stomach with her right palm. "Uh, Winston," she called out, "I do believe I'm fixin' t'puke."

Winston hurried her out the side door of the church and down three steps. She lost every bit of the breakfast from the café right there in the grass. She sat on the stoop. "Water," she said like a croaking frog. "I need me some water."

Winston walked her to the pump well. The cold liquid splashed onto a wooden platform as he pumped the handle. Lacey dunked her head under the flow. The cold water caused her to gasp. She held out her hands and poured handfuls of the liquid into her mouth, then spit it out. Finally, she took a drink and rubbed water over her face before stepping back into the grass and laying down. "Gotta sleep, Winston."

Brandon and Sheriff Kuhler stopped in every shop along the street asking questions, but no one had noticed any strangers riding through town. He poked his head into the hotel. No one stood at the front counter, so he went inside the small lobby and rang the desk bell.

"Hello, mister," an elderly matron greeted him. "Would you like a room for the night?"

"No, ma'am," Brandon said tipping his hat. "I would like to ask you a question, though."

"At your service," she said and arranged a stack of papers on top of the counter.

"Have you rented a room to a group of men in the past day? They have a lady with them." He swallowed hard. "A beautiful lady with the prettiest eyes, violet eyes, and gorgeous long…." His voice caught for a second. "Brown hair with…curls…long curls."

"I sure did," she said with a wink. "They checked out maybe 30 minutes ago, maybe a little less."

"Excuse me," said a voice from behind.

Brandon turned to see a well-dressed woman sitting in a parlor chair with a book in her hands.

"I doubt the girl she's talking about"…she pointed to the cashier…"is the girl you're looking for."

Brandon walked toward her. "What makes you think it wasn't her?"

"Well, when that group you asked about walked through here, I heard that pretty young lady say she was getting married today." The lady shrugged her shoulders. "Maybe they're still at the chapel."

"Married? No, then it's not Lacey," Brandon said. "She wouldn't be getting married."

The woman put her book down. "Lacey, you say? Yes, that's what they called her…Lacey. Such an unusual name."

"Where's the church?" he asked, stumbling over the words, and ran out the door in the direction the woman pointed.

"What's wrong with your woman?" the preacher asked Winston as Percy and Simon were helping to prop the bride into a standing position.

"She's a heavy drinker," Winston said, holding Lacey tight against his side, "but I love her all the same."

"May we get started now?" the preacher asked with a frown pointed in Lacey's direction.

"Sure 'nuff, I'm ready any time ya'll are," Lacey said as she reached to swat an imaginary bug from the clergyman's shoulder.

"Dearly beloved," the minister began. "We are gathered here to join —"

"The HELL you are!" A voice like roaring thunder had crashed through the front doors of the church and stormed up the center aisle.

"Who is that?" Simon asked as he hurried to step aside as the thundercloud bound down the aisle, glaring at Winston the entire way.

"You made it here just in time for her funeral," Winston said with a smirk. "I mean wedding…I think."

Brandon noticed Lacey's enormous pupils and his eyes darkened to near black as he delivered a near-deadly blow to Winston's face. He was on top of him in a second, ready to throw a punch to finish him off, when the sheriff sprinted up the aisle and pulled him from a charge of murder.

"Leave this to the law, Brandon. Leave it."

"Miss Fronie," Lacey hollered as Brandon carried her inside the boardinghouse. "Miss Fronie!"

"Lacey," Fronie shrieked as she came around the corner with a lit candle, pulling a robe over her shoulders. "Heaven's, girl, what happened to you? Where have you been?"

"It's a long story, Fronie," Brandon said. "Right now, I want to get Lacey to bed so she can get a good night's sleep. Can you help her for a minute?"

"I wouldn't have it any other way. Let's go."

Brandon carried Lacey up the steps and placed her on the bed. "I'll be on the other side of the door while you get her changed." He stepped out, stood with his back flush against the closed door, and exhaled a sigh of relief.

Fronie helped Lacey get comfortable in bed and gathered items for a quick freshen up. When she turned back, Lacey had fallen asleep.

She whispered, "Bless your heart, dear one. I can only imagine what you've been through." She worked quickly and when finished, pulled the hem of her clean nightgown down, and tucked the covers under Lacey's chin. She bent to kiss her forehead. "Rest, angel," she said before stepping into the hallway.

"Asleep," she told Brandon. "But I suggest you wake her, or they'll be hell to pay for the both of us." She blew him a kiss and said goodnight.

Brandon rolled his shoulder around the edge of the doorframe and watched Lacey sleep while he gathered his emotions. He was Lacey's protector, and she could have been killed.

In that moment, his heart bursting with love, he made a vow: *I will protect you for the rest of your life.*

randon sat on the bed and whispered Lacey's name. She turned her head. As she opened her eyes, she gasped and held up her hand so they could, palm to palm, experience the transfer of heat from one to the other and back again. For in this moment, with a love so great, they became one being. Her tears wet his cheeks, his dampened her hair. They spoke at the same instant. "I love you."

As they embraced, they each lay their free hand to caress the other's hair, gentle strokes, loving whispers, forever promises. Brandon gathered her in his arms, and they rocked as if the sweetest lullaby played softly in the background. Neither spoke. They didn't need words when a love as great as theirs shouted to the heavens, echoed off paradise, and reverberated back to settle for eternity within their hearts. Two bodies, one flesh. Forever. Brandon kissed his sleepy angel goodnight and walked from the room. He gently closed the door.

"Lacey, dear," Emma entered her room before breakfast and pulled a chair next to the bed. She swept a stray hair from Lacey's cheek and took her hands. "Miss Fronie and I were so worried about you.

"I'm fine, Emma," Lacey said and stretched the sleep away. "I have so much to tell you. I don't know where to begin."

Sheriff Kuhler appeared in the doorway. "Glad to see you back, young lady. I've been all over this county and the next… looking for you."

Lacey sat up further in bed. "I saw Horace get shot. How's he faring?"

"The bullet only grazed his arm, Miss Kendall. Doc Petitjean tended him, and Horace went on home to recuperate."

"Seems Horace didn't take too kindly to my engagement to Brandon," Lacey said. "He hid me away and thought he could convince me to marry him."

"Horace Sparker?" the sheriff said with surprise. "Horace kidnapped you?"

Lacey chuckled and looked at Emma. "This is gonna sound strange, but yes, Horace kidnapped me long before Winston Beaumont and his hoodlums did." Lacey grinned. "I feel worse for Horace than I do for me. Perhaps I went a bit too far in showing him I wouldn't make the fine, delicate wife he had envisioned."

"Regardless, Lacey." Emma glanced at the sheriff. "He must be punished. What he did was wrong."

"What he did was wrong, but he never hurt me, and I sure put the hurts to him. What's done is done, and now I just want to focus on Brandon and our wedding." Lacey held back a chuckle and could hardly wait to tell Emma about her fashionable hoop dress and the fried wild onion and popcorn soup.

"I'll mosey on out to Horace's place and have a talk with him all the same, Miss Kendall," the sheriff drawled and headed for the door. "But if you don't have a mind to press charges against him, there isn't any more I can do."

After lunch, the sheriff knocked on Lacey's open door and stuck his head inside. "Ladies," he said. "I just left the Sparker place and looks like Horace took off. His cabin is emptied out and there was an envelope tucked into the door with your name on it."

Lacey reached for the envelope and tore it open. She pulled out a note and read it in silence. "It is reimbursement money for Brandon's bogus trip, along with money for me to buy a new dress with fitted sleeves and tiny 'lil buttons on the cuffs."

Sheriff Kuhler and Emma stood in wonder as Lacey clenched the note and doubled over in laughter.

"Your leg is healing up nicely," Doc Petitjean remarked after removing the splint and examining Lacey's leg. "Just a bad twist."

"Good afternoon, Doc," Fronie said as she came bustling into the room. "How's our patient doing?"

"She'll be good as new in no time," he said and patted Lacey's arm before standing to take his leave. He stopped at the door. "Use that leg a little each day, Miss Kendall, and see how it works for you. Let me know if it gives you problems."

"I will, Doc, and thank you," Lacey said and handed her empty dinner plate to Miss Fronie.

"Did you hear that, Lacey, good as new in no time," Emma said gaily.

"That's the best news I've heard all week," Lacey said. "Tomorrow, I'm gonna —"

"You're going to take it easy and let me take care of you," Miss Fronie interrupted as she fluffed Lacey's pillow. "You've been through a terrible ordeal and you need to recuperate."

The two women took their leave, and Lacey giggled, thinking of the ordeal she put Horace Sparker through. She figured it would be a cold day before he got a wild notion to steal himself a woman. Settling into the softness of the covers, Lacey daydreamed about her upcoming wedding until she fell fast asleep.

Minutes after she finished breakfast, there was a knock on her door. "Who is it?"

"Your future husband," Brandon said as he opened the door and pointed to it. "Why isn't your door locked?"

"I guess Miss Fronie forgot to turn the lock when she left." Lacey sat up in bed and squealed as she held her arms open for an embrace.

"I was so worried about you," Brandon said as he held her close. "When I found out Horace's telegram was a fake, I had this terrible fear something was wrong, and it involved you."

Lacey was glad that when Miss Fronie came in to remove her breakfast tray, she had helped Lacey brush her teeth and slip into a peach dress with an ivory eyelet neckline.

"It has been an interesting few days," she said with a wink.

"I can hardly wait to get my hands on him and find out why he sent a fake telegram."

"You may have to wait a long time to do that, Brandon," Lacey said and motioned for him to hand her a glass of water.

"Why is that?"

"Have a seat, dear," Lacey patted the side of the mattress. "This may take a while."

"He did what?" Brandon's voice boomed throughout the building after Lacey told him what had transpired. "I'll kill the miserable son of a —"

"Brandon." Lacey attempted to calm the fury. "Please listen to me. No real harm was done, and Horace left town. He even left money to reimburse your trip."

"I'll promise you one thing. If that weasel sets foot in my line of vision, I'll be the last sight he'll see before being introduced to the devil."

"I truly don't think Horace will be back in New Harmony again," Lacey said as she threw her legs over the bed.

"What are you doing?"

"Doc said he wants me to use this leg a bit. He thinks it may not be broken."

"Now, that is good news," he said embracing Lacey in a giant bear hug. He stood and headed for the door, turned, and lifted his index finger. "Don't move, I'll be right back."

"Where are you going?" She attempted to peer around the corner and into the hallway.

"Stay put," he said. "I told you, I'll be right back."

She dangled her legs off the side of the bed and waited.

He returned a few minutes later and scooped her into his arms. "What are you doing?" she giggled.

"We're going for a short buggy ride," he said and carried her down the steps.

Miss Fronie met them in the foyer. She held the door open with a basket handle dangling from one arm, a blanket over the other. The aroma of sausage frying up in a skillet filled the air.

"Have a nice picnic," she said with a wink as Brandon took the basket handle with two fingers and walked through the open door. He helped Lacey into the buggy seat and sat with his thigh pressing into hers.

"A picnic sounds delightful," Lacey said, smoothing the skirt of her dress, allowing a part of her hand to touch against his thigh. His muscled leg caused a shiver to race down her spine. She let her hand linger for a few heavenly seconds.

"The mere idea of spending time with you sounds wonderful to me," Brandon said as he laid his hand over hers.

"I missed you," she said, brushing a stray hair from Brandon's forehead. "I never want to be away from you again."

He lifted her hand and kissed the inside of her palm and the tips of each finger. "I missed you, Lacey."

Brandon halted the two horses past a grove of trees near South Sunday Creek. he hopped from his seat and walked to Lacey's side, offering a hand to assist her. "My lady," he said as she stepped from the buggy, causing a chuckle to escape her lips.

"This is a beautiful spot for a picnic," Lacey said as she viewed the lush green banks of the creek holding in the clear lazy water.

Brandon grabbed the blanket and basket of food from the buggy. "Where shall we sit?" He looked for a flat spot of ground.

"Over there looks nice." Lacey pointed toward a grassy area surrounded by wildflowers. "And stop acting like I'm helpless," she said taking the blanket from Brandon's arms. "Doc said to use this leg more, and I intend on doing just that."

Lacey took off across the grass, half-limping, half-walking to lay the blanket on a nice flat area. She pulled the four corners out straight and motioned for Brandon to set the basket down.

"Come on," she said and took his hand. "Let's go down to the creek."

They walked to the water and stood hand-in-hand listening to the babbling of the stream and sounds of little critters and flying insects. Brandon wrapped his arm around her shoulders and pulled her close. He chuckled, recalling a day at South Sunday Creek when he made her so angry, she could've bitten the head off a nail.

"I know what you're thinking about," Lacey said and gave his arm a soft pinch.

"I truly wasn't spying on you that day. And I would've hollered if you'd given me half a chance before you stripped out of your clothes."

"All right, Brandon, enough said." She squeezed his arm. "Unless you want me to get mad all over again?"

"I think about it often." He laughed and jumped aside to avoid a blow.

"Yeah, you better get away," she said teasing. "Are you hungry, because I could eat the south end of a north bound mule."

"You should be pretty easy to feed, then."

This time she sank a playful punch to his arm.

"Let's see what Fronie packed for our lunch," Brandon said and led her back to their blanket.

Lacey sat and opened the lid, peeking inside. "Fried sausage and biscuits with two pieces of thick corn bread."

"Well, I didn't give Fronie much time to throw a lunch together for us," he said. "Looks like we got the leftovers from breakfast." He patted the blanket beside him. "Sit down, sweetheart. There's something I want to tell you."

"Is everything all right?"

"More than all right. The past few days were the longest, most miserable of my entire life. God, how I missed you." He rubbed the tips of her fingers as he spoke and leaned toward her to place his hand behind her head and pull her close. He kissed her forehead and whispered, "I love you and, I need you to know when I say I love you, those aren't words I have ever told a woman before. Just you."

"You've never been in love before, with anyone?"

"Never. And I never thought I would be." He half-chuckled. "To tell you the truth, when I first saw you, I thought you were the most beautiful woman I had ever seen."

"Really? You thought I was beautiful?"

"I did. Until you opened your mouth." He fell back onto the blanket, laughing.

Lacey dropped on her elbow to lay at his side. She poked the tip of his nose with her index finger. "Funny, very funny."

"I'm sorry, Lacey. You had a wagon load of backwoods vocabulary." He laughed again and held his hands up. "Have I told you today how much I love you?"

"All right, you're forgiven. And you can never tell me enough how much you love me. Never." She leaned in for a kiss. "You're my first love, too. I've never been in love, and I will never love so deeply again. My heart is yours…forever."

"There they are," Rueben called as Brandon and Lacey walked through the door of the boardinghouse. "Come in and have a seat."

Brandon followed Lacey into the parlor and chose a chair next to hers. "Something on your mind, Rueben?" he asked as Fronie appeared from the hallway with a tray holding a carafe of coffee and four cups.

"I'll grab two more cups," she said and turned on her heel.

Rueben stood and cleared his throat. "Luke should be here any minute," he said glancing toward the stairway. "I sent him upstairs to fetch Emma."

"Is something on your mind, Pa?" Lacey asked and shot Brandon a grin.

Luke and Emma walked in holding hands and laughing over some shared secret neither was willing to share. Luke sat and pulled a still giggling Emma into his lap.

Fronie returned with a large coffee carafe and after pouring drinks, she sat in a wing chair next to Rueben.

Rueben stood and reached his hand to Fronie. They swung their hands like teenagers as Rueben cleared his throat and said, "There ain't no use in beating around the bush. Me and Fronie here." He bent to kiss the hand he held. "We is getting hitched."

"That's wonderful, Pa." Lacey said as she rose to give them each a hug. "I had a feeling there was something going on between you two."

Brandon chuckled at Lacey's comment, and rose to give his congratulations.

"This family alone is gonna keep Reverend Thomas from doing any fishing this summer," Luke said as he shook his pa's hand and gave Fronie a clumsy hug.

Matthew punched Pa in the arm and said, "Now, I ain't wanting no more brothers or sisters."

Pa punched him back. Harder.

The next afternoon, Lacey arrived at the building site with a basket brimming full of food. "Anyone hungry?" she called. She spotted Brandon and her pa placing a window in the front room. She set the basket full of fried chicken and cornbread in the back of the wagon.

"Where are Jeremiah and Matthew?" she asked. "Don't tell me those boys got outta work again today?"

"Last time I saw 'em, they were headed that way," Pa said, pointing toward the trees.

Lacey planted her hands on her hips. "We'll see about that," she said cupping her hands around her mouth to holler. "Jeremiah …Matthew get your tails over here!" Her calls were met with silence. "I'm gonna scrounge the boys up, and we'll have lunch," she said over her shoulder. Lacey reached the old smokehouse and touched the edge of the burned doorframe. She turned as a rustling of leaves interrupted her thoughts.

Jeremiah came crashing through the trees, his entire body covered with mud. Matthew zigzagged behind him, his fingers gripping the handle of a hog-slopping bucket.

"I thought you boys were supposed to help Brandon and Pa with the cabin," she said sternly. "Where's Luke?"

"Luke's setting posts behind the cabin," Matthew called as he chased Jeremiah around the charred brick of the smokehouse.

Lacey followed the laughter and peeked around the side of the building.

Jeremiah managed to get the bucket away from his brother and proceeded to dump it onto Matthew's head.

"Ouch," Matthew yelped as he put his hands up. "What did you put in that bucket? Rocks?"

"Big baby," Jeremiah prodded. "Ain't nothing 'cept mud I dredged up from South Sunday Creek."

"Yeah, then where'd all these rocks come from?" Matthew groaned as he scooped a handful of the muck and sifted through it with his fingers.

Lacey stepped closer and offered a hand to help Matthew stand. She looked at the mess in his palm, and gasped. Every ounce of blood running through her body pumped triple-time.

"What?" Matthew asked as he looked at his sister's wide-eyed expression. "You sure 'nuff have a funny look on your face."

"Jeremiah, go…hurry now and go get Brandon and Pa," Lacey said. She crouched next to her brother. "I mean it, now, hurry!" She looked directly into Matthew's hazel eyes. "Brother dear, what you're holding in your hand is gonna change all of our lives."

Matthew curled his lip. "Huh?" He looked at the nuggets in his palm and back to his sister.

"Gold, Matthew," Lacey whispered and fingered the small chunks. "This here is gold!"

Brandon came running toward them, Luke, and Pa on his heels.

"What's happened?" Pa said, nearly out of breath. "Lacey, what's wrong?"

Lacey stood. "Men," she said. "Today is a day none of us will ever forget." She opened Matthew's palm. Expressions of shock enveloped each face as the realization hit them.

Two weeks later, Lacey walked downstairs and peeked over Brandon's shoulder. She kissed his cheek. "I think you are as excited about this home as I am."

"I am happy, completely happy." He drew her close for a kiss. "Have you talked to Emma about her and Luke's plans?"

"I spoke with her earlier this morning," Lacey answered. "Luke hired a contractor to build on the east side of South Sunday Creek, and Pa says Matthew and Jeremiah are ecstatic about moving into your cabin after the wedding."

"I feel like I'm living in the middle of a boomtown," Brandon said with a chuckle. "All of this new construction taking place."

"It's gonna feel more like that all the time," Lacey said.

A broad smile crossed Brandon's lips as he shook his head. "And to think it was the bumbling duo of Jeremiah and Matthew who found the gold."

"Incredible, simply incredible," Lacey said at the thought of her two lazy brothers doing something productive.

"I can't believe it," Lacey said the day before the wedding. Tears streamed down her face as she stood and marveled at their new cabin. "It is so perfect, Brandon."

"It's a wonder it got finished in time," he said bending to pick up a stray nail. "With all the additions we made, I was a little concerned. Without all the extra help," he said, as the last of the building crew pulled out of the lane, "it wouldn't have happened."

Lacey and Brandon held hands as they walked through their new home. Brandon stopped at the door to the bedroom and spoke in Lacey's ear. "Tomorrow," he said huskily as he held her close. "Tomorrow we won't have to part at bedtime." Brandon kissed the top of Lacey's head and showered kisses on her cheeks before claiming her lips. "Tomorrow, Lacey," he whispered to her smiling face as he took a slow backward step and retreated down the hall. Brandon called over his shoulder, "I want to get some measurements before I take you back to Fronie's. I'll only be a minute."

Lacey entered the bedroom and stood with her back against the door. She touched her fingertip to lips that continued to burn with fire and dreamed of tomorrow.

The second Lacey woke on the morning of her wedding day, her heartrate quickened, and a wide smile parted her lips. She tossed the covers aside and scurried to open the curtains. As soon as she drew them apart, the sunlight washed over her face like a blush. Not a cloud was present in the bright blue sky and the warmth of the sun reminded her of melting into Brandon's loving embrace. She opened the window and inhaled a deep, refreshing breath of air as the room basked in the early morning sunshine.

She picked up her hairbrush and sat on top of the covers, careful not to snag her nightgown with the bristles, and brushed her hair until it glistened and fell around her shoulders in soft curls. Several times, she placed her hand over her heart to confirm it truly did beat as fast as a rabbit when chased by a hungry hound.

After bathing in a hot tub prepared by Miss Fronie, she drew her hands, as if pressed together in prayer, to her lips and gazed across the room at her wedding dress. She stepped toward it. Rachael had designed every single stitch. Lacey had never allowed herself to imagine, not in her wildest dreams, she would become a lady, much less be the wearer of such a fancy wedding dress.

With a light touch, she ran her fingers over the bodice. Fitted with the narrowest of folds, tiny stitches were hidden within each vertical line. The tiny pearls Rachael had sewn randomly into the delicate fabric twinkled like stars cast from a ray of sunshine.

Emma knocked softly on the door and came in to help Lacey dress. She lifted the gown over Lacey's head and fastened the four small, covered buttons on each wrist.

"Goodness sakes," Lacey said into the mirror, reaching to pull the sweetheart neckline upward. She'd never shown the top of her breasts before. Well, except when she worked at the saloon, she thought with a shudder. Rachael picked up the veil draped over the bed and placed it beautifully on Lacey's head, the soft lace framing her delicate face. A knock sounded on the door.

"Lacey," Pa said. "Are you ready, darling?"

As she opened the door, she flared the skirt of the gown and twirled in a circle. "Whaddya think, Pa?"

"I declare, Lacey girl," he said, shaking his head. "You're the prettiest darn lady I've seen since, well, since your ma on *our* wedding day."

"Oh, Pa. Thank you," Lacey said as a tear rolled down her cheek.

"None of that on your big day," Rueben said, brushing the tear away with his thumb. "Don't you go thinking your ma ain't seeing you on your wedding day." He pointed upward. "You best believe she's watching and is proud of her sweet girl."

"Thank you, Pa," she said and placed her hand on his arm so he could escort her to the church.

♡ ♡ ♡

"Lacey, you look so pretty," Rachael said as she took Lacey's arm and led her and Rueben into a small room at the back of the church. She closed the door. "You two wait here until the ceremony. We do not want Brandon to see you before the wedding starts. It's bad luck." Rachael fixed Lacey's veil, and left to find a seat.

Lacey took a deep breath and blew it out slowly. "This is the happiest day of my life, Pa." She fingered the crucifix dangling from her ma's necklace.

The chapel overflowed with the townsfolk eager for the wedding, but also the buffet and dance that followed the ceremony.

Flossie Hutter sat on the organ bench and as she played the first note, Lacey placed her hand on Pa's arm and walked through the opening doors and toward the man of her dreams, feeling like a true lady in her beautiful wedding dress.

Her gaze settled on Brandon and she noticed a sparkle and realized it was a single tear trailing down his cheek. In moments, the love of her life would stand beside her holding hands and making forever promises. Yes, Brandon Lee Chandler, the Tomboy of Calhoun County will promise to love, honor, and cherish you all the days of her life.

Had she ever experienced such a pure joy? She reckoned never.

When Lacey reached Brandon, Rueben put his daughter's hand into the hand of her soon-to-be husband and the two stepped to the altar together. Reverend Thomas blessed Brandon and Lacey's union, blessed two gold bands, and joined the couple together for eternity with the words, "I do."

Laughter and the voices of the wedding guests echoed from one end of town to the other. Miss Clemmie long since forgave Lacey for her mishap and offered her café for a succulent buffet and reception after the wedding ceremony. The newly married couple walked hand in hand to greet loved ones and friends as a fiddler played a lively two-step.

The evening passed quickly and soon it was time for the newlyweds to make their exit. They said goodnight to their guests, and Brandon escorted Lacey to his buggy. They reminisced about the day, laughing, and unable to stop touching and kissing as they traveled.

Brandon halted the buggy in front of their homestead and jumped down from his seat. He held Lacey's hand as she stepped from the buggy and swept her into his arms to carry her across the threshold of their new home. He ensured she stood steady on her feet as he gazed into her eyes. "I love you, Lacey. God, how I love you."

"Brandon," she whispered on tiptoes to kiss him, "I love you with all of my heart and soul."

Brandon took her face in his hands and kissed her deeply. "I will be right back," he said when he released her. "It will take me ten minutes to pasture the horses."

"I'll be ready for you," Lacey said and watched as he hurried out the door.

She danced as if floating on a cloud to their bedroom and hurried to unbutton the top few covered fasteners down the back of her wedding dress and along the cuffs. After removing and hanging the beautiful garment, she dressed in a white satin sleeping gown with crisscross ties in a corset bodice. She remembered when she'd found the frilly, feminine gowns and blush worthy lingerie too girly and had considered throwing it all away. Now, she wished she could thank her aunt for all the life-changing influences she had on her and would never know. *Then again, who knows, maybe she does.* She said a silent prayer. After brushing her hair and allowing it to fall down her back in soft curls, she pulled the bed sheets and quilt to the end of the mattress and turned when Brandon entered the room.

"You look beautiful, Lacey. My dear, you have made me the happiest man in the world." He walked to his bride and pressed a hand on either side of her waist. "Lacey Autumn Chandler," he said and drew her close, "I love you more than I ever knew it was possible to love another."

Lacey looked into Brandon's eyes. "My heart is so full of love, I feel it's gonna burst clear outta my chest."

Brandon bent to kiss the top of her head before curling his index finger under her chin and lifting her face upward to place wispy kisses on her forehead, eyelids, cheeks, and the tip of her nose. Her pulse quickened as he touched his palms to the sides of her face and continued to press feather-light kisses on her lips before his kisses became longer and more demanding. A warmth permeated from his body, through her lips, and out the tips of her toes. She returned his kisses, first slow and soft and then with a fevered passion that matched her husband's.

She took a deep breath and stepped back, searching his eyes as he removed his shirt, revealing his broad, muscular chest. She touched his bare shoulders and sensed a shiver run through his body. He took her hand, kissed her palm, her wrist, and up the length of her arm to reclaim her full lips to his, both with a growing need as the seconds passed.

He moved to cradle her in his arms and laid her gently atop their marriage bed.

ood morning, angel," Brandon whispered as Lacey's eyes flickered before opening.

With a lazy smile, she reached to touch his cheek. "Good morning, yourself," she said in a sleepy voice, stretching her arms over her head.

"Did you sleep well?"

"I did, but I can't seem to wake up this morning." She noticed Brandon staring intently at her. "What are you looking at me like that for?"

"I know a way to put you right back to sleep," he said with a devilish grin, reaching under the covers.

"Brandon Chandler." Lacey giggled and placed her hand over his. "It's daylight."

Brandon's expression grew serious. "All the better to see you with, my dear," he whispered hoarsely and planted kisses on his wife's neck.

After Lacey put the breakfast dishes away, Brandon cracked the front door open and raised his voice loud enough for her to hear in the kitchen. "Whenever you're ready to go, I brought the buggy around."

"Let me grab my shawl," Lacey said and headed toward the bedroom. "I'm so excited. I can hardly stand it."

"Are the envelopes ready?" he asked, walking through the front room.

"Yes, they're on the kitchen table. Why don't you tuck them into your pocket?" Lacey's voice grew close as she re-entered the kitchen. "All right, ready to go."

Brandon walked toward his wife and took her in his arms. "Have I told you today how beautiful you are?"

Lacey tilted her head back and smiled as she said, "Only about a dozen times."

"Not enough." He teased and brushed his lips over hers. "You look beautiful, sweetheart."

"You're gonna spoil me rotten, Brandon Chandler," Lacey said as she nestled her hand through the crook of his arm as they walked onto the front porch.

"That is my intention, dear," he said and helped her into the buggy.

Brandon grabbed the reins. "Where to first?"

Lacey's eyes grew wide. "Adam and Sarah's. I can't wait another minute to see the expression on their faces when we tell them." She could hardly sit still as they rode through the valley.

♡ ♡ ♡

Adam and Sarah walked outside, and Lacey and Brandon returned the elderly couple's waves.

"Everyone heard about your good fortune, you two," Adam said as he shook Brandon's hand.

Tears wet Sarah's cheeks as she and Lacey embraced for a hug. "We're so happy for you. Come in and join us for a piece of blackberry cobbler," she said, motioning them toward the house.

"We'd love to, Sarah," Brandon said," but we have a lot of ground to cover today. In fact, that is why we came by to see the two of you." He took Lacey's hand and reached into his pocket with the other.

"We want to spread our good fortune with our loved ones, and those who helped to bring us together."

Sarah glanced at her husband as Brandon handed Adam a sealed envelope.

"We're going to be on our way and then you can open it," he told Adam. "Accept it with our love and blessings."

Brandon squeezed Lacey's hand as he helped her back into the buggy.

"Have a wonderful day," Lacey called with a giggle as they waved and rode away.

They stopped in the pasture and turned to see Adam and Sarah embrace. Adam was swinging Sarah in a circle, her feet dangling off the ground. They appeared to be laughing and crying at the same time.

Then, they paid a visit to Rachael, Miss Clemmie, Miss Fronie, Jimbo, Thelma, and Bobbi Sue.

Reverend Thomas had stood speechless as he told the couple, "I not only envision a new church, but the many donations to the poor and sick the money will benefit for years to come."

"I wish I could be there when everyone back home in Rock Springs opens their envelopes," Lacey said on the ride home. "I can almost envision the looks on the faces of Miss Aimee, Sue Ellen, and Mary Margaret, not to mention Deputy Leroy and Sheriff Billy Ray for all the grief I caused over the years."

After a late lunch, Brandon took Lacey's hand and led her onto their wide front porch. They stood arm in arm at the railing and glanced past a meadow of wildflowers. From this distance, the many workers looked like ants scurrying back and forth. Lacey clasped Brandon's hand. Butterflies played tag in her stomach. She envisioned the completed structures and the grand opening of:

The Lacey Autumn Chandler
~ School of Proper Decorum ~

REFERENCES

Anonymous. (1827). *The American Toilet, Virtues for Girls in the American Toilet*. New York: Imbert's Lithographic Office.

Godey, L. A. (1864). *Godey's Lady's Book and Magazine*. Philidelphia: Punon Knaccuk.

Ruth, J. A. (1882). *Decorum: A Practical Treatise on Etiquette and Dress of the Best American Society*. Chicago: Union Publishing House.

NEW HARMONY, MONTANA

1874

eremiah Levi Kendall's eyeballs nearly popped from their sockets. He slapped his right hand over his heart and sure enough, it raced like a rabbit chased by a coon dog. Strutting within range was the biggest turkey he'd ever seen. Never mind that folks said he could cast a shadow over a grizzly bear, this giant of a man drew in a mouthful of air and willed himself not to gasp. Just a minute earlier, he'd pulled an arrow from its worn leather quiver and put it to the string. He'd pulled it back a time or two to test his arm and now, in range of his arrow, was a prize gobbler. A split second before releasing the arrow, a shrill cry cut through the air and sent the turkey hightailing it into the brush.

"What in Sam's hell?" Jeremiah stood his full six foot eight inches and looked toward the tree line. *A woman? Child? Baby? Baby animal?* He silenced all movement hoping to hear a repeat of the sound and figure out what the hell caused him to lose the biggest gobbler he'd ever laid eyes on.

He fought the urge to gather his gear and return home. No, he couldn't ignore the cry. It wouldn't be proper. Plus, if what he heard was a wailing baby or a lady screaming for help, it wouldn't be right to leave.

He walked in the direction of the cry, the sweet, fruity fragrance of freesia and hyacinth minimizing the wild rose and sweet pea scattered among trees of cottonwood and green ash. He noticed a shoe print and stooped to trace his finger over the outline of a narrow moccasin. He couldn't figure why a woman, most probably Cheyenne, since their reservation was the closest, had wandered this close to a settlement? A twig snapped. He steadied his quiver and crouched low, freezing in place beside a large bush. Although he'd come across one set of tracks, that didn't mean the woman traveled alone. He craned his neck to see what lay ahead. What had he heard? He supposed it could have been an injured animal, a hawk maybe, but more than likely it was a decoy to flush him out and steal him blind. Once again, he heard the shrill cry that had sent a chill up his spine and the turkey running for cover. All senses on alert, he listened to the unmistakable, high-pitched wail of a newborn baby.

He stepped around the bush and remained keen for signs of danger as he pushed aside low-lying limbs and fern trails. He froze when he saw, not 10 yards ahead, an Indian woman squatted with her back leaning into a mighty Ponderosa pine. A newborn lay nestled in the crook of her left arm. Unsuccessful, he bunched his legs toward his taut belly and screamed as if ablaze with firewater. The woman, intent on her task, didn't notice Jeremiah. Until she did. The look in her eyes left no doubt she was prepared to kill. Problem was, Jeremiah wasn't ready to die.

ueben Augustus Kendall had a purpose. He sank to his knees beside the feather bed he'd purchased just yesterday at the General Store in Miles City. It slept like the one he'd shared for over 20 years back in Rock Springs, Nebraska, with Lacey and the boy's ma, Mary Anne, the only woman he'd ever loved. His shoulders rose as he took a deep inward breath and ran a rugged, age-spotted hand through salt and pepper whiskers, seemin' more salty every day. A heavy sigh accompanied his shoulders downward.

Mary Anne Kuhl. She'd been the prettiest girl in Rock Springs, Nebraska township. He'd first spotted her on the playground, giggling on the swing set as she grasped the frayed ropes that held a red, paint-chipped seat. She'd throw her head back and stretch her legs out straight on the down swing, revealing worn-out spots on the soles of her shoes.

When he'd turned sideways in his classroom seat to pass the first grader a paper, he had marveled over her unusual eye color. He'd figured violet and if that weren't pretty enough, they'd cast sparkles like when the sun hit his boyhood fishing hole at Britches

Creek. She'd worn a lazy smile spread over crooked teeth, and he'd known right then and there, one day, he'd marry the cute girl with the little brown shoes.

He'd knelt the same way fifteen years ago after Mary Anne died giving birth to their stillborn, Pearl Rae. A piece of him died alongside. When life spiraled out of control, he hunkered down on his knees and talked to his maker. God knew him better than any creature on earth, and he figured he may as well go straight to the top, savin' time that way. He removed his well-worn black 10-gallon hat and held it over his heart.

> *Dear Lord,*
>
> *I'm fixin' to ask a mighty big favor. I got down on my knees, even, 'cause I want you to see my sincerity. Well, truth is, sincere and downright desperate.*
>
> *This here grief I'm fixin' to squabble about concerns that woman, Fronie Helfrich, over at the boarding house. My hellion daughter, now a lady—Lacey calls her Sour Fronie after the trouble she had with the woman when she boarded with her a spell. Well, she's taken a cotton to me, Lord. I don't mean to sound unchristian-like, but she doesn't fall anywhere near this side of, well, let me say she'd have to slither up a few ladder rungs to reach homely. I ain't tryin' to be mean. Just speakin' the truth.*
>
> *Here's the problem. We'd talked about gettin' hitched but gall darn if ever since, she ain't showed me a wicked side of her akin, well, akin to the devil. Not only that, but for the most part, she's fearful mean.*

Hell, a workin' man could bail hay with the fork in her tongue, and kid you not, Lord, her breath could drop a razorback sow. She bats her eyes at me like a toad in a hailstorm which is more aggravatin' than a horsefly nippin' on a bull's rump.

I'm here to ask for divine intervention. Git her off m'rump, Lord. You gotta keep me from killin' the woman and spendin' my last days behind bars. Amen.

acey Autumn Chandler heard the cabin door swing wide and startled as it smacked the front room wall with a tremendous thud. This thwack was followed by the sound of her husband's cowboy boots clip-clopping wildly toward the kitchen, hollering her name as if an outlaw had hog-tied a lit stick of dynamite to his—

"Lacey, where the hell are you? The cabin … the cabin is on fire!"

She leaned her backside against the cookstove and crossed one bare foot over the other, a long-handled fork clenched in her right hand as he entered the kitchen in a full run, skidding to a stop when he saw the source of the fire.

"Bacon's 'bout done fryin'," she said in her lazy twang. "How do you want your eggs this mornin'?" She turned back to the stove and scooted several charred slices of pork to one side of the cast iron skillet.

"Uh, smoked?" Brandon walked up behind his bride and wrapped his arms around her waist. He snuggled close to kiss the nape of her neck. "How is my lovely wife this morning?"

Her shoulders hitched up to protect her from a tickle. When she cracked four eggs, along with several jagged pieces of shell into the bacon grease, he reached to unhook a spatula from the wall beside the stove. "How about I take over from here?" He gave her a gentle nudge. "And you set the table?"

"The a … a … 'umm table?"

"Yes." He did a half turn. "We'll want to eat at the…what in Sam's hell is—"

"That there?" Lacey pointed at a long-tailed varmint with pink nostrils. "Don't tell me you aint never seen no possum?"

"Of course, I've seen possum. Just not possum with a bullet hole in its head lying on my kitchen table next to the butter."

"And honey, next to him is two squirrels and three rabbits. When I checked traps, reckon 'bout four or so this mornin', them five critters was waitin' for me, proud as you please. That ole possum, I shot him on the walk back."

"You got out of bed at four this morning to check traps?"

"Reckon, I did," she said with a shrug. "And, after we eat, I'll skin 'em and draw up a nice cold saltwater bath to draw the wild out of them hares. Last thing we need is rabbit fever." She grabbed the possum by its tail and walked to stand beside Brandon. "Which do you reckon you'll be wantin' come supper time?"

"Well, it sure as hell isn't going to be possum, I guarantee you."

"You've not had the pleasure of my possum stew, so don't go saying you don't want it when you ain't never had it. Reckon I could boil up a pot of possum sweetbreads with turnips 'n taters iffin'—"

"Rabbit. Let's have rabbit this evening. That sounds mighty good. But, for now, can you take the critters out of the kitchen? Maybe leave them outside, so we can eat breakfast at the table?"

Lacey swiped her foot under the table to retrieve her boots, then gave each a few tugs and a yank up to her calf while balancing on the opposite leg. "See you in a minute, honey," she said and scurried out the back door with the critters.

When she returned, Brandon had filled their plates. He pulled Lacey's chair out and motioned for her to sit.

"Well, thank you, Mr. Chandler."

He pushed her chair forward.

"A thinkin' woman would sure think you was sweet on me. Can I expect you to be such a gentleman at every meal?"

He kissed her offered cheek. "You turn into the vixen I saw between our bed sheets last night and you'll never see such a gentleman." Brandon winked and pointed his fork at her, ready to devour his food. "After breakfast, I plan to devour your—"

The two startled when a young girl with a face full of freckles and two fire-red pigtail braids bounded into the kitchen and plopped on the floor. She tossed the braids over her shoulders, untied grimy shoelaces, and pulled filthy, hole-ridden, dirt-caked boots from her feet. She took a deep whiff inside each and crinkled her nose before propelling them across the floor.

"Phew-ee, betcha I know what's stinkin' in here." The heels hit the baseboard with two solid clunks. She cocked her head back and moaned while rubbing her feet. "Ahhh, this sure feels good and smells 'jis like a bouquet of daffodils. Ain't that right?"

Acknowledgments

Critique groups are essential for learning the craft and growing as a writer. The unique perspectives of others, the awesome suggestions, the encouragement from those passionate souls who not only love to write but truly *must* write. Every day.

A huge thank you to the members of my critique groups who have become extended family: Diane How, Jeanne Felfe, Donna Reed, Nicki Jacobsmeyer, Denise Judd, Brad Watson, Rose Callahan, Doug Osgood, Bob Weismiller, Tom Klein, and our greatly missed Phyllis Borgardt. You all contributed to *Lacey's Lessons of Love* good old-fashioned spit-shine.

Thank you to Gabriela Pereira, a dear friend and 'instigator' of DIY MFA where you get the knowledge without the college. Your knowledge made a difference. Big. Huge. MEGA!!!

Thank you Judith Briles for giving Lacey her wings to soar. You are the ultimate book shepherd and your knowledge and wisdom astound me.

Rebecca Finkel, book designer extraordinaire, you ripped open a sack of creativity and splashed it onto Lacey's covers and pages. You ROCK!

A very special thank you to Diane How and Jeanne Felfe for setting personal time aside and going above and beyond.

To Carol Kimberlin, Norma Eifert, Carolyn Evans, Patricia Wright, and Skip Cassoutt for your friendship—and all the fun on game nights. Love those Lake Ridge rules!

Thank you to Sharon Will, beta reader. Fran Nelson, a ray of sunshine, and to Caroline Moore, who gives of herself daily.

And to Joan Matlock. My forever friend.

Discussion Questions for Lacey's Lessons of Love

1. What was your favorite part of Lacey's Lessons of Love? Why?

2. Were the characters believable? Did you have a favorite? Which one(s) and Why?

3. When Lacey finds the bat in the keg of sausage gravy ... did she handle it appropriately? Should she have done it differently? What would you have done?

4. When Lacey dealt poker, should she have allowed Brandon at the table? Should she have agreed to his proposition? Why? Why not?

5. Brandon humiliated Lacey when she was typing. What could she have done to prevent it? Should she have had a different reaction than what she did? What would you have done?

6. Miss Aimee prepared Lacey for the trip to Montana. Was Miss Aimee helpful? Was Lacey's reaction reasonable? Should something have been done differently? What?

Lacey's Lessons of Love is the perfect romantic comedy read for a book club or yourself. Fun, full of surprises, outrageous, ornery, cozy, discovery of self, and a romp.

To bring author Tammy Lough to your book club, contact her at:

TammyLoughBooks@gmail.com

636-452-2395 (636-4-LACEY-K)

www.TammyLough.com

Bring the *For the Love of Lacey* series and
author **Tammy Lough** to Your Book Club

RomCom is fun to read ... and even more fun to talk about. Just ask the RomCom Expert Tammy Lough. You will laugh, as she reveals how she sets up the frame of each book. You will delight in the antics that Lacey gets herself into. And you will love how Tammy writes.

Her books are the ideal beach, porch read, and curl up and read to do a drop in and drop out for several hours of reader delight.

From her wheelchair, Tammy's imagination is in high gear ... and so is her personality. She would love to join your Book Club from her shabby chic cottage to spark up your next gathering with Lacey stories, her books, and to answer your questions.

To bring author Tammy Lough to your book club, contact her at:

TammyLoughBooks@gmail.com

Meet Tammy Lough

 **Tammy** is an award-winning author of over 75 published works who loves creating women's fiction bursting with humor, romance, and moxie aplenty.

She is a member of Romance Writers of America, Saturday Writers, a Chapter of the Missouri Writers Guild, Southwest Writers, and Women Writing the West. And she is honored to write as the romance columnist at the mega-popular website for writers, *Gabriela Pereira's DIY MFA.*

Tammy calls Missouri home. She is the proud mom of David and Christopher Lough and has three cherished grands, Riley, Brianna, and Mason.

You can connect with her through her website:
www.TammyLough.com

And definitely follow her humor and Lacey's moxie at:

TammyLough, Author

@TammyLoughBooks

Lacey's
CIRCLE of LOVE
TAMMY LOUGH

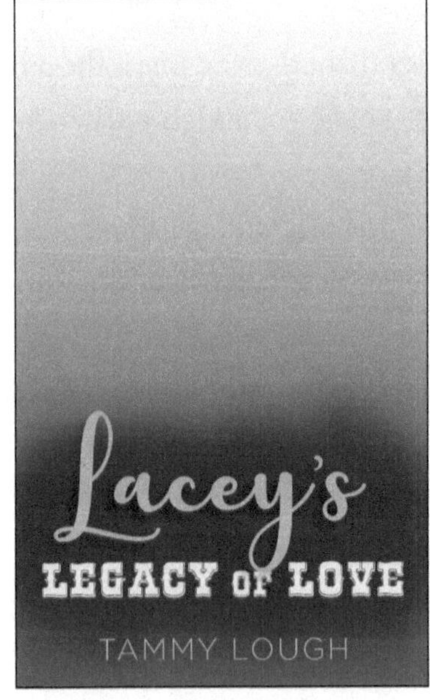

Lacey's
LEGACY of LOVE
TAMMY LOUGH